MW01122653

Drum Beat:
The Chester Drum Casebook

Drum Beat:
The Chester Drum Casebook

Stephen Marlowe

Five Star • Waterville, Maine

This collection of stories is a work of fiction. Names, characters, places, and incidents are either the product of the author's imagination, or, if real, used fictitiously.

First Edition
First Printing: June 2003

Published in 2003 in conjunction with Tekno Books
and Ed Gorman.

Set in 11 pt. Plantin by Elena Picard.

Printed in the United States on permanent paper.

Library of Congress Cataloging-in-Publication Data

Marlowe, Stephen, 1928–
    Drum beat : the Chester Drum casebook /
Stephen Marlowe.
1st ed. Waterville, Me.: Five Star, c2003.
        p. cm.
      ISBN 0-7862-4315-5 (hc : alk. paper)
        1. Private investigators—Washington (D.C.)—
Fiction. 2. Detective and mystery stories, American.
3. Washington (D.C.)—Fiction.
PS3563.A674D78 2003
813'.54–dc21   2003049087

Dedication

*To Deirdre
who was in one
and to Gary
who enjoys them*

Table of Contents

Prelude:

A Fast Drumroll

by Bill Pronzini

When Stephen Marlowe introduced Washington, D.C.-based private investigator Chester Drum in the mid-1950s, both the traditional private eye tale and the tough-and-sexy paperback original were at or near the height of their popularity. The first six Mike Hammer novels by Mickey Spillane were runaway bestsellers; Ross MacDonald's Lew Archer was well-established, as were Thomas B. Dewey's Mac, Wade Miller's Max Thursday, and Brett Halliday's Michael Shayne, among others. Softcover publishers were selling millions of copies annually by well-known professionals and such discoveries as John D. MacDonald and Richard S. Prather. Of the dozens of new detective characters who were born each month in paperback editions, most had exploitative, lackluster careers and passed on with little notice. Only a handful made any kind of lasting impact, and fewer still were innovative enough to enter the pantheon of distinguished fictional sleuths. Chet Drum was and is one of that rarified number.

The reason for Drum's success is two-fold. First: Unlike his contemporaries, nearly all of whom plied their trade in a large, urban U.S. environment, his "beat" was international and the cases he investigated of a far-reaching, often volatile political nature. While he maintained an office in Washington—and, later, another in Geneva, Switzerland—his cases took him to such global locales as Iceland, India, Russia, Spain, France, Italy, and South America. And second: Drum's creator is both a writer of considerable talent and a lifelong globetrotter himself. The respected critic Anthony Boucher, reviewing one of the early Drum novels in the *New York Times*, said that "very few writers of the tough private-eye story can tell it more accurately than Mr. Marlowe, or with such taut understatement of violence and sex." He might have added that Marlowe's depictions of foreign backgrounds, the result of first-hand experience, are as vividly rendered as they are authentic. And that Chet Drum is a fully realized character, believable as both man and detective—intelligent, tough when he has to be, compassionate yet unsentimental.

The first Drum novel, *The Second Longest Night*, appeared in 1955. Notably, the publisher was Fawcett Gold Medal, the first of the paperback houses to specialize in original, male-oriented category fiction. (Not "pulp fiction," a term that has been grossly misused since the Tarantino film, but rather an apotheosis of the true, pulp-magazine fiction of the '30s and '40s. The best of the softcover originals published by Fawcett, and such others as Lion, Dell, and Avon, were rough-hewn, minor works of art, perfectly suited to and representative of their era.) Between 1955 and 1968, Marlowe produced twenty Drum novels for Gold Medal, resulting in aggregate sales of several million copies. One of these, *Double in Trouble* (1959), was a collaboration with Richard S. Prather, in which Drum joins forces with Prather's Shell Scott to solve a common case. Despite the lurid titles of some of the early entries—

Killers Are My Meat, Homicide Is My Game, Peril Is My Pay—all are literate, fast-paced, action-oriented without being overly violent, sexy without being sex-laden, and compulsively readable.

Although he was still in his twenties when he created Chester Drum, Stephen Marlowe was already an established professional writer. ("At the age of eight," he has been quoted as saying, "I wanted to be a writer and I never changed my mind.") In 1949, after graduation from William and Mary, he joined the staff of a prominent New York literary agency and soon began to sell science fiction to *Amazing Stories* and other leading pulp magazines of that era; most of these, as well as a number of adult and young-adult s-f novels, appeared under his birth name, Milton Lesser.

By the mid-1950s, he felt he'd done as much as he wanted in the s-f field and was beginning to concentrate on suspense fiction. He became a regular contributor to such digest-sized, hardboiled crime-fiction magazines as *Manhunt* (where the first Drum short story, "My Son and Heir," was published in 1955), *Accused, Hunted,* and *Pursuit.* His first suspense novel, *Catch the Brass Ring,* appeared as an Ace Double paperback in 1954; several other non-series novels followed, under the Marlowe byline and as by C. H. Thames; the most accomplished of these is the unfortunately-retitled *Blonde Bait* (Avon, 1959, as by Marlowe). In addition to the Drums, he also wrote two other series: a pair of private eye tales as by Andrew Fraser, and four enjoyable novels featuring a team of investigators for "Ripley's Believe It or Not" as by Jason Ridgway.

When changing tastes and editorial policies brought about the cancellation of the Drum series in 1968, Marlowe turned to more ambitious suspense novels with international settings and complex themes. These include *Come Over, Red Rover* (1968), *The Summit* (1970), and *The Cawthorn Journals* (1975), the last named a chilling narrative set in Mexico that explores the reality of magic, the nature of evil, and the corruption of power.

His literary interest and intent metamorphosed yet again in the 1980s, when he began a series of brilliantly conceived, meticulously researched novels exploring the lives and personalities of genuine historical figures. *The Memoirs of Christopher Columbus* (1987) became a critically acclaimed international bestseller, as did *The Lighthouse at the End of the World* (1995), a seminal study of the tortured genius, Edgar Allan Poe, and *The Death and Life of Miguel de Cervantes* (1996), which he considers the best of all his novels.

Marlowe's horizons may yet change again; the novel he is presently writing is contemporary in setting and different in theme from anything else he has done. "The last thing you want," he says, "is to feel jaded by or with your work. The *New York Times* once called me the most prolific mystery writer in the United States. I said, 'Good Lord, I don't want to be the most prolific anything; I would love to be the best.' "

Drum Beat marks Chet Drum's first appearance in print in nearly thirty years. Five (of a total of eight) of his short cases open the collection. The first of these, the eponymous "Drum Beat" (*Ed McBain's Mystery Book*, 1961), set on a plane flying from Duluth, Minnesota, to Washington, D.C., generates a remarkable amount of suspense in a mere 1,000 words. "Evan Hunter (Ed McBain) phoned me at noon one day when I was living in a New York suburb," Marlowe recalls, "and said he needed a short-short to fill a hole for his magazine that was to go to bed that afternoon. I wrote it in about an hour, drove into the city, and gave it to him. To date, what with anthology sales in various countries, TV sales in ditto, it has earned more than I was paid for any of my early novels."

"Baby Sister" was also written on request, for a 1965 anthology of detective stories entitled *Come Seven, Come Death*; it's a tale of two beautiful sisters, one of whom is an ultra-expensive whore, and both high and low life on the French Riviera. "Chester Drum Takes Over," the last and arguably the best of all the Drum shorts (and coincidentally also Marlowe's last piece of short fiction), originally appeared in *Ellery Queen's 1973 Spring-Summer Anthology*; its locales are the Italian Alps and Switzerland, its central plot component the covert sale of military hardware to Israeli agents. "Wanted—Dead and Alive" (*Manhunt*, 1963) deals with treachery and sudden death among members of an American film crew aboard a car ferry traveling the Adriatic between Italy and Greece; and "A Place to Visit" (*Alfred Hitchcock's Mystery Magazine*, 1968) involves smuggling and the gypsies of Spain's Costa del Sol, a favorite European locale of Marlowe and his wife, Ann.

The final entry in these pages, *Drum Beat—Dominique*, is the author's choice as the best of all the Drum novels. First published in 1965, set in Paris in the spring, the French countryside, and the Italian frontier, it is in Marlowe's words "a good mix of Drum material: trouble in high places, atmospheric background with noir undertones, understated violence. And on rereading it I found Drum's emotional involvement a plus." Other virtues include sharply drawn characters, several harrowing scenes (including one in the Paris Flea Market), and a surprise-filled denouement.

These six selections provide ample evidence of why Chet Drum's adventures were so popular in the '50s and '60s— and why they earned his creator a well-deserved Private Eye Writers of America Life Achievement Award in 1997. Stephen Marlowe has gone on to other pursuits, but the crisp prose, richly observed backgrounds, and timeless storylines of the Drum saga remain fresh and vital, and offer a new generation of readers the same high level of entertainment.

Petaluma, California

Drum Beat

The big man sitting next to me in the window seat of the turboprop that was flying from Duluth, Minnesota to Washington, D.C. looked at his watch and said, "Ten after seven, Drum. We're halfway there. If I were running away and out over the ocean somewhere, they'd call it the point of no return."

"You're not running away, Mr. Heyn," I said.

He smiled a little and agreed. "No, I'm not running away."

And then the ticking started.

Heyn's eyes widened. He'd been living with uncertainty and fear too long. The physical response was instant: the widening of the eyes, the sudden rictus of the mouth, a hand clutching at my wrist on the armrest between us.

The wordless response said: You read the papers, don't you? This wouldn't be the first bomb planted aboard an airliner, would it? And I'm a marked man, you know I am. That's why you're here.

I stood up quite calmly, but a pulse had begun to hammer in my throat, as if in time to the ticking.

For a moment I saw the deep blue of the sky beyond Heyn's head and then on the luggage rack over it I saw the

15

attaché case. It wasn't Sam Heyn's. Heyn's was next to it, monogrammed.

The ticking came from the unmarked case. It was very loud, or maybe that was my imagination. It sounded almost like a drum—each beat drumming our lives away and the lives of forty other innocent people in the turboprop.

I looked at the attaché case. I didn't touch it. Time-rigged, sure; but who could tell what kind of a spit-and-string mechanism activated it? Maybe just lifting it from the rack would set it off.

A minute had passed. Heyn asked, "Find it?"

I nodded mutely. A little boy squirmed around in the seat in front of Heyn. "Mommy," he said, "I hear a clock."

Mommy heard it too. She gave Heyn and me a funny look. Just then a stewardess came by with a tray. She stopped in the aisle next to my seat, in a listening attitude.

"Is that yours?" Her smile was strained. "With a clock in it, I hope?"

"It's not mine." I squeezed near her in the narrow aisle. Close to her ear I said softly, "It may be a bomb, miss. That's Sam Heyn in the window seat."

Her back stiffened. That was all. Then she hurried forward to the cockpit. Heyn looked at me. A moment later over the PA a man's voice said:

"Whoever owns the unmarked attaché case above seat seventeen, please claim it. This is the captain speaking. Whoever owns . . ."

I heard the ticking that was like a drum. Faces turned. There was talking in the cabin of the turboprop. No one claimed the attaché case.

Sweat beaded Heyn's forehead. "When, damn it?" he said. "When will it go off?"

The captain came back. He had one of those self-confident, impassive faces they all have. He looked at the attaché case and listened to it. A man across the aisle got up to speak to him.

"Sit down, please," the captain said.

Then a voice said, "Bomb . . ." and passengers scrambled from their seats toward the front and the rear of the cabin. In the confusion I told the captain quickly, "My name is Chet Drum. I'm a private investigator bringing Sam Heyn here to testify in Washington before the Hartsell Committee. If he can prove what the Truckers' Brotherhood's been up to in the Midwest, there's going to be trouble."

"I can prove it," Heyn muttered.

I stared at the attaché case. I heard the ticking. It didn't look as if he'd get the chance.

"We could unload it out the door," the captain told me.

"Cabin's pressurized, isn't it?"

"So?"

"Who the hell knows how it's rigged? Change of pressure could be enough to set it off."

The captain nodded. He raised his voice and shouted, "Will you please all resume your seats?" Then he said, "If we could land in a hurry . . ." His face brightened. "Jesus, wait a minute." He looked at his watch. "Seven-nineteen," he said. Nine minutes had passed since the ticking started. "All we need is four thousand feet of runway. There's a small airport near New Albany . . ."

He rushed forward. Seconds later we were told to fasten our seat belts for an emergency landing. The big turboprop whined into a steep glide.

The attaché case ticked and ticked.

We came in twice. The first time the wind was wrong, and the captain had to try it again. Buzzing the field, I saw a windsock tower, two small lonely hangars and three shiny

17

black cars waiting on the apron of the runway.

Three black cars waiting for what?

I felt my facial muscles relax. I smiled idiotically at Sam Heyn. He frowned back at me, mopping sweat from his forehead. "Well, well, well," I said.

He almost jumped from his seat when I reached over his head and lifted down the ticking attaché case. The man across the aisle gasped. We were banking steeply for our second run at the field. I carried the attaché case forward and through the door to the cockpit.

The copilot had the stick. The captain looked at me and the attaché case. "Are you nuts or something?"

"I almost was."

He just stared. The flaps were down. We were gliding in.

"Keep away from that field," I said. The copilot ignored me.

I did the only thing I could to make them listen. I smashed the attaché case against a bulkhead, breaking the lock. The captain had made a grab for me, missing. I opened the case. There was a quiet little clock inside, and a noisy big one. The little one had triggered the big one to start at seven-ten. That was all.

No bomb.

"They knew your route," I said. "They figured you wouldn't dare ditch a time bomb, knew you'd have to land here if you heard it ticking at seven-ten. Three shiny black cars waiting at an airport in the middle of nowhere. They're waiting for Heyn." I pointed. "If you radio down below, you can have them picked up by the cops."

It was seven thirty. "I never want to live through another twenty minutes like that," the captain said.

Neither did I. But Sam Heyn would get to Washington on schedule.

Baby Sister

She was wearing one of those no-back bathing suits that have finally managed to chase the bikini off the French Riviera. Prone on the hot sand the way she was, with her back a tawny tanned color, and the whole glorious length of her stretched out indolently, she looked nude from the waist up. She wasn't. Those no-back suits have collarbone hugging necklines—not that I could see her collarbones at the moment.

"And yesterday?" she asked me, raising her head. She was sweating in the heat and the sun, and there was sand on her chin. Her long hair was almost exactly the same color as her suntan, but with golden glints in it. Her green eyes were staring at my bare feet. A couple of inches from her outstretched left hand on the sand was a pack of Gauloise cigarettes. I nudged it toward her hand with my big toe, squatted in front of her, lit the cigarette that she had lazily placed between her lips, and said:

"Yesterday your little sister bought a couple of simple little frocks at a couturier named Madame Florissant, right here in Cannes a block off the Croisette. They weighed in at a thousand new francs each, and she took them as is, without alterations. That was the afternoon. In the evening—"

"A thousand new francs each, *Mon Dieu,*" said Caroline Thevenin. A thousand new francs is two hundred bucks American folding money.

"In the evening," I went on with my report, "she picked up an American sailor named Huggins in a café on the Croisette. They ate at the Carlton and took a cab to the casino, not the municipal one on the waterfront but the private joint up the road toward Nice."

"She won? She won for a change?" Caroline Thevenin asked hopefully.

"Huggins won a couple of hundred at what you French call 'le craps.' Your little sister Gaby dropped a bundle. She was looped on Cordon Rouge champagne, but not so looped they wouldn't take her dough. She lost at chemin de fer, lost more at vingt-et-un, and really did a swell job at roulette."

"How much?" Caroline asked, sitting up and brushing sand off the sleek black front of her bathing suit.

"Four thousand."

"Francs? New francs?"

I shook my head. "Dollars."

"*Mon Dieu,*" Caroline said again.

"Then Huggins took her to her suite at the Carlton and hopped the launch back to his ship. It's a cruiser," I added irrelevantly. "Rocket-launching variety."

"At least he did not spend the night," Caroline said. "Perhaps I should be happy for small favors."

But I had to scotch that too. "They have a date for tonight. Huggins has a gleam in his eye."

A shadow came between me and the sun. I looked up and saw Raoul Duplesis. "Stop her," he told Caroline in

French. "Stop her, or at this rate she will go through all your savings in a month."

"It's been quite a shock to Gabrielle," Caroline said, defending her younger sister. "She will come to her senses."

"Yes?" said Raoul with a sarcastic smile. "Tell me when."

"Raoul, it is my money." Raoul was putting his foot in it, but either didn't want to or hadn't read the signs. Caroline Thevenin's green eyes had gone hard, and the throaty purr of her voice was a danger signal.

But Raoul persisted. "Not only does she spend your money like vin ordinaire, but you pay M. Drum five hundred nouveau francs a day to watch her do it. This must stop. I, Raoul Duplesis, tell you so."

"You, Raoul Duplesis," said Caroline sweetly, "are a parasite."

Duplesis grinned down at her arrogantly, his white teeth flashing against his bronzed skin. He was a muscular specimen about my height, which is six-one, and my weight, which is one-eighty-five. Our lines of work, though, differed. I am a private eye, international variety. Raoul Duplesis is a pimp.

"I am an artist," Duplesis said, still grinning down at her. He laughed. "Perhaps you might say, a ghost artist."

Duplesis was a third-rate surrealistic dabbler who had done a lazy canvas a month the last couple of years. Caroline Thevenin had signed her name to all of them. None sold; none was good enough. Every now and then she'd get rid of a batch by burning them, claiming, when her kid sister Gaby came down to the Riviera for a visit from the finishing school in Montreux where she was stashed, that they had sold.

For a couple of years this had kept Gaby, full name Gabrielle Thevenin, happy. Big sister was a talented artist keeping her in school by painting up a storm. But then one night a couple of weeks ago she had walked in on Caroline while big sister was plying her trade.

Caroline was the most expensive beeznis girl on the French Riviera. A beeznis girl is a whore.

She charged five hundred francs a night, lived frugally, except for what she paid Duplesis, and had salted away a pile in the Credit Lyonnais branch bank here in Cannes. Wisely, in case anything happened to her, it was a joint account in her name and her sister's. But learning Caroline was a high-class whore instead of an artist had come as a shock to Gaby. She had reacted with a grim and compulsive determination to spend all her sister's hard-earned dough in a hurry. She had cleaned out the account, opened a new one in her name only and was having herself a ball as only a ball could be had on the French Riviera. My job was to see that she didn't get hurt in the process.

"It is time you went to the police," Duplesis said. "The little thief will make us both paupers, chérie."

But Caroline Thevenin and I had been all through that. If she went to the cops about the dough, and if there was a stink, that would be the end of the finishing school in Montreux.

Caroline got mad, and when Caroline got mad it really was something to see. She sprang up from the sand, all five-ten and thirty-six, twenty-four, thirty-six of her, placed her hands on her hour-glass hips, stood about two inches from Duplesis all the way from their jaws to their bare toes, and bawled at him like a fishwife.

"Yes? You dare to call my little sister a thief? And what are you? A pimp when I found you, and that is what you will be again, because of what use are your paintings to me

now?" That much I could understand, and then the French
got too fast and furious for me, and too tough for Duplesis
to take, because it ended with him stepping back and hitting Caroline in the face open-palmed, deftly and contemptuously, once forehand and once backhand, before I could
get between them, grab Duplesis' wrist, lever his arm behind his back in a hammerlock and shove him stumbling
across the sand.

Naturally, all that brought a crowd, the men looking
speculatively at Caroline, the women angrily at Duplesis
and curiously at me. Duplesis had had enough, at least for
now. He slunk away like an old Mack Sennett villain,
heading for the beach-café of the Martinez Hotel.

"He could be right," I told Caroline gently. "If she keeps
it up, the kid's liable to break you."

Unexpectedly there were tears, but not of anger, in the
big green Thevenin eyes. "Let her get it out of her system.
She will. I know it. She is all I have."

I was having a Pernod with Senator Hartsell at the sidewalk café outside the Hotel Carlton. It was almost dusk but
still hot, and a heat haze half-obscured the high peaks of the
Maritime Alps beyond the curve of the bay. Looking beyond the heavy traffic moving sluggishly along the
Croisette, I could see a launch leading its white wake toward shore from the big cruiser anchored a mile or so out
on the water. If Huggins were aboard, and I thought he
would be, I was about to start earning my daily wage.

"Kind of messed up your vacation, didn't I, Chet?" the
Senator chuckled. I had done some investigatory work for
the Hartsell Committee in Bonn and Paris and, afterwards,
opted for a week in the sun. Senator Hartsell had suggested
Cannes.

"I never miss an opportunity to get rejuvenated by Caroline Thevenin when I'm on this side of the big pond," he had said in Paris. "That girl is incredible. There ought to be more like her—she keeps an old coot like me young."

Senator Hartsell had spent just one night at his rejuvenation cure. The next morning he'd looked like a pallbearer at his best friend's funeral. "Double dang it all to hell and back," he'd told me, "Caroline's heart just ain't in it." Then he had dumped Caroline's story in my lap. "Damned if I know what to do. Do you?"

"What does the lady want done?" I had asked, going for the bait.

Senator Hartsell had smiled his cagiest political smile. "Well now, son," he had suggested, setting the hook, "why don't you kind of ask her?"

Caroline Thevenin's green eyes and sultry voice had further hooked me, which is how and why I'd become her profligate kid sister's bodyguard. So far the body, which could compete with Caroline's though on a different scale, had needed no guarding.

"Here comes Huggins," I said at the café outside the Carlton. A red-haired, freckle-faced kid in a white sailor suit was approaching our table. He passed it striding jauntily on his way to the Carlton entrance.

"Rien ne va plus," intoned the croupier in a bored voice as, with a flick of the wrist, he sent the little ivory ball spinning on its way.

I stood about six feet from Gaby Thevenin at the big betting table. She had been playing eight and eleven steadily and stubbornly, a hundred new francs on each at a clip. She was watching, without any real interest, as the roulette wheel slowed down and the ball, whirling in the opposite direction, bounced into a slot.

"*Vingt et rouge,*" said the croupier disdainfully, as his sidekick raked in the chips. Gaby watched him as if he were a man raking leaves. She had dined with Huggins at a deluxe joint on the Croisette with, if anything, less enthusiasm. It was his money they spent at the restaurant, not her sister's.

"How much you drop?" Huggins asked in a loud whisper. He had a balloon glass of cognac in his hand, and he'd made the short trip to the casino bar several times before. He was more than a smidgen drunk and beginning to show it.

"I do not know," Gaby said. "Ten thousand new francs. Or perhaps twelve."

Huggins whistled. "Jesus, where'd you get it?"

They were speaking English, Huggins with the flat accents of Kansas, and Gaby as if she were translating French literally, word for word. She had very black hair and gray eyes and was wearing a white, low-cut off-the-shoulder gown that showed the smooth creamy curves of her throat and shoulders and thrust her breasts up and out pneumatically for inspection. I was not beyond inspecting her somewhat lecherously. She was really something.

"My sister is a famous artist," she said, answering Huggins' question. "You have heard of her? Caroline Thevenin?" She laughed, not quite bitterly.

"No," said Huggins.

"Permit me," said an old codger in a white dinner jacket standing on the other side of Gaby. She had been matching Huggins drink for drink, but seemed to be holding it better than the sailor was. She turned on the old guy slowly.

"Yes?"

"Did you say Caroline Thevenin?"

"Yes, I said Caroline Thevenin."

"And that she is an artist?"

"But yes," said Gaby sweetly.

The old guy laughed a couple of asthmatic wheezes. "Well, my dear," he said, "you of course have your name for it and I have mine."

Gaby turned back to Huggins. "With your permission," she said, still sweetly, plucking the balloon glass of cognac daintily out of his hand the way you pluck a flower off a stem. Then she hurled its contents in the old guy's face.

A pair of casino guards dressed like the customers in dinner jackets began to close in, but the old guy didn't make a fuss. He shrugged a very French shrug, wiped his face with a monogrammed silk handkerchief and bet on three numbers and black.

"*Rien ne va plus,*" said the croupier.

Huggins looked very pale under his freckles. "Let's get the hell out of here," he said.

Gaby shoved the rest of her chips out on the table. "*Pour le personnel,*" she said, and the chips disappeared down the trap.

After that, Huggins and his date went pub-crawling.

They wound up, at three a.m., in a dingy dive on a cobbled road that leads up past Super Cannes to the three Corniches. Their taxi driver, a beefy man with a heavy beard-shadow on his sullen face, was having a demi and playing dominoes at a corner table with the patron. They seemed to know each other, which should have set the alarm bells jangling inside my head. But by three a.m. it was a tired old head and I told myself, okay, so he suggested this dive for a nightcap and maybe the patron will give him a slice of the take. No reason to call out the Sûreté over it.

My own taxi driver was waiting outside. I'd shared his vigil in the dark and empty back streets of Cannes outside half a dozen other dubious bistros, but this time I'd decided to join the party—if discreetly, at a table of my own. Huggins had had a lot to drink and looked ready to pass out. Gaby, still matching him drink for drink, looked as fresh as the orange blossoms they cultivate for perfume in the hills above Cannes.

Gaby said something I didn't hear. Huggins said, in sad and well-lubricated disbelief, "You mean you're really not going to bed with me?"

The girl patted his hand, smiled and shook her head. "I am sleepy and would like you to take me back to the hotel." She added unnecessarily, "Where I will sleep—alone."

But first she headed for the W.C. Huggins watched her pretty butt, tight in the white dress, wag off in that direction. Then he sighed, told the patron, "We'll have one for the road, I guess," lurched to his feet, and went to the can himself.

Instead of filling their glasses at the table, the patron brought them behind the zinc bar and took a long time sloshing bad brandy into them. While this was going on, the taxi driver hunched his shoulders at one end of the bar and spoke softly and quickly into the telephone there.

The patron returned the glasses to the table. The taxi driver stuck a cigarette on his lower lip, lit it and waited. Gaby returned from the W.C. first. Nobody looked at her, though they were Frenchmen and she was well worth looking at.

I was wondering what they would have done after Gaby and Huggins drank their mickeys when the sailor returned to the table. Roll them? Then why the phone call?

Huggins sat down. "You sure?" he asked Gaby, raising his glass.

"You are nice, Harry. But yes, I am sure."

By then I was standing over their table. Gaby stared at me with some slight interest. Huggins had a hard job focusing.

"Bedtime," I said brightly and in a clear voice. I wanted the patron and the taxi driver to hear me. If I didn't have to mention the mickeys, there was still the chance I could get Gaby and her escort out of there without a fight. "I'm a friend of your sister's," I told Gaby. "Time we were heading back, Miss Thevenin. I've got a car outside, and we can drop your friend at the dock on the way."

Gaby's eyes narrowed with anger. "We have our own taxi," she said coldly. She snapped her fingers in front of my face. "I do not give this for a—friend of my sister."

"Look," I said, "I'll explain it to you outside, but—"

"I want no explanations from you. I want nothing to do with a watchdog sent by Caroline. The next time you are— together, tell her that."

"You've got it wrong," I said.

Huggins stood up unsteadily, the drink still in his hand. "You heard the lady. Beat it."

When I remained where I was, he took an awkward swipe at me with his free left hand. Half the brandy spilled out of the glass in his other hand. I shoved back, seemingly as awkwardly, and managed to spill the rest of it. In my follow-through I leaned a hard elbow on the table, dumping Gaby's glass. The brandy spread across the table, some of it dripping on her white gown.

"Clumsy oaf!" she cried, and Huggins took another poke at me. I let him have that one for free. It was a left hook

28

that had a lot of weight behind it, but it lacked snap. When it connected with the side of my jaw, I pretended to be more hurt than I was. I staggered back against the wall and stood there with my arms and head hanging.

Huggins' face hovered close. "Had enough, mate?" He was grinning, pleased with himself. Over his shoulder I saw the patron hand Gaby a dishtowel. She went to work on her gown. The taxi driver wasn't anywhere in sight. I heard the door slam.

When Huggins repeated his question, more truculently, I nodded but said, "It looks like you lost your cab."

Huggins grinned again, cockily. "We'll take yours, mate. Any objections?"

I said I had no objections. Huggins seemed disappointed. I'd been an easy target for a left hook, and he was spoiling for a fight. Maybe he thought showing her his prowess was one way into Gaby's bed.

He paid the patron and left with the girl. I dropped a few franc-notes on the table, but the patron stood between me and the door. He held a stick the size of a billy in his hand.

"A moment, monsieur," he said. "Spilling their drinks, that was no accident." I was twice his size, but he didn't look scared. Why should he? I had a glass jaw, didn't I?

"Out of my way, Frenchy," I said in English.

He brought the billy up and then down. I caught his wrist in mid-air and squeezed until he dropped the stick. Bending his arm back, I forced him to his knees. He made a squawking sound.

"Who'd the driver phone?"

No answer.

"Was it Duplesis?"

Same no answer. I bent the wrist further, and his face blanched.

"Oui. Oui, Duplesis. My arm, you will break it."

"What's his first name?"

". . . Raoul."

I dropped his arm and ran for the door. The early morning air was cool and smelled of the sea. I saw a Citroën 2CV parked at the curb, and both taxis. They were getting into the wrong one, their own Simca instead of the Peugeot that had brought me.

"Hold it," I shouted, going for the Magnum .44 in its clamshell holster under my left arm. By then I was three steps outside the door and running. I heard a whisper of sound to my right. The darkness split wide open, suddenly blazing brightly. I fell into it.

My own taxi driver was leaning over me anxiously in the back seat of the Peugeot. My head felt as if it had jumped off a cliff with no help from the rest of me.

"They gone?" I tried to sit up. The driver's face went around and around.

"Perhaps it would be better if monsieur did not try to talk." But the spinning face nodded. "They have gone."

"In the other cab?"

"Yes. I know a doctor who—"

"What about the Citroën?"

"A man came in it, just as they emerged from the bistro. It was this man who hit you. With a gun, I think."

I felt for my own Magnum. It was still holstered.

"Then he followed the other taxi, monsieur."

"How long ago?"

"Fifteen minutes. Certainly no more than twenty."

"Get me to a phone."

I leaned back, aware of movement, the rumble of tires over cobblestones, the sound of a motor. Then I was outside, staring at a street-corner phone booth and wondering what I was supposed to do there. The driver supplied a jeton. I dropped it in the slot and asked the operator for Caroline Thevenin's number.

"Allo?"

"Drum. Where's Duplesis live?"

"Raoul? But why?"

"He took the kid. I got sapped. Where's he live?"

I heard the sharp intake of her breath, but she let me have his address. It was a few blocks in from the Croisette on the way to Nice.

We made it in less than ten minutes.

Raoul Duplesis had his pad in the caretaker's cottage of a big estate. We had to drive up a gravel road lined on either side with palm trees. The Peugeot stopped a good hundred yards from where we saw light up ahead.

"Monsieur, you have your business, but I, I am only a taxi driver."

I peeled a wad of franc-notes from my wallet and gave them to him. "Right. You stay here. If you hear gunfire, go for the gendarmes. Fast. Okay?"

When he nodded, not liking it but agreeing to it, I went crunch, crunch, crunch up the gravel road. I was beginning to feel better. I might even be able to take another one of Huggins' creampuff punches without falling through the floor.

The wind was making a racket in the palm fronds which I hoped would cover the crunch of gravel under my shoes. When I got close, I saw two windows, the one to the left of the door shuttered, the one to the right open to the sea breeze. A small lamp was lit behind the translucent curtains in the right-hand window, but very bright light pierced the slits in the shutters of the other one. It was so bright that it could have come only from a photo-floodlamp. I scowled. Raoul Duplesis, pimp and artist, had turned into a photographer.

I paused at the open and dimly lit window, listening. Heard only clattering of the palm fronds and the thumping of heartbeat. I went over the sill with the Magnum in my hand.

It was a small bedroom. The bed linen was turned back and had been wrestled with recently by an uneasy sleeper, but the bed was unoccupied now. There was a door opposite the window, partially ajar, and a brilliantly lit hallway beyond it. I took off my shoes, left them on the window sill and padded like a second-story man into the hallway.

At the far end I saw a doorway. A man with his back to me was silhouetted there against the glare of floodlamps. He seemed the right size to be the driver of the Simca taxi. He had his arms outstretched, holding the doorjamb on either side. He never heard me come up behind him. Either I was cat-quiet or what was going on inside the room had all his attention.

Holding the Magnum butt first, ready to use it if he moved, I looked over his shoulder.

Three photo-floods lit the large room brighter than day. There was a big sofa on the far wall and on the sofa was draped of all things a leopard skin and on the leopard skin was draped Gaby Thevenin. Nothing at all was draped on her. Her small nude body was magnificently proportioned and on her face she wore a dopey smile that, when the pictures were taken, might make her look either drunk or satiated or both. She was not quite out, but she'd been drugged to the eyeballs.

A hand and an arm came into my range of vision. They

were attached to Raoul Duplesis, who was wearing white ducks and an Apache shirt. He lifted Gaby's chin. Her head lolled back, and he rearranged it for a good mug-shot. Then he tilted her torso so that the high, firm breasts were half in profile. Then he calmly arranged her left leg just so, showing pelvic shadow at the juncture of the sleek thighs.

What he had in mind was obvious. A few shots like that, a few prints shown to Gaby afterwards, the threat of showing them to the head mistress at the finishing school in Montreux, and Gaby would meekly hand over her sister's dough.

Duplesis stepped back, raised the 35 millimeter camera hanging from his neck, squinted through the viewer and took a picture.

"Mon Dieu," gasped the man in the doorway. "But she is really something."

What happened then happened very quickly. Duplesis turned to stare at his confederate irritably and saw me. I socked the taxi driver behind his right ear with the butt of the Magnum. He dropped to his knees and pitched forward on his face. Duplesis threw something at me. At first I thought it was the camera, but he wouldn't throw that, not with the film in it. What he threw was a lightmeter, and it caught my left temple solidly. I swayed and went down, the Magnum squirting from my fingers. Duplesis ran at me and over me, a gun in his own hand. I turned over, caught his ankle and spilled him. We both got up. He'd lost his gun too. He bolted through the hallway, into the bedroom and out the window. I was right behind him.

I brought him down twenty yards along the gravel road with a flying tackle. We rolled over and over. Once I tasted gravel in my mouth and once Duplesis almost got away, but then I was straddling him and banging his head back and forth with short, chopping blows from both fists until he stopped struggling.

"Get up. You will get up," a woman's voice said. A hand grasped my shoulder. It was a soft woman's hand, but not gentle. I got up and saw Caroline Thevenin. Ranged on either side of her with hostile looks on their pretty faces were three other beeznis girls.

"It is you," Caroline Thevenin said.

I pointed down at Duplesis. "Camera," I panted. "He was taking pictures of Gaby." I explained why, and she called him some choice names in French. Her sidekicks chimed in while Caroline Thevenin got the camera, opened it and exposed the film.

"And Gaby?" she asked, suddenly alarmed.

"Inside. Doped but otherwise all right." All of a sudden I had an idea. "And you'll find a buddy of Duplesis'. Sapped."

"*I* will find? And you?"

I gave her the Magnum. "The guy on the floor ought to keep. But if he doesn't, you'll have this."

"I don't understand."

"Gaby," I said. "Get her out of there, take her home, feed her plenty of coffee and call a doctor. When she comes to, tell her I called you. Just called you. You and your friends did the rest. If you can get her to believe that, she might have a change of heart."

Caroline Thevenin nodded, smiling, and spoke rapidly in French. Then all four beeznis girls strode, very beeznis-like, toward the cottage.

I waited among the palms until they returned. Two of them were carrying Gaby, wrapped in the leopard skin. By that time Duplesis had climbed unsteadily to his feet.

"You will leave Cannes in the morning," Caroline told

him. She said something else. I didn't hear it, but whatever it was, it was a man-sized threat. Duplesis looked at her, and at the Magnum in her hand. "You will never come back," she said.

He nodded and scurried back toward the cottage with his tail between his legs.

I was sitting at a café on the Croisette with Caroline Thevenin the next day.

"Want another?" I said.

She looked down at her empty glass. She'd already told me that Huggins had been found wandering dazed on the Croisette. He'd been slugged and left at the side of the road.

"And Gaby," she'd said with a smile over our first drink, "Gaby gives me back the money, and once again it is in a joint account. She does not think beeznis girls are so bad, thanks to you."

Now Caroline held her hand over the empty glass. "No. No more drink now. The afternoon grows late, and I must get ready."

"Ready?"

She gave me the full, dazzling Caroline Thevenin smile. "Why, yes. For tonight."

"Tonight?"

"Tonight I will—pay you."

Chester Drum Takes Over

"Signor Drum? Signor Chester Drum?"

I looked at my watch. One in the morning and a small bit. I had drifted off in bed with a book face down on my chest. A stiff wind was lashing cold March rain against the windowpanes.

"Or a sleepy facsimile thereof," I said into the phone.

"Prego, signore?"

"Yeah, this is Drum."

"One moment, please," she said in English. "For Domodossola, Italy."

I lit a cigarette and jacked myself partially upright. The book slid off my chest and thumped on the floor. Well, I thought, at least they'd come back as far as Domodossola. It was better than I had expected, with Vinnie Hatcher running things, Domodossola was the first town of any size on the Italian side of the border, down over the Simplon Pass. It was four hours from the bedroom of my apartment if you drove like hell. I thought there was a pretty good chance I would be driving like hell.

"Mr. Drum?" Another girl's voice, not the operator. The connection was sharp. She could have been calling from a phone right here in Geneva.

I admitted my identity again.

"This is Miss Sabra. We're in Domodossola, on the way back."

"I know where you are," I said. "What's up?"

"Trouble. The worst kind of trouble." Her voice was twanging like a taut bowstring. She was all keyed up for a scream.

"You mean the deal's off?"

"No. We left Rome this morning and got this far. The Grand Hotel in Domodossola. We had an auto accident. Mr. Shalom couldn't go on. You knew about his heart."

I smiled a little at the corny noms de guerre. Miss Native-of-Israel and Mr. Peace.

"And of course you can't risk a doctor, is that it?"

"A doctor wouldn't help," Miss Sabra said flatly. "He's dead. He died a half hour ago. What are we going to do?"

I thought for a minute, wondering why Vinnie Hatcher couldn't tell her what to do. He was right there. "Do corpses give you the willies?" I asked.

"I am a lieutenant in the Israeli Army," Miss Sabra said. "I'm not squeamish."

"Okay. Get him in the car. You sit in back with him, like he's sleeping, and Hatcher drives you back over the Simplon into Switzerland. What's the problem? They don't make a big thing about the frontier between Italy and Switzerland. You'll be in Geneva before breakfast."

"Mr. Hatcher smashed the car. That's why we stopped here. You'd better speak to him."

"The next voice you hear . . ." a man's voice said after a slight pause. "Hi, Chet old buddy."

He sounded pretty drunk.

"Hello, Vinnie," I said. "Can you rent a car?"

"In the middle of the night in Domowhat's-its-name? We need you, old buddy. With chariot."

"How'd it happen?"

"A guy passed me coming into town and I kind of wandered into a ditch. Busted the front axle."

"I should be there in four hours," I said. "Lay off the sauce, will you?"

"Who pays for the damages?" Vinnie whined. "I don't have that kind of insurance."

"We'll discuss it with Miss Sabra later. Just lay off the sauce."

"I am cold stone disgusting sober," Vinnie said.

He wasn't, but I told him, "Stay that way. Tell Miss Sabra four hours. I'll see you."

I hung up and dressed in a hurry. I needed a shave, but no one was going to stop me at the border, either coming or going, for that. I loaded five cartridges into the Smith & Wesson Magnum .44 and shoved it into my raincoat pocket. The car that forced Vinnie into the ditch could have been driven by an Arab.

Two packs of cigarettes, and no time for coffee. Forty minutes on the autoroute to Lausanne and then three hours and some to reach and cross the Simplon Pass into Italy. I went downstairs and ran a couple of blocks through the rain to where I'd parked my VW in front of the big Gothic church. I always park there, and they never ticket the heap. Maybe they figure I'm clergy, which is a laugh in my line of work. I'm a private detective, same as Vinnie Hatcher. Only most of the time I don't drink on the job.

Hatcher came to the door of one of the rooms they'd taken in the hotel in Domodossola with a half-empty bottle of Strega in his hand.

"Four hours right on the nose," he said.

39

"I told you to lay off the sauce. Where are they?"

"Room 207. Right down the hall. It raining or snowing on the pass?"

"Raining, but that could change."

Hatcher raised the bottle toward his face. I slapped it out of his hand, caught it in mid-air, and took it past him into the bathroom and poured it out in the sink. He got a big hand on my shoulder while I was doing that, and I turned and slapped it away as I had slapped the bottle out of his hand.

We looked at each other, a full half minute of it. Then Hatcher shrugged and smiled. "Okay, boss," he said, mockingly. "Anything you say, boss."

"Be ready to roll in ten minutes"

"I'm ready right now."

Vinnie Hatcher was a big man, palely blond and freckled, with washed-out blue eyes and a face dames would find attractive, complete with broken nose and a mean prow of a jaw. He was maybe 35 or 40. He had been a captain in Uncle's Army, running the counterintelligence show at a base in Germany until they'd given him the boot for such as falling down dead drunk on the floor of the officers' open mess about five times too often. He'd drifted into private work in Switzerland, as more than one American had, including me, because American corporations with European headquarters in Geneva, Zug, and Lausanne pay pretty good rates for private snooping. Word was on the Rue de Rhone that his drinking problem was getting worse. He'd probably needed Miss Sabra's assignment for eating money. Or drinking money.

Miss Sabra did not open the door to my knock. "Who is it?" she said.

"Drum."

That wasn't enough for her to be sure of the voice. "Say something else."

"I just poured half a bottle of Strega down the sink in Hatcher's room."

She opened the door. Black raincoat, unbuttoned, and the butt of a cigarette clenched nervously between thumb and forefinger. A high-cheekboned face and the dark eyes enormous, but looking tired and defeated now. Short black hair, cut so she'd have no trouble with it under an Israeli Army helmet, if dames in the Israeli Army wear helmets. She was 25, give or take a year or two, pretty, and stacked in an intriguing lean and hungry way. I didn't know her real name.

She shut the door behind me. We were in a small sitting room dominated by one of those wild Venetian glass chandeliers in about fourteen colors.

"Where is he?"

"On the bed."

I went inside and pulled the sheet back. He was a small bald man in his sixties, wearing gaudy pajamas. Face gray now, grayer than a face ever gets unless it belongs to a dead man. I raised one arm by the wrist. Miss Sabra started to say something, then changed her mind. I let the arm drop. Stiff, and it would get stiffer. Rigor mortis was just setting in.

"Where are his clothes?"

She pointed to the armoire. I went over and got his trousers and wrestled him into them. Shoes on the bare feet and an ancient, not-quite-threadbare trenchcoat finished the job. I threw the rest of his stuff into his canvas suitcase.

"What kind of passports are you carrying?"

"American," she said, looking at me defiantly.

"They any good?"

41

"They got us across the border once."

"Stamped?"

"No."

They rarely stamp passports at border crossings in Western Europe these days. All they want is a quick look at the date.

"Deal all set?" I asked.

"Yes and no."

"You'll burn your hand," I told her.

She looked down at the butt of the cigarette and crushed it out in an ashtray. Her fingers were stained yellow from the tar. She lit another cigarette.

"He was nervous," she told me. "It's against the law, where he gets the parts, to sell arms to Israel. Of course the fact that everyone is selling arms to the Arabs so they can have another try at—"

"Skip the politics," I said.

"You don't like us, do you?"

"Miss Sabra," I said, "none of my best friends are Arabs."

"Why are you angry with me then?"

"Because you hired me and I set the deal up for you and then you fired me and got Hatcher."

"It was a mistake. I admit that."

"Okay, forget it. I'll get you back across the border. How'd it go with Mr. Milo?"

Milo was an expatriate Greek dealer in jet-plane parts. He had a police permit to stay in Italy. At the moment he could go nowhere else, which meant that he'd had to see Miss Sabra and Mr. Shalom in Italy, if they arranged a deal for the sale of military hardware the Israelis needed to keep their Air Force flying. Prove that Miss Sabra and Mr. Shalom had been in Italy, and Milo might find himself cut off at the source of supply, which would put him out of business. He sold for cash on the barrelhead and he didn't care who he sold to as long as his profits ran in the neighborhood of 200 percent. But the possibly senile, possibly paranoid president of the country of origin was mad at Israel. If it could be proved that Milo sold to Miss Sabra and Mr. Shalom he'd have to look around for another commodity, such as guano or eiderdown feathers.

"Mr. Milo was worried because he was our obvious contact," Miss Sabra said.

"You paid in advance?"

"We had to."

"Check?"

"Cash. A great deal of money. The hardware will be shipped from Naples to Haifa in a Greek freighter later this week, disguised as agricultural equipment."

"With the customs people paid to look the other way."

"Of course. But if it is learned that Mr. Shalom and I were in Italy, the deal is off. That's what Milo said."

"We'll cross over in a few hours. What are you worried about?"

"We have to cross the frontier with a dead man."

Miss Sabra's face crumpled suddenly, and she was crying. She looked very young and defenseless. I felt awkward.

"I'll get you across," I said. "He'll be in his own bed in Geneva in the morning. You'll have a death certificate saying he died in Switzerland. Take it easy."

"You don't understand."

"Pull yourself together," I said harshly. I wanted to get going.

She went on crying. Her voice keened against the damp lapel of my raincoat. "My parents died during the first war

43

with the Arabs, when I was a baby. He—he was like my own father."

I patted her shoulder stiffly, not knowing what else to do. I wished we were in the car and driving up the Simplon Pass.

There was a knock at the door. "What're you guys waiting for?" Vinnie Hatcher called.

The first part of it was easy because the Grand Hotel in Domodossola was grand in name only and because it was still this side of six in the morning.

I went down the service stairs and found the back way out through the kitchen. It was dark and smelled of garlic and olive oil. I ducked outside and around the block through the heavy rain to drive the VW behind the hotel, then took a peek into the lobby before returning to Hatcher and Miss Sabra. An old night porter in a black uniform with the crossed keys of his calling on the left lapel was snoozing in his lodge. The reception desk was deserted. Satisfied, I returned to the service stairs and climbed them.

The door was open and Hatcher's head appeared in it.

"Miss Sabra pays your bill," I said. "You and me take him down the back way and put him in the car. Then you go back for the bags."

Hatcher looked at me. "Just like that?"

"There's nobody here but us chickens."

Miss Sabra went away before we tackled the body. Even in the few minutes that had passed, it had grown stiffer. We propped it between us like a drunk, an arm on my shoulder and an arm on Hatcher's shoulder. The legs trailed like logs. The shoes dug a furrow in the worn rug in the hall.

Hatcher began to pant right away. All that drinking had

taken his wind. "He weighs a damn ton."

"It's just two flights down."

We got him down the stairs and through the kitchen and to the car. Hatcher kept him from falling while I opened the door and pulled the back of the seat forward. Then I went around to the other side and got in, and Hatcher pushed and I pulled, and pretty soon Mr. Shalom was sitting in one corner in back like a wooden Indian.

"Get the bags," I told Hatcher. "I'll drive around front."

"Will he fall?"

"I don't think so, but what if he does?"

"Sure, just us chickens."

Hatcher took off and I chauffeured Mr. Shalom to the front of the hotel, lit a cigarette, and waited. The body remained seated in an upright position. I kept the motor going and watched the windshield wipers thumping back and forth. It was still dark.

Miss Sabra ran out. "The porter," she said. "He insisted on getting our bags."

Hatcher and the porter came out together. The old man was burdened down with Mr. Shalom's canvas bag, an overnighter for Miss Sabra, and Hatcher's flight bag. I hoped they would all fit under the hood of the VW. Otherwise we'd have to move the body to get at the luggage space behind the rear seat.

I yanked the hood release and got out and opened the snout of the VW. Canvas bag first, and then the overnighter. I stuffed Hatcher's little grip in and slammed the hood down. It wouldn't lock. I got the flight bag out and tried again. The lock caught. Miss Sabra had climbed into the back of the car with the dead man. I dropped the flight bag at her feet and got behind the wheel alongside Hatcher.

"Buon viaggio," the man said. Hatcher gave him some change.

"Arrivederci," I said.

I started driving.

"A thousand francs," Hatcher said. "Or maybe fifteen hundred."

"For what?"

"To fix my car."

"Work it out with Miss Sabra after we get to Geneva."

"She has the dough on her. I want it now."

"I'll give you the money later," Miss Sabra said.

"No. I want it now."

I heard her sigh from the back seat and her hand appeared with money. Hatcher took it and her hand went away.

The road starts climbing as soon as it leaves Domodossola. You turn left and there is a steep rise and then a switchback and you see the few early-morning lights of the town as you turn and start climbing again. *Sempione*, the sign says. Sempione is Simplon in Italian, and, unless you want to drive through the tunnel of the Grand St. Bernard, where the border guards are snug and dry and might give you more of a once-over, it is the way to go.

I took the Italian side of the pass in second gear. The road was potholed after the winter snows and the early spring thaw. We rumbled and bounced along, reasonably warm with the heater and defroster going. I was chain-smoking and wished I had a drink. That was nothing compared to what Vinnie Hatcher was wishing. He couldn't keep his hands still. The sweat stood out like droplets of oil on his face. He was staring straight ahead and seeing nothing and blinking rapidly.

I glanced at the rearview mirror every now and then. Miss Sabra sat very still, not quite in contact with the dead man but close enough to keep him from falling across the seat if a turn dislodged him. Her eyes were shut.

Ten kilometers this side of the frontier the night dark gave way to a dirty gray dawn. The rain had changed to snow, which seemed to fall from a point ahead of our head-lights and move horizontally toward us and around us. There was snow on the high crags to our right and snow falling into the still-dark chasm to our left. We turned into a long narrow valley that followed a riverbed and then there were patches of snow on the road, and soon more snow than pot-holed frost-buckled blacktop, and finally all snow, fresh powder a couple of inches deep and ours the only tire tracks on it.

"You got chains?" Hatcher asked.

"Yeah, but we ought to be able to make it without them."

"You're the jock."

With the weight of its engine in back over the rear wheels, the VW surged forward. A low cloud hung over the road and enveloped us like thick white smoke. I took my foot off the gas pedal to slow down and stared through the windshield. I could see almost nothing. The road curved to the right gradually and then very sharply.

I turned the wheel hard and we fishtailed a few yards and found traction again. I heard movement in the back seat and took a quick glance at the rearview mirror. The wooden Indian had fallen across Miss Sabra's lap. She was trying to right him and biting down hard on her lip, her eyes tight shut.

"He's so cold," she said. "He's so cold."

★ ★ ★ ★ ★

They gave us no trouble on the Italian side of the frontier. A man poked his head out of the shack and said in very bad French that I had to hand in my gasoline carnet. That was no problem, since they had given it to me on the way down from Switzerland. It entitled me to a tourist rake-off at gas stations in Italy. I handed it over and we were waved ahead. Nobody even looked at our passports.

We drove for a while through the high timberline no-man's-land between countries. I threw away my empty pack of cigarettes and started a fresh one.

Ahead a big Swiss flag was flapping in the wind and snow. The road widened into four lanes and went under a big roof on stanchions and I followed a yellow arrow to the control point. A tall Swiss border guard in a loden cape and a big campaign hat came out as I rolled the window down.

"Grüss Gott."

"Grüss Gott."

He had taken a look at the license plate first. I didn't like that. If you have a foreign plate, they will glance at your passports, ask if you have anything to declare and expect a negative answer, look at your car papers, and send you on your way. If you have a Swiss plate they will examine your luggage. If you have, as I had, a Swiss "Z" plate—the "Z" standing for temporary resident—it could go either way.

"Passports."

I had already collected the passports. All four, including the two ersatz ones, were American. That was good. Four people in a car in the wee hours of the morning ought to be from the same country.

He held the passports under the brim of the big campaign hat and flipped through them. He handed them back.

"Green card," he said in French.

48

That was to establish the fact that I was carrying the right kind of international insurance for the car. I gave him the little green booklet and he flipped through that, too, and found the date and nodded and returned it to me.

"Have you anything to declare?" he said. He sounded bored. I was glad he was bored.

I was about to say no.

Vinnie Hatcher beat me to the punch. He said, "Oui, monsieur."

I had my hand in the pocket of my raincoat and the butt of the gun in it and the muzzle against Hatcher's thigh before anyone said anything else. What happened next would depend on how scared Hatcher was. If he was calm enough to realize that the gun would do me as much good here as an extra pack of cigarettes, we were all through.

"Yes?" the border guard said, in English this time and a little less bored.

Hatcher stared past me at the blur of a face under the campaign hat. He looked on the point of speaking. A muscle in his cheek twitched. I jabbed the gun against him hard, wondering what the hell I could declare now that Hatcher had opened his mouth—assuming he would say nothing else.

"Yes?" the border guard said again. There was a light in the window of the office behind him and a few other guards sitting around a table, probably waiting for their buddy to return to their card game.

"Wrist watch," I said, poking my left hand through the rolled down window and showing him the watch.

He looked at it. "But it is Swiss."

"Bought it in Italy."

He gave me the sort of look that said what he thought of

anyone foolish enough to buy a Swiss watch in Italy and pay the duty both places.

"You have a receipt?"

"I lost it."

"How much did it cost?"

"Twenty-five thousand lire," I said. "They told me it was a bargain."

He looked at the watch. He hadn't asked me to take it off yet. If he did, I was all through because then I'd have to take my hand off the gun. Even if he didn't, I was all through if he kept us much longer because Hatcher, even if he was scared blue, as apparently he was, would begin to get the idea I was helpless.

"Twenty-five thousand lire," he said. "Then in that case there is no duty."

Twenty-five thousand lire is less than fifty bucks.

"Anything else?"

"No," I said, fast.

The campaign hat moved toward me and looked past me at Hatcher and then moved to the side back window for a look at Miss Sabra and Mr. Shalom. The face under the campaign hat grinned. "Sleeping," it said.

"We had a long drive."

"From where?"

"Rome," I said.

"Welcome back to Switzerland."

A big hand touched the brim of the campaign hat, and I put the car in gear and we were in Switzerland.

I drove maybe five kilometers through the snow, past earth-moving equipment and steamrollers and a sign that said to watch out for road work, though the workers hadn't arrived on the job and probably wouldn't today now that it was snowing. I found an overlook with a fine view of a dense cloud and pulled off the road.

Hatcher gave me a quick frightened look. "What are you going to do?"

"Talk," I said.

"So talk."

"You insisted on payment to repair your car in advance," I said. "But you didn't stay back there to get it done. That should have told me."

"Told you what?"

"Not to mention driving into a ditch in the first place. I ought to break your back."

Hatcher just licked his lips.

"You were going to declare a dead man, weren't you? That's why you came with us. That would have been one way of proving Mr. Shalom was in Italy."

"I didn't."

"Get out of the car," I said. "And don't try to make a run for it."

He got out and I got out with the gun in my hand. I frisked him and found his own hardware. It was a Luger. Something small and hard was in his raincoat pocket with it. I jammed the Luger into my own pocket.

"Who are you working for?"

"A guy," he said. "A guy in Geneva."

I hit him.

"I swear I don't know his name. He wanted the deal stopped, that's all. Like by accident, without any involvement on his part. You know?"

"No, tell me."

"An accident, so the cops would come. But then Shalom got sick so I figured that would be even better. He had a bad heart. He'd need a doctor."

"Only he died."

"And the girl called you."

By then he was over his fright and smirking. He still had us, short of my killing him. All he had to do was reach a phone and say a dead man had just been transported across the border. He could even wait until we reached Geneva to do that and someone would check with the frontier station where the guard would remember the old man sleeping in the back of the car, and it might not be enough to prove anything in a court of law but it would be enough to make Mr. Milo call the deal off. Not as good as the accident in Domodossola, not as good as a dead man at the border itself, but plenty good enough if Milo was as nervous as Miss Sabra thought he was.

I wasn't in this deep enough to kill Hatcher. I had just been hired to do a job. I felt sorry for Miss Sabra, but there was nothing I could do.

"Is it going to be all right?" Miss Sabra asked from the car.

I didn't know what to tell her.

"Do we get to drive on now, boss?" Vinnie Hatcher smirked.

On one of those hunches that are all you have left I said, "Let's see what else is in your pocket, Vinnie."

"There's nothing," he said.

But he stood still while I reached into his pocket again and found the small hard something and withdrew it.

That left me holding a small unlabeled pill bottle in my hand—dark green glass, a plastic screw-on cap, and a single pill inside.

I unscrewed the cap one-handed and held the bottle out toward Vinnie. "Take it," I said.

"Are you nuts or something?"

"Take it, I said."

He shook his head.

"What is it?"

"Pep pill, for when I'm not drinking."

"You're not drinking now. Take it."

He stood there in the snow, looking at the bottle and the single pill. He shook his head.

"What kind of heart disease did Mr. Shalom have?" I asked the girl.

"Angina."

"He have pills for it?"

"A glycerin compound. You put them under the tongue. They always worked before."

"You have them?"

"Yes."

"Let's have a look."

She handed a pill bottle out the front window on the driver's side, a bottle the same size as Hatcher's but amber instead of green. There was a label from the Pharmacie Principale in Geneva.

Most of the time, if you can pop a pill in your mouth, angina is a painful but not a fatal disease.

The little white pills were the same size as Vinnie's.

"Could he have switched them on you?" I asked.

"I—yes!" Her dark eyes narrowed. "I was nervous. I dropped the bottle. He picked it up and opened it for me. He could have had his own pill ready."

"That's crazy," Vinnie Hatcher said.

He said nothing else for about ten seconds. Then he said, "What the hell, I'll take it, if it will convince you. I didn't kill the old man."

He took the green bottle. He swallowed the pill.

"See?" he laughed. "Quick-acting poison. I'm dead only don't know it."

"It probably is a pep pill," I said. "Not giving Mr. Shalom his own medicine was enough to kill him. If he couldn't be found in Italy alive, you decided he'd be found there dead."

Hatcher said nothing.

"Didn't you?"

Hatcher shrugged. "You'd have a rough time proving that in court. Can we get in out the hot sun now, boss?"

He still had us, and he still knew it.

Miss Sabra asked, in a very calm voice, "Are you quite sure that was the way it happened, Mr. Drum?"

"I'm sure, but I can't prove it."

In the same calm voice: "Would you stand aside, please, Mr. Drum?"

I looked at her. She had a small handgun. Later, before I disposed of it, I learned it was a Berretta.

Vinnie Hatcher looked where I was looking. He turned and started running, and the small handgun made a flat sound and spurted orange, just once. Hatcher kept running three more steps to the edge of the overlook, out of control now and either hit or not hit, and struck the guard rail with his legs and went on over headfirst, soaring for an instant, completely clear of the ground, and then down into the low cloud and gone in it. A few seconds later we heard him striking rock and bouncing and striking again out of sight far below.

I didn't say anything. I got back into the car and shut the door on the other side and on my side. I started driving. We went through a short tunnel and met our first traffic coming up the other way, a rattling little 2CV Citroën. It went past and there was a water runoff from the roof of the tunnel and we were through that and out the other side. It was snowing harder.

Finally Miss Sabra said, "Are you going to report this?"

"Give me your gun," I said.

She gave it to me, and I shoved it in my pocket. She didn't ask any more questions.

It was like the pep pill all over again. If she hadn't hit him, he'd have gone over the guardrail under his own steam. No matter what it said in the papers in a week or a month, after they found the body.

"You sure are a lousy shot," I said. "You missed him by a mile."

Wanted—Dead and Alive

I was drinking an ouzo-and-water on the aft deck of the car-ferry *Hellas* and watching the lights of Brindisi fade into the Mediterranean darkness when a stocky figure came toward me, lurching slightly with the ship's roll.

"What the hell are you doing aboard?" I said.

"Did I ever say I wouldn't be?"

"Wife see you yet?" I asked.

"In the lounge. A real touching scene. She was looped. As usual."

That made two of them, I thought. Sebastian Spinner's lurch hadn't been all ship's roll. He was gripping the rail hard with both hands to keep the deck from tilting.

"What about the hired gun?"

"Christ, no. If he's aboard, I haven't made him." Spinner sighed ruefully. "Provided I remember what the sonofabitch looks like." A foghorn tooted in the bay, sounding derisive.

Sebastian Spinner was producer-director of *Lucrezia Borgia*, which was being filmed on location all over Italy. Twenty-five million bucks, not Spinner's money, had been pumped into it so far. The studio was near bankruptcy; the picture still wasn't finished and never would be if Spinner's wife kept wandering all over the map, with or without whatever stud struck her fancy at the moment.

It seemed even less likely that the picture would be finished if Spinner's wife, Carole Frazer, who was playing La Lucrezia, wound up dead on the twenty-six hour steamer trip between Brindisi, Italy, and Patras, Greece. Neither Spinner nor I would make book that she wouldn't. Spinner had hired a Neapolitan killer to hit her in the head.

I'd first bumped into Sebastian Spinner in Rome a couple of weeks ago, when I'd blown myself to a vacation after the Axel Spade case. It was a party, the kind they throw in Cinecita or Hollywood, where somebody dressed to the earlobes always gets tossed into the pool, where an unknown starlet named Simonetta or something like that peels to the waist to prove her astonishing abundancy and where guys like me, if their luck is running bad, get hired by guys like Sebastian Spinner.

"Drum?" he'd said, scooping a couple of martinis off a tray and handing me one. "That wouldn't be Chester Drum?"

I admitted my guilt.

"The private dick?"

"Not very private if you keep shouting it like that."

Spinner laughed phlegmily and clamped my arm with a small, soft hand. He was a stocky bald man, and his face and pate were shiny with sweat.

"They say you're the best in the business," he said, and added modestly, "I'm the best in my business. Sweetheart, if we get together it could be you're gonna save my life. Though sometimes I ain't so sure it's worth the trouble." Spinner was alternately egotistic and self-deprecating, a typical Hollywood type who made me glad I usually worked out of Washington, D.C.

He steered me outside and we drove off into the hot Roman night in his low-slung Facel Vega. He said nothing until we'd parked on the Via Veneto and took a curbside table at Doney's.

"Somebody's gonna hit my wife in the head," he said then. "Christ, they kill her and there goes *Lucrezia Borgia*, not to mention twenty-five million bucks of Worldwide Studio money. If that happens, they wouldn't give me a job sweeping out the latrine of the second unit of one of those goddamn grade Z epics made with the Yugoslav army."

I asked: "How do you know somebody's going to kill your wife, Mr. Spinner?" I asked it politely, the way you do with a loquacious drunk.

Spinner recognized my point of view and didn't like it. "On account of I hired the guy," he said indignantly, and then I was all ears.

A few days before, while they were shooting on location outside of Naples, Spinner had gone up to Vomero on a bat. You couldn't blame him. His wife was sleeping with Philip Stanley, her leading man, and everybody knew it.

"I was sitting in this trattoria in Vomero," Spinner said. "I was gassed to the eyeballs, and all of a sudden it was like that Hitchcock gimmick where two guys meet on a train and . . . You remember the film, don't you?

"Well, I met me a mafiosa type and we started in to talking. I ain't usually the jealous type. *Merde,* I been married six times, what's an extracurricular roll in the hay more or less matter, it's a free country, I get yens too. But Carole's been spreading it around, and her middle name ain't exactly discretion and this Stanley bastard practically rubs my face in it. No dame's gonna make Sebastian Spinner wear neon horns.

"That's what I tell the mafioso type, and he nods his head and listens, and pretty soon, like, I'm foaming at the mouth, and finally I shut up. That's when he says, 'For five thousand dollars American I will kill her,' and that's when I say, 'For five thousand dollars American you got yourself a deal,' and the swifty cons me into giving him half of it in advance and walks out of the trattoria after I tell him when the best time to hit Carole in the head would be."

"When would it be?"

He told me about her upcoming trip to Greece. "On the boat," he said. "They got a ferry that runs from Brindisi to Patras. Carole hates to fly."

I watched the traffic swarming along the Via Veneto and being swallowed by the Pinciana Gate. "I take it you sort of changed your mind."

"You bet your sweet life I did. What goes with *Lucrezia Borgia* if Carole gets hit in the head? You tell me that, pal."

"Okay, call your gun off. What do you need me for?"

"I can't call him off."

That got a raised eyebrow from me.

"I don't even know his goddamn name, I'm not sure what trattoria in Vomero it was and he had a face like all the other little swifties who'll sell their own sisters for a thousand lira in Naples. Kee-rist, I need a drink."

"Maybe he just let you talk yourself out of twenty-five hundred bucks," I suggested. "What makes you so sure he intends to go through with it?"

"Nothing, sweetheart," Spinner admitted with a slightly sick smile. "Nothing at all. Maybe he *is* laughing up his sleeve down in Vomero. Don't you think I know that?"

"So?"

"So maybe on the other hand he ain't."

I went down to Naples for a few days and prowled all the

dives in Vomero without any luck. I got to Brindisi half an hour before the *Hellas* sailed. Now, on the aft deck of the car-ferry, I told Spinner:

"Look. Sober up and stay that way. I'll watch your wife, but if the guy's aboard maybe you'll recognize him."

A voice, not Spinner's, said: "I say, old man, don't you feel a bit of a horse's ass following us?" and a man joined us at the rail. In the light streaming through the portholes of the lounge, I recognized Philip Stanley. He was a big guy, about my size, in a navy blue blazer with gold buttons and a pair of gray flannel slacks. He had a hard, handsome face going a little heavy in the jowls, and his eyes held that look of smug, inbred self-satisfaction they seem to give out along with the diplomas at Eton and Harrow and the other public schools that turn out the members of the British Establishment. Actually, he had grown up in a Birmingham slum, and it had taken him all his life to cultivate that look of supercilious disdain.

"Sweetheart," Spinner said, "I never dreamed Carole would pack her playmate for the trip. Maybe she's slipping if she don't think she can do better in Greece. A lot better. They're pretty torrid in the sack, those Greeks, what I hear."

Stanley laughed. "Better than you she can always do, at any rate. But tell me, old boy," he asked dryly, "would you be speaking about those Greeks from personal experience?"

Spinner took a drunken, clumsy swing at him. Evading it easily, Stanley grabbed his wrist and levered the plump man a few staggering steps along the deck before letting go. Spinner fell down and leaped up again as if he had springs in his shoes.

I got between them, and Spinner said gratefully, "Hold me back, Drum. Hold me back, sweetheart. Every mark I put on his face'll cost Worldwide half a million bucks."

Stanley snickered, and neatly turned his broad back, and walked away along the rail. Spinner shuffled toward the door to the lounge. I lit a cigarette and followed the Englishman. A few more minutes away from Carole Frazer wouldn't hurt. Spinner would have the sense to keep an eye on her until I showed up.

"Got a few minutes?" I asked Stanley.

"Twenty-five hours to Patras," he said, leaning both elbows on the rail and staring down at the frothy white wake. "But just who are you?"

"Drum," I said crisply. "Worldwide front office."

"I never heard of you."

"You're not supposed to—until I land on you with both feet."

"Meaning?"

"Meaning if I can't get some assurance *Lucrezia*'ll be in the cutter's room inside of six months, the front office is half-inclined to chuck the whole works."

Stanley straightened and turned suddenly in my direction. He looked worried. "Are you serious?"

"Sure I am," I said. Though with his rugged Anglo-Saxon good looks Philip Stanley was about as far from a hungry little Neapolitan killer as you could get, the more I knew about the principals in the case the better I'd be able to handle whatever developed. "The director's been throwing a bat all the way from the Italian Alps to Calabria, and between takes the stars go hopscotching from bed to bed all over Europe. You think maybe Worldwide's wild about that?"

"I'll admit I've slept with Carole," Stanley said, "but—"

"Admit it? Hell, everybody knows it."

"But I had hoped to keep her somewhat closer to the set by doing it."

"That's what I like about you box-office big-shots. Your modesty."

"I am afraid you misunderstand," Stanley said, and a tortoni wouldn't have melted in his mouth. "Naturally I've gotten a certain amount of publicity as Carole's leading man, but I am not, as you put it, a box-office big-shot. I will be, if we ever finish *Lucrezia*. Otherwise I'll just be another not-quite-matinee-idol knocking at the back doors of Cinecittà for work."

Him and Sebastian Spinner both, I thought. The only one who didn't seem to mind was Carole Frazer.

"Damn it all," he went on, "why'd you think we're languishing a year behind schedule? Because I've slept with Carole? That's nonsense, old boy. I don't have to tell you the woman's a nymphomaniac, if a lovely one. But if it isn't me then it's someone else, and that's only the half of it. Carole was rushed to London three times for emergency medical treatment, and each time, as I also don't have to tell you, it was some psychosomatic foolishness. Why, she's only appeared in half a dozen crucial scenes so far, close-ups, and virtually every far shot's been done by her stand-in. We have a great deal more footage of the stand-in than we do of Carole. If you doubt my word, ask Spinner. And Dawn Sibley's no mere double, she's a fine actress in her own right. Sometimes I think it would be simpler all around if we were to chuck Carole and let Dawn do *Lucrezia*. I don't stand alone. Ask around, old boy, and then tell *that* to the front office. Most of us want to see this film completed as much as you do. But unfortunately it was conceived as a vehicle for Carole."

After that long tirade, he had nothing else to say. I

watched him walk across the deck and inside. For a little while I listened to the rush of water under the hull-plates. Brindisi was a faint and distant line of light. Overhead a gull, nailed in silhouette against the starlit sky, screamed and flapped its wings once. When I looked again, only a glow remained on the horizon in the direction of Brindisi. I carried my empty ouzo glass to the lounge.

At a big table near the bar, Carole Frazer was holding court. She was wearing black tapered slacks and a paisley blouse that fondled her high breasts without hugging them lasciviously. A casual lock of her blond hair had fallen across her right eye and right cheek. A languid smile that did not quite part her moist red lips was the reward her suitors got.

There were about a dozen of them, most of them dark and slender Italians and Greeks with intense eyes and gleaming teeth. Any one of them, I realized, could have been Sebastian Spinner's little swifty from Vomero. He'd be as easy to single out as a fingerling in a fish hatchery.

"Ouzo," I told the barman, and he poured the anise-flavored liquor and added enough water to turn it milky. His hand was not steady on the carafe, and he sloshed a little water on the bar. In the world that Hollywood made, Carole Frazer was an institution. He was staring at her bug-eyed. I couldn't blame him. Seen close, her blond beauty was really scorching.

Spinner sat alone at a table nearby. He was drinking scotch and darting small, anxious glances at the men clustered around his wife. Each time he'd shake his head slightly, and his eyes would flick on like a snake's tongue. He had trouble keeping his head off the table. He was very drunk.

I went over to him and sat down. "Any luck?"

"Nope. Maybe he's here. Maybe not. I can't tell them apart, bunch a goddamn Chinamen."

"Lay off the sauce," I suggested, "and you won't see double."

Carole Frazer called across to us in her throaty purr of a voice. "Mister, if you can make him do that, you're a better man than his psychiatrist. Who are you?"

"I'm his new psychiatrist," I said, and she laughed, and then she lost interest in us as the dark heads bobbed and the white teeth flashed all around her. She lapped up male adulation the way a thirsty kitten laps up milk.

Pretty soon Spinner told me, "Gonna hit the sack. It's no use. You'll keep an eye on her?"

I said that was why I was here, and he lurched across the lounge toward the companionway that led to the *Hellas'* deluxe staterooms. A while later Carole Frazer got up and stretched like a cat, every muscle of her lithe body getting into the act. The Italians and Greeks went pop-eyed, watching. She patted the nearest dark head, said, "Down, boy," and, "Arrivederci" and went in the direction her husband had gone. But that didn't necessarily mean she was going to find him. After all, her leading man Philip Stanley was aboard too.

Finishing my ouzo, I went in search of the purser's office. It was located in the first class entrance foyer. A kid in a white uniform sat there reading a letter and sighing.

"What's the number of Carole Frazer's stateroom?" I asked him.

"Kyros," he said smoothly, "the next time you see the lady, why not ask her?"

He smiled. I smiled and studied half a dozen travel brochures spread out on the counter. I picked one of them up. In English, French and Italian it described the delights of a motor trip that could be made from Athens to Delphi and back in a day.

"How much?" I asked.

"Depending on whether you wish a chauffeur or a self-drive car, kyros—"

"No. I mean the brochure."

"That is free, kyros, compliments of the Adriatic Line."

I pocketed the folder and dropped a fifty-drachma note on the counter. "Fifty?" I said. "That seems fair enough."

"But I just—" he began, and then his eyes narrowed and his lips just missed smiling. "De Luxe Three, starboard side," he said without moving his mouth, and returned to his letter.

The starboard deluxe companionway ended at a flight of metal stairs going up. At the top was a door and beyond that a narrow deck above the boat-deck, with three doors numbered one, two and three spaced evenly along it. There were wide windows rather than portholes, all of them curtained and two of them dark. Faint light seeped through the third. It was Carole Frazer's cabin.

Looking at it, I liked the setup. Door and window both outside, on this deck. If I spent the night here, nobody could reach Carole Frazer without me knowing it. I listened to the throb of the ship's engines and looked at my watch. It was a quarter to one. I sat down between the door and the window of Carole Frazer's stateroom. The bulk of the Magnum .44 in its clam-shell rig under my left arm was uncomfortable. I shifted the holster around a little, but that didn't help. No one has ever invented a shoulder holster that is comfortable, just as no one has ever invented any other way of wearing a revolver the size of a Magnum and hiding it when what else you are wearing is a lightweight seersucker suit.

For about an hour I kept a silent vigil. Nobody screamed, no Vomero swifty came stalking upstairs, nothing happened except that the *Hellas* covered another twenty-five miles of Adriatic Sea.

And then I heard voices. The only thing that wasn't deluxe about the half-dozen deluxe state rooms aboard the *Hellas* was the soundproofing. Well, you couldn't have everything.

"Awake?" a man asked.

"Uh-huh."

"Like another drink?"

"My head's spinning right now."

"Just one more? With me?"

"All right."

Silence while Philip Stanley and Carole Frazer had a post-nightcap nightcap. Like any private dick, I'd been called a peeper more than once. Like any private dick, I'd never liked it. I'd done my share of peeping—or anyway listening—but never outside a woman's bedroom. The one kind of work I don't do is divorce work. But if the hired gun was going to make his move, it figured to be during the night. "Peeper," I muttered sourly under my breath, and remained where I was.

"Oh, Phil," Carole Frazer said, and her voice was more throaty than it had been in the lounge. "When you do that—"

"What's wrong, don't you like it?"

"You know I do. I love it. But I'm so—drunky. Head going around and 'round."

Another silence. Then he laughed, and she laughed and said, "Phil, you amaze me." She called him a brief Anglo-Saxon word that is usually not a term of endearment, but her voice made it sound endearing. Then she laughed again, deep in her throat, and then she said, "You keep this up, you're going to screw yourself right into the wall," and then after that there was silence for a long time.

I must have half-dozed. I blinked suddenly and realized that the night had grown cooler and I had grown stiff from sitting in one position for so long. I glanced at the luminous dial of my watch. After three o'clock. It would be dawn before long, and still no sign of the Vomero swifty.

There was a faint click, and the stateroom door opened enough for Philip Stanley to poke his head out and take a quick look to left and right. The one way he didn't look was down, where I was sitting. His head popped back inside, and the door shut softly. I remained where I was.

The door opened again. This time Stanley came out. He was carrying a suitcase, and from the way his shoulder slumped it looked heavy. He took it to the rail, set it down and placed a coil of rope on top of it. I froze, absolutely still. If he turned right on his way back to the stateroom he would see me. If he turned left, he wouldn't.

He turned left and went inside again. What the hell was he up to?

In a few seconds he reappeared with Carole Frazer cradled in his arms. He was fully dressed. She wasn't dressed any way at all. She mumbled against his ear. He set her down, gently, next to the suitcase. For a while longer I sat there like someone who had walked in on the middle of a movie and didn't know what the hell was happening on the screen or why. Stanley tied the rope to the handle of the suitcase, uncoiled the rest of it, took two turns around the suitcase, passed the rope through the handle once more, took four or five turns around Carole Frazer's body under the arms, passed the rope through the handle a third time and knotted it.

Carole Frazer mumbled again, faintly complaining. She was as drunk as Bacchus. He ignored her until she said, "It's cold out here. I'm cold. What's the matter with you? I don't—"

He clipped her once, behind the left ear, with his fist, just as I started to get up in a hurry. I had the Magnum in my hand.

"Need some help with your package?" I said. "Kind of heavy for one man to get over the rail."

The gun meant nothing to him. He cried out once, hoarsely, and came for me. The big Magnum could have ripped a hole the size of a saucer in him, but I didn't fire. When you get trigger happy you're not long for my line of work, despite any evidence to the contrary on TV.

Stanley lunged as a bull lunges, horns and head down, going for the muleta. I took his head in chancery under my arm, and his weight slammed us both against the wall. It jarred him loose. I was stiff from my long vigil, and he was fighting for his life. What I'd seen was attempted murder, and he knew it. He butted me. My teeth clicked and my head jolted the wall a second time. He stepped back, almost gracefully, and kicked me in the gut. Right around there I began to wish I had used the gun.

But by then it was too late. We hit the deck together, Stanley on top, me trying my best to remember how to breathe and Stanley clamping a hand like a Stilson wrench on my right wrist so I couldn't use the Magnum. I cuffed his head, somewhat indolently, with my left hand. He cuffed mine, harder, with his right. I tasted blood in my mouth. At least I had begun to breathe again, and that was something.

All of a sudden the Magnum went off. The big slug hit the window of Carole Frazer's stateroom, and glass crashed down all around us. I judo-chopped the side of Stanley's neck. His weight left me as he went over sideways. I got up before he did, but not by much. His eyes were wild. He knew that shot was going to bring company.

He swung a right that sailed past my ear, and I hooked a left that hit bone somewhere on his face. He dropped to his knees and got up and dropped to them again.

I heard footsteps pounding up the metal staircase. Stanley heard them too. Two faces and two white, black-visored caps appeared. Stanley did not try to get up again right away. There was a dark and glistening stain on the deck below him. He stared down at it, fascinated. He touched his throat. Blood pumped, welling through his fingers.

The two ship's officers saw the gun in my hand and remained where they were.

A shard of flying glass had hit Stanley in the throat. The way the blood pumped, an artery had to be severed.

"There a doctor aboard?" I said, going to Stanley. "This man needs help in a hurry."

But he got to his feet and backed away from me. Who knows what a guy will do when he's a little drunk, and half-crazy with fear, and in danger of bleeding to death?

"Keep away from me," he said.

"You crazy? You won't last ten minutes bleeding like that."

Smiling faintly he said, "I'm afraid I wouldn't come on very well as a convict, old boy."

Then he took a single step to the rail and went over.

They stopped the ship. They always do, but it rarely helps. We covered another mile, and turned sharp to port, and came back. Three life-preservers were floating in the water, where the ship's officers had thrown them. But

Philip Stanley was gone.

On deck after lunch and after I'd made and signed a deposition for the *Hellas'* captain, Spinner said: "I don't get it. You think I'm nuts or something? There was this little swifty in Vomero. I know there was."

"Sure," I said. "Stanley hired him, but his job ended in Vomero."

"Stanley hired him?"

"To make you think you'd hired yourself a killer. If your wife had disappeared during the crossing, you'd have kept your mouth shut about the possibility of foul play if you thought your own man had done it."

"Why did Stanley want her dead?" Skinner squealed.

"Because the picture was more important to him. He got scared they'd never finish it, the way Carole was carrying on." I lit a cigarette. "Hell, he told me last night how he wanted Carole's understudy to take over. She almost did."

Carole Frazer joined us on deck. She was wearing a bikini and stretched out languidly in the bright, hot sun. She didn't look at all like a girl who'd almost been murdered a few hours ago.

"Watch the sun," Spinner warned her. "La Lucrezia's pale, baby." He sighed. "That is, if you're gonna do the picture after what you been through."

"Do it?" Carole asked sleepily. "But of course I'll do it, darling. The publicity will be marvelous."

It was, and after our night aboard the *Hellas*, Carole Frazer settled down to work. They made *Lucrezia Borgia* with a new leading man. Carole Frazer's up for an Oscar.

A Place to Visit

The sign outside, in big white letters, said *Pepe's*. That much, in keeping with the geography, was Spanish, but the rest of the place was Greenwich Village with maybe a little Soho thrown in.

The canned music, as I opened the door and entered the dim interior, was a beatnik caterwaul. The waiters all wore tight white duck trousers, scarlet shirts tied at the waist and peroxided hair. A drunk in the corner, wearing a Hemingway beard, a baseball cap and a pair of steel-rimmed glasses low on the bridge of his nose, was shouting something about a bullfighter. Three modishly dressed types at the bar were discussing the current occupant of the White House in disparaging terms. A girl, not quite drunk, sat on the end stool fiddling with a pair of castanets and saying "ole" over and over again without spirit.

She wasn't the girl I was looking for. Nobody paid any attention to her, or to me, Chester Drum, until I hoisted myself up on a stool and said, "Pepe."

"Not here," one of the peroxide boys told me. "You're drinking?"

"Beer."

"One cerveza coming up."

He plunked the bottle and a glass down in front of me, and a chit that said I owed Pepe sixty pesetas, muchas gracias. Sixty pesetas is a dollar. Pepe is the diminutive of José, which is Joseph in Spanish. The girl I was looking for was living here in Torremolinos, in the south of Spain, with an American expatriate named Joe Cummings.

I said, "Señor Cummings charges a lot of dough for a bottle of beer."

The peroxide boy shrugged.

"You can always do your drinking elsewhere, amigo. We got class. You pay for class."

". . . madman with a cape," pontificated the man with the Hemingway beard, "but did anyone ever see him do a single decent *natural* to the left?" He was talking to himself.

The girl at the end of the bar went on clicking her castanets.

A bad Spanish imitation of the Beatles took over on the canned music.

I finished my beer. "When do you expect him?"

"Pepe?"

"Pepe," I said.

"He comes and he goes."

"I'll wait," I said.

Waiting earned me another beer and another one of Pepe's IOUs. It was swell beer.

An old man wearing one of those electric blue work jackets you see all over Spain, a pair of dirty white ducks and a beret came by sweeping the floor with a twig-broom. He was dark enough to be a gypsy, and he was the only Spaniard in the joint.

The door opened and a guy wearing the red and white

team colors strolled in. He was big and his blond hair was no peroxide job.

He had wide-spaced, mean-looking eyes and a complexion as pink and soft as a baby's bottom. Still he managed to look tough.

He slapped the old man's back. "Glad to see you're minding the store, partner," he said in English, and laughed, and went around to the business side of the bar.

"No comprendo," the old man said contemptuously.

The big blond guy moved down the bar to where the girl sat alone with her castanets. "You're drunk, Fran," he said. "I told you not to hang around here when you're drunk."

"I had a few," she protested.

"I say you're drunk. The Guardia could lift my license on me."

"I am not drunk."

"Beat it," he told her.

She stared at him with inebriated defiance.

"Drinks are on me," he said with a small smile, picking up her chits and tearing them in half. "Now blow."

"Well, in that case," she said, and lurched toward the door and through it. The three modishly dressed types snickered.

The peroxide boy whispered something to the big blond guy, and he came over to me. "You wanted something special?"

"Pepe? Joe Cummings?"

"So?"

"Joyce Addams," I said quietly.

"Never heard of her." The wide-spaced eyes narrowed.

"You got together in San Sebastián a couple of months ago," I said slowly. "You stayed at the Hotel Plaza in Madrid for the Festival of San Isidro. You drove down here by way of Granada, and she's been here ever since."

"Sorry, wrong number," Joe Cummings said.

"Her father hired me to bring her back to Geneva, no questions asked," I said. "She goes to the university there."

He laughed. "Been cutting a lot of classes, hasn't she?"

"No questions asked," I repeated.

"Better check with the operator," he said. "Or hey, have you thought of the Yellow Pages? They're full of dames who want a free ride in the south of Spain or the south of anywhere."

The three modishly dressed types, who had been listening, snickered again.

"This is the part that hurts," I said, "because ordinarily I wouldn't do it this way. I've got a blank check of her old man's in my pocket. It's yours, filled in with a reasonable figure, if she drives back with me tonight, and that's the end of it."

"What's a reasonable figure?" he asked, now showing some interest.

"I thought you never heard of her."

"I'm just curious."

"It could go as high as a grand," I said. My client, who was loaded, worked for an American government agency in Geneva, had his eye on a big political appointment and couldn't afford adverse publicity, had told me I could go as high as five thousand.

"Okay. I heard your pitch. I don't know your pigeon. Now get lost."

"You're making a mistake," I said.

"I'll take it up with my tax accountant."

He didn't offer to pay for my drinks. I paid and went out the door into the plaza that was lighted as bright as day. If he wanted to do it the hard way I'd go along with him.

Torremolinos had grown from a fishing village to a jet-set watering place, but that still didn't make it any big city. I decided I could find Joyce Addams without any help from the guy she was keeping house for, but I didn't like it. Her old man had insisted on no fuss and no publicity. Well, she was his daughter.

"Señor."

I turned around. The old Spaniard who had been sweeping the floor of Pepe's was behind me.

"You will continue to walk," he said. "Turn at the first street to the right. It is dark. Then we can talk."

I followed his instructions. The street was dark all right. It smelled of charcoal, garlic, and the sea. I heard the old man's shuffling footsteps. "The señorita," he said in Spanish, "every day she cries. She wishes to go home."

"Then why doesn't she?"

"He will not allow it."

"Where is she?"

The old man said nothing.

I sighed. "All right, how much?"

The old man spat on the pavement. "Nada. For nada, señor. I only wish to know that you are the man who can do it."

I saw no way I could establish that fact. "Her father thought so," I said. "He sent me over a thousand kilometers to find her."

"A thousand kilometers," the old man said musingly, and I realized I had said exactly the right thing. "It is like the other end of the world. He must have much faith in you."

"Where can I find his daughter?"

The old man's thoughts were elsewhere. "His partner," he said. "I am his partner. It must be so, as no foreigner can commence a business in Spain otherwise. But he treats me like dirt. You have seen? And of course the money all goes to him. Yet should the Guardia Civil learn of his various enterprises, señor, I too would be punished."

"Where is she?"

"That also is her problem. She knows, so he cannot let her go. Sooner would he kill her. That is clear, señor. Every day she cries. Every night."

I said nothing.

He walked away from me and then came back. A match flared and he was smoking. "A thousand kilometers," he said. "The father must have great faith in you. You are norteamericano also?"

I said I was an American.

He let out a long breath. "In the old days, before this of the bodega called Pepe's, I worked as a gardener in my village of Churriana, in the mountains. The Americans who stayed there were always good to me. Sí, sí, they were. It meant much to me. But the one who calls himself Pepe, he is an abomination."

"Then help me," I said.

He was going to, of course, or he wouldn't have followed me, but he had to wait for anger to trigger courage. I waited with him. Finally he said, "With the gypsies. On the beach. You walk down the Calle San Miguel to the mill tower, and follow the steps down to the water. There you will see caves where the gypsies live. Ask for the gitano named Rafael. And you understand as well that we never spoke?"

I said I understood.

"Then vaya con dios, hombre."

His footsteps shuffled away.

Caves pockmarked the sandstone face of the cliff. Outside each one, a cook-fire was smoldering to ash. Along with the sea breeze I smelled frying fish and saffron and olive oil. A high tenor voice shouted a flamenco lament at the dark sky. There was no moon but the stars were bright.

Half-seen gypsies directed me to the cave of Rafael. They were just shadows in the night, and they wanted to stay that way, but as I passed I left whispers in my wake. It wasn't every day, and sure as hell not every night, that the gypsies had visitors.

A pregnant woman was frying fish in a pan outside Rafael's cave. The olive oil spattered, and she drew a hand back from it. She looked up at me with dark, steady eyes. Large gold earrings swung from the lobes of her ears. In the firelight her face was dark and seamed, but still drawn tight like old parchment over the fine bone structure. I decided she once had been pretty. Gypsies, particularly gypsy women, age fast.

"I'm looking for Rafael," I said in Spanish.

"There is no one here who calls himself that, señor."

"How do you call yourself?"

"I have no name."

"Whose cave is this then?"

"The cave of my man," she admitted grudgingly.

"Does he have a name?"

"Yes."

"Rafael?"

"Go away, señor."

The gypsies are secretive, and their lives are weighted down with superstitions ten centuries old. To know the name of a gypsy, if you are a stranger, is to have power over him.

"Tell Rafael I came from Pepe. Pepe, the norte-americano."

She took the large pan of fish off the fire, set it on a rock and disappeared barefoot into the cave. I lit a cigarette and waited.

In a few minutes she was back. She replaced the pan on the fire. Right away the olive oil began to sizzle. She sat hunkered down near it like an Indian squaw.

She said, very softly, "Is it the girl?"

"What about the girl?" I said.

"You will take her away? Señor Pepe wants her back?"

"Maybe," I said.

"It would be well, señor," she said. "The girl does not belong here."

"Why doesn't she leave?"

The woman looked up at me. "Have care, señor," she said slowly. "You do not come from Pepe if you ask that."

I realized I had made a mistake, and then I wasn't so sure. The gypsy woman said, "Take the girl and go then, with my blessings. But have care." She got up suddenly and grasped the lapels of my jacket. "Every day it is more. The way my man looks at her, the way he must touch her every chance he gets—I know what he is thinking. I know what it is he wants." Her hands dropped to her belly, that was big with child. "I have this. Always I have this. Tell my man that you are from Pepe, as you told me. You are an estranjero, otherwise what would you be doing here? Then take the girl and go."

I started toward the entrance to the cave.

"I do not want to be responsible for killing her," the woman said to my back.

The walls were rough-hewn, but there were old, almost threadbare carpets on the floor. The light of candles revealed a few battered old chairs, a table, even an armoire. I heard a baby crying somewhere. Low doorways with curtains hanging across them led to other rooms. I was in an apartment carved from the soft sandstone of the cliff.

"Anybody home?" I said brightly in English.

A curtain parted and a man came out. He was wearing rags, and he was filthy. He hadn't shaved in a week. His skin was gypsy-dark and his eyes, sunk deep in a narrow skull, were shrewd and calculating. As he approached me I began to smell him.

"The girl," I said curtly. "Where is she?"

He shrugged one shoulder. It was more like a twitch.

"Come on, come on," I said then in Spanish. "Where is she?"

"You are from Señor Pepe?"

"Of course not," I snapped at him. "The Guardia Civil sent me."

He opened his mouth and revealed three yellow fangs. A sound emerged. I realized he was laughing. He jerked a large and dirty thumb toward the curtain behind him. He made the sound that he thought was laughter again. "That is good," he said. "The Guardia."

I passed through the curtain and saw Joyce Addams.

She was sitting on the edge of a bare mattress and wearing a skirt and blouse that had seen better days. A candle burned on a table near the bed. She pouted at me, the same sulky and spoiled pout that I knew from the picture I carried in my wallet. She was a lithe little brunette, twenty years old, very pretty, and at the moment trying to affect a go-to-hell look in her eyes but she was scared blue.

"I don't know you, do I?" she said quickly. "I guess I don't recognize you without the peroxide job. I'm not much good at recognizing Pepe's boys without their peroxide jobs. It's good for business, he says. It gets the swish trade of which there is gobs in Torremolinos, he says. You can't tell one of Pepe's boys without . . ." She began to cry.

"Who has your passport?" I asked. "Pepe or the gypsy?"

"What? My passport?"

"Your father sent me. I'm getting you out of here."

She was still crying. I patted her shoulder and made comforting sounds. I felt awkward.

She blew her nose, hard. She looked up at me and put on the brittle act again, or tried to. Her voice broke a couple of times as she spoke. "Pepe has it. Trust Pepe to know how to turn a buck. After he kills me, he'll sell it. Doctored, of course. You can get a thousand dollars for a valid American passport."

"I'll remember that for when I go broke," I said. "Why should he want to kill you?"

She gave me an impatient look, as if my not knowing her life was in danger was somehow denigrating. Then her eyes opened wide and fixed on something over my shoulder. I started to turn, but the room was small and the gypsy Rafael was both quiet on his feet and very fast, and what I did was turn toward something that smashed against the side of my head.

The candle guttered, or maybe it was just me. Whatever happened, I was in no condition to question.

A voice said, "His name is Chester Drum. He's a private detective licensed to operate in—"

Another voice cut that one off. "I can read. Hand it over." The second voice belonged to Joe Cummings.

I opened an eye and saw a ceiling the way a ceiling looks when you are very young and have been on a carousel too long. I shut the eye.

"There's water if you want," Joyce Addams said.

I touched my head and brought away a sticky hand. I

swung my legs to the side of the bare mattress, where someone had thoughtfully deposited me, got them over the side and leaned toward the floor with my head between my knees. After a while I lurched to my feet and made it to the curtain hanging in the doorway. I pulled the curtain aside. Joe Cummings and one of the peroxide boys and the gypsy were out there. Cummings had my wallet. He gave it to the peroxide boy. He was preparing to leave.

"See you later," he said to no one in particular. "About midnight?"

The gypsy, in English that would have won no elocution prizes but still English, said, "Midnight, sure. What about the girl?"

"Both of them," Cummings said.

"Got you, boss," the gypsy Rafael said, not liking it, and I knew how I had been made so fast. Who would have thought the gypsy understood English?

Cummings looked at me, grinning. "I saw my tax accountant," he said, and went out. The peroxide boy pointed a gun at me. It was a Luger. "You get to go back inside with sweetie-pie," he said.

I let the curtain drop.

"It's crazy," Joyce Addams said in what for her was a subdued voice.

She cleaned my blood-matted hair with a damp cloth. I sat back on the mattress feeling sick but not moribund, smoking a cigarette and staring up through the smoke at the rough-hewn stone ceiling.

"I mean," she said, "everything was so predictable. I'd finish school, and there was this boy back home, my father liked him, he's going to be a lawyer, but he's so damned stuffy. I just couldn't stand it, really. Everything was all mapped out for me. I didn't like school anyway. I'm not very good at school. I took off."

"You took off," I said.

"Hitchhiking south, complete with rucksack. After a few days I wound up in Spain. San Sebastián? I was never in Spain before."

"San Sebastián," I said. "Where you met Pepe."

"I was in a bar, alone. I shouldn't have been, not a girl, not in Spain. They began to make a fuss. Joe came along and after that it was all right. I was feeling wild and free, you know? I mean, in New York or Geneva I never would have let myself get picked up at a bar. It's why I ran away, I guess."

She looked away from me. "I went back to Joe's hotel with him. I never—"

"Look," I said, "save it. You don't have to tell me the story of your life."

She didn't hear me, or didn't want to hear me. "I was smashed, really smashed. I didn't even know what I was doing. Joe saw to that. Spanish brandy all night. Boy, that Fundador. Anyway—"

"You stayed with him. You came down here. Okay. How did it begin to go sour?"

"I was drunk off and on, mostly on, till we got here. It was my revolt with a capital R. You know? Just the opposite of the life I'd led."

"What you needed was a low type. Joe is a low type. I get you."

"You don't have to be cynical. You don't understand me at all."

"Your father didn't pay me to understand you."

"Sometimes you sound just like him. My father."

"Look, Joyce," I said patiently, "the sooner you tell me what kind of trouble you're in, the sooner—"

"That's what I'm trying to tell you. You're not even listening."

"I mean right here. Right now. Joe's going to kill you, you said. I want to know why."

"I'm getting to it."

I looked at my watch. It was eleven-thirty. "Get to it now."

"I guess I came to my senses. I mean, if I didn't want to lead the kind of life my father had in mind, that didn't mean I had to—well, you know. I had an argument with Joe. I said I was leaving and he said he couldn't care less. That didn't bother me—much. A clean break and all, you know. But then Joe said I was going just the way I came— one skirt, two blouses, a pair of jeans and the rucksack on my back. I started getting mad.

"I followed him that night, after Pepe's closed. I don't know why. I was curious. He was always spending half the night somewhere. He went to the beach. There was a boat. A bunch of gypsies began unloading things, wooden crates. They took them up the beach to a truck. One of the cases dropped on the rocks and broke open. It was full of cameras."

"Sure," I said, "and maybe the others had automotive parts and Swiss watches and like that."

Her eyes widened. "How did *you* know?"

"Spain's a smuggler's paradise," I said. "They get the contraband in Gibraltar and sell it on the black market here."

"I went right up to Joe and said if he didn't at least give me air fare back to Geneva, I was going to snitch on him. He got real mad. 'You shouldn't have seen this,' he said. 'You shouldn't have said that.'

"One of the gypsies wanted to kill me on the spot. He

had this big knife and he kept looking at it and looking at me. But Joe shook his head, no. He said there was no hurry. He took me here and talked to me. He said, 'Look at the position you put me in. You can blow the whistle on me any old time, can't you?' I was scared, but I was still mad. I've got this temper, you know? I said it was for me to know and him to find out if I ever told on him. It's crazy, but it was almost like a game, arguing with Joe like that here in the cave. Finally he said, 'Okay, baby, you asked for it,' and went away. That was last week. They haven't let me out of here since. The old man keeps looking at me and trying to paw me, and the old lady doesn't like it, and they have four children and the old man has a gun and the only thing Joe can do is kill me. He's got to, you know?"

She sat there, watching me. She'd told it all like a small child who'd run away from home, maybe took a streetcar to the end of the line or something, and then got hungry and used her pocket money on an ice cream and then walked home and got sent to her room without any supper, tired, hungry, but proud of her exploit.

When I said nothing, she gulped a couple of times, and the second gulp became a sob, and she said, "I'm scared. I'm so scared. I just wish it never happened, not any of it. I'm twenty, I ought to feel all grown up after what I've been through, but it was all a mistake and I feel like a little girl. Take me home. Please, you've got to take me home."

Pepe, I thought, might have his own ideas on the subject.

Midnight came and went, and then it was one o'clock, one-thirty, and pushing two.

I got up and pulled the curtain aside. The gypsy Rafael was seated at a table with a plate in front of him and fish tails on it and a gun alongside his fork. Near his right elbow stood a bottle of wine, almost empty. Rafael took a swig. He was a little drunk, but not so drunk that he didn't look up at me and raise the gun and shake his head. I let the curtain drop.

One of the peroxide boys showed up at two-thirty. He looked tired. His white ducks were wet almost to the hips.

"All right, let's get moving," he said in a bleak voice. There aren't a whole lot of people who like to commit murder.

The boat was riding at anchor about fifty yards out in the surf. In silhouette against the starlit night, it was a fair-sized cabin cruiser. Its inboard engine was throbbing powerfully. It would be a big engine, of course; big enough to outrun the Guardia patrol boats if it had to; big enough to take us a few miles out in jig time, drop us, and still make it back before dawn. Not that when it got back would be of any importance to us.

Half a dozen gypsies were hanging around, their trousers wet. They had been unloading contraband. At first their presence surprised me, and then I realized that taking Joyce Addams for a ride had probably been their idea more than Pepe's. Life is cheap in Spain and cheaper still among the gypsies, and they were hanging around to see that Pepe did what they thought had to be done. After all, it was his mujer who could put the finger on them.

We reached the edge of the surf. It lapped up at the sand and hissed back out to sea.

One of the gypsies approached me. He said politely, "Your shoes, señor."

I just looked at him, not getting it. He smiled. It was not an unfriendly smile at all. He pointed down at his bare feet.

"Where you are going," he said, still in that polite voice, "you will need no shoes."

"What?" I said.

"But I, I need shoes. For a favor, señor?"

It hardly makes sense that you can laugh at a time like that, but I managed it as I bent down and removed my shoes. He took them from me gravely with a little bow. He tried them on and laced them. He took a few tentative steps forward and back. He began to smile. "They are a good fit. I thank you, señor."

The Guardia, I thought. Maybe a Guardia foot patrol would come along the beach. But I knew they wouldn't. Contraband runners from Gibraltar have to worry only about the patrol boats, unless they miss a payment at the local Casa Cuartel.

A voice called across the water: "What's holding you up?" It was Pepe.

Joyce came close and looked at me. She was trying hard not to cry. I was trying hard to smile. Once we were on that boat, and once it began to move, I knew we were dead.

The peroxide boy motioned with his Luger. He and the gypsy Rafael moved out into the surf with us.

When we were still about twenty feet from the boat, a figure leaned over the side and heaved up at the anchor line. It didn't have far to come. There was a slight splash and the anchor clanged on board. By then we were thigh-deep in water. The surf was gentle but the footing uncertain. Shells and sharp rocks cut my bare feet.

Joyce stumbled. I moved toward her, but the peroxide boy waved me off. "Rafael can handle it. He likes to."

"Keep your filthy hands off me," Joyce said. The gypsy snickered.

The boat was bobbing as we neared it. Waves lapped its

hull. Two figures were leaning toward us from the cockpit—Pepe and a young gypsy. I was standing up to my hips in water that reached Joyce's waist. Rafael was still holding her.

"Easy does it," Pepe said. "He comes first."

I looked at the peroxide boy. He stood just far enough away so I couldn't go for him. He jerked the muzzle of the Luger toward the boat.

"All I came here for was the girl," I said slowly, looking up at Pepe. "Your business is your business. We could fly out of Malaga tonight."

Pepe glanced at the young gypsy, who shook his head slowly. "It's too late for that," Pepe said. "They'd cut my throat. Better come aboard."

"You're making a mistake."

"Move!"

I grabbed hold and pulled myself up over the side and into the cockpit. It was awkward work, starting in hip-deep water. Pepe got a grip on my jacket and yanked. The young gypsy on board stood nearby with another Luger, his legs planted unnecessarily wide against the slight rocking motion of the boat.

I got to my feet in the cockpit. It wasn't a huge boat, maybe a thirty-footer, and the three of us made a crowd in the small open area behind the cabin. I looked forward and saw a figure standing at the wheel with his back toward us, ready to take her out—another of the peroxide boys. I faced starboard again and saw Joyce's head, her hair drenched from her ducking, appear over the side.

Suddenly it dropped back out of sight, and she cried out. She had lost her footing. The young gypsy with the gun started to laugh.

Rafael was grinning, half-helping, half-fondling Joyce as

he levered her up to where Pepe could get hold of her.

The young gypsy was staring down at them. "Now there," he said in Spanish, "is a man who enjoys his work."

Rafael pawed at Joyce and lifted her.

"Damn it, cut the comedy," Pepe said.

The young gypsy began to laugh. Rafael, with a final prodigious effort, heaved Joyce aboard.

There was a moment's confusion as, soaking wet, she got slowly to her feet.

The young gypsy was still laughing when I hit him.

He slammed back against the padded bench in the rear of the cockpit. I was on him before he could get up. I got the Luger and shouted to Joyce. "Get down flat!"

She dropped obediently to the floor of the cockpit and I waved Pepe back to where the young gypsy was. "Hands all the way up," I said, "and keep them there." He obeyed. I moved to the port side of the cockpit.

A shot rang out. It was the peroxide boy in the water. He hadn't hit anybody, but now I heard yells from the beach. I aimed for his shoulder and let one go with the Luger in my hand. He screamed and flopped into the water, gun and all. Rafael was floundering back through the surf toward the beach. I saw a line of foam and dark shapes approaching us fast: the gypsies from the beach.

"Take her out," I shouted to the peroxide boy at the wheel. He just stood there.

I fired past his head. The windshield shattered, spraying him with glass. I was leaning against the gunwale on the port side of the cockpit, trying to look port and aft at once.

"Take her out now," I said. "Fast."

The engine roared. The boat began to move.

I watched the beach and the gypsies fade behind.

★ ★ ★ ★ ★

We stood a couple of hundred yards offshore and the big manmade mole that gave Malaga its harbor, ten miles up the coast from Torremolinos. I could see the lights of ocean-going ships in the harbor, and the city lights of Malaga beyond, strung along the hillside above the bay.

"This is where you get off," I told Pepe.

He looked at me. He licked his lips. "You're crazy," he said. "You can't."

"Why can't I? You can swim, can't you?"

"The gypsies. I told you. They'll slit my throat."

Joyce looked at him steadily. There was something in her eyes that I hadn't seen there before. "I wonder what they'll find when they do," she said quietly.

They went over the side one at a time, the gypsy with a sneer, the peroxide boy stiffly, his face frozen with fear, Pepe with a last pleading look at Joyce.

I put the spotlight on them while they were swimming. In a few minutes they clambered up on the mole, then they were gone and I cut the light and made my way forward to the wheel.

The lights of Malaga grew ahead of us, and spread out, and became a city.

Drum Beat—Dominique

One

For a guy who once held down the number two spot in the protocol section of the State Department, Jack Morley had come a long way—all of it in the wrong direction.

I walked right past his table on the terrace of the Café Rotonde a couple of times without recognizing him. What I saw was a shabby drunk who needed a shave, a haircut and, chances were, a bath. He was wearing what looked like somebody's cast-off safari jacket. It was a couple of sizes too big for Jack and made his neck look like a rooster's. You couldn't blame me for not recognizing him. The last time I'd laid eyes on Jack Morley had been a couple of years ago in Washington. Handshaking a pair of Middle Eastern diplomats into Blair House, he'd been turned out in his usual go-to-meeting outfit—camel's hair topcoat, white silk scarf, dark worsted suit and Homburg. He resembled then everybody's idea of what the boy voted most-likely-to-succeed at Harvard turned into ten years later.

Any resemblance between that Jack Morley and the drunk trying his best not to knock over the table while he got a glass of Pernod to his mouth outside the Café

Rotonde on Boulevard Montparnasse in Paris was purely coincidental.

I got a table near the lottery booth, ordered a drink and looked across Boulevard Raspail to the traffic island, where Rodin's statue of Balzac, considered obscene even by the French until they gave the bronze old man a bronze cloak, was now half-hidden by the branches of a chestnut tree. I looked at my watch. It was a quarter to eight of a warm evening, and Jack Morley already was fifteen minutes late. I decided to give him until I finished my whiskey-and-water, and then go up to the Raspail Vert for some bouillabaisse.

If it had worked out that way, none of this would have happened the way it did. But as I asked the waiter for my check, a big and not quite frowzy-looking blonde drifted over to my table, jerked a thumb in the direction of the shabby drunk and asked in an accent that was British but not BBC, "He wants to know are you Mr. Drum."

I looked where she was pointing and still failed to recognize Jack. I glanced back at the blonde. She was big without being fat, with a Devon milkmaid's overabundant figure, rosy cheeks and china-blue eyes. Her streaky blonde hair was long and combed in no particular fashion or maybe not combed at all. Her mouth was a sullen red pout.

"I'm Drum," I admitted. "Who's your friend?" She had been sitting with the shabby drunk.

"He's *your* old friend Jack Morley," she said, somewhat indignantly. "Who else might he be?"

I went over to Jack's table. The waiter brought a third chair.

"Chet, you old son of a gun," Jack Morley said. His eyes were bloodshot and seemed oddly vulnerable without the dark, shell-rimmed glasses. But his grin, finally, was the same. He stuck out a moist hand. I could feel a tremor in the fingers when I shook it and his head was shaking too, slightly, on the scrawny neck.

Only a banality could have covered my shock over how much Jack Morley had changed. "Long time no see," I said.

"God, it's good to see you. Have a drink?" The waiter took our orders. "I wrote you as soon as I read in the *Paris Trib* you were opening an office in Geneva. Going international, huh?" he said, a shade enviously. "Trying to put the Pinkertons out of business?"

"More and more of my cases take me to Europe. I decided I might as well have a place to hang my hat."

"One-man office?"

"I got a guy who holds the fort for me in Washington while I'm here, and vice versa." I said that uneasily. I had the notion that Jack was going to ask me for a job, and while I would have snapped up the old Jack Morley as a partner, the Jack Morley sitting on the café terrace with me was another matter.

He must have sensed my uneasiness, because he said: "I'm still with the government, you know."

"I didn't know. I heard you left State."

"It got kind of tough around Washington after Betty and I broke up. I guess you heard about that."

"It surprised the hell out of me," I said. "You and Betty were my candidates for the golden people."

"With feet of clay," Jack Morley said, and took a big bite out of his new Pernod. The blonde patted his hand. She managed to look sulky and bored at the same time.

"This is Jill," Jack said. "Jill Williams. She's a dancer."

"Used to be, ducks," said Jill Williams.

Then Jack and I spent a few minutes talking about old times. We'd gone through the FBI Academy together, then each served out a two-year hitch with the Bureau before I decided to hang out my private detective shingle and Jack took the State Department exam. It seemed like a long time ago.

"The reason I wrote you in Geneva," Jack said, and got a box of Gitanes out of his pocket and lit one tremblingly. He looked nervous and unsure of himself, and ducked behind the protective façade of the past again. I waited through a stream of remember-whens and I-wonder-what-happened-tos, and all the while Jack was chain-smoking and gulping Pernod.

"I told you he was a great guy, my old buddy Chester Drum," he told Jill finally, and it embarrassed me. To Jack I was something of a hero.

"Let's wait and see, ducks, if he'll do it for you," Jill said dryly.

Jack said the same line again, and then dropped his option on it again. "The reason I wrote you in Geneva." He cleared his throat, grinned, allowed his hand to be patted by Jill once more and said, "Jack and Jill, kind of comical, isn't it? The Left Bank Mother Goose bit?"

Jill gave me a pleading look, and I liked her for her frankness. She wanted Jack to get on with it. Hoping to help him do that, I took a stab: "What kind of work you doing for Uncle Sam these days?"

Jack laughed self-deprecatingly. "I'm a ghoul," he said.

"Oh now, Jackie, you have a perfectly respectable job," Jill said.

"Yeah, but I'm still a ghoul." He shrugged. "Hell, a job's a job. I work for the Army. Adjutant General's office, Graves Registration branch. I go around looking for dead men. Told you I was a ghoul."

"Stop that, ducks, you stop it now," Jill said.

"Time was," Jack explained, "when Graves Registration had a whole mess of field investigators. They worked out of an office here in Paris, on Rue Marbeuf. They followed every lead they could get their hands on, and some of them were pretty hairy, all over Europe and North Africa. You see, the Army never shut its books on men missing in action during World War Two, even though it's been almost twenty years since old Adolf blew his brains out. Well, most of the MIA's have been accounted for to the satisfaction of the Department of the Army and the next-of-kins, and the whole mess of field investigators has been reduced to a team of three custodial ghouls who poke around Europe tracking down dead men and, as I said, I'm one of the ghouls. That's what I do for the government these days." He laughed. Jill didn't laugh. "I guess I'll never make Secretary of State," he said.

Jill took up the refrain this time and completed it. "The reason Jack wrote you in Geneva, Mr. Drum, is he needs your help."

"On a little matter," Jack said.

"I don't think it's so little," Jill said.

"I can't pay you," Jack said uncomfortably. "I don't have a hell of a lot of dough these days. I mean, I'll pay your expenses, of course, but I couldn't touch those carriage-trade rates of yours."

"It's very expensive living in Paris," Jill said.

Jack laughed again. "She means I blow my salary on Pernod."

"What kind of help do you need?" I asked Jack.

He looked at Jill. She nodded encouragement.

"Well, I'm supposed to be a blackmailer," Jack said.

"Come again?"

"A blackmailer. I'm supposed to be one."

I said: "Are you?" and the way I said it made Jill smile gratefully.

"Not that I know of," Jack said.

"Who are you supposed to be blackmailing?"

Jack finished his latest Pernod, ran a hand over the beard-stubble on his jaw, took a deep breath and said: "A United States Senator."

I said nothing. Jack elaborated: "Senator Clay Bundy."

"Well," I said, "you sure think big in this new line of work of yours. How'd it come about that you're supposed to be blackmailing him?"

"Bundy's convinced I am. Only I'm not."

"So I gathered. But what are you supposed to be black-mailing him about? Is the Senator ripe for that kind of plucking?"

"You bet he is," Jack said promptly.

"What's he done?"

Jack looked at his big blonde. "I can't tell you. I haven't even told her. I just can't, that's all. Take my word for it, he's ripe. He's in Paris these days, you know. Some kind of Armed Services junket, ties in with his committee. Maybe it'll come out when you see him—I mean, if you do. But I can't tell you. I've got my conscience to live with."

I let that ride for the moment. "What do you want me to do?"

"Look at me," Jack said bitterly. He tapped his right cheekbone with a fingertip, drawing attention to his blood-shot eye. Then he extended his hand to show me the tremor in the fingers. "I'm halfway to being a goddamn rummy. When I get excited I get the shakes all over. I can't go and see him. Not like this."

"Stop your drinking," I suggested.

"I will, I will," Jack said quickly and almost devoutly.

"I've got to. I realize that." He took a long sip of Pernod. "One of these days I will. I swear I will." He shuddered slightly. "One of these days."

"And right now you want me to convince Senator Bundy you're not blackmailing him? How the hell can I unless you give me the dope on it?"

"I never met Bundy. The Senator never met me."

I stared past Jack's shoulder and watched a pretty girl wheeling her motorbike down the steps to the Vavin Metro station near the corner. It was almost dark by then.

"What I want," Jack said, "is for you to impersonate me and convince the Senator I'm innocent. You come on all full of confidence and—well, honesty. And I don't. You could convince him if anyone could."

"Not me. I couldn't play Jack Morley. I've bent elbows at a few cocktail parties in Washington with Senator Bundy. He knows me."

Jack's beard-stubbled face turned pale and little beads of sweat popped out on his forehead. "Oh Jesus," he said, "I was counting on you."

Back in our FBI days, Jack had been one of my closest friends. Now, looking at him, looking at what had happened to him, it was as though the old, urbane, devil-may-care Jack Morley had died.

"No," I said, "hold it. I'll see Bundy for you, but I'll see him as myself."

"Well, if you're a friend of his, that could work out great."

I didn't bother to say it was a long way from having had a few drinks with a high-pressure politician like Bundy to being his friend. I said, "It could work out great if I knew more about it."

Jack shook his head.

"Listen," I said, "there aren't a whole hell of a lot of

ways you can get yourself mixed up in a phony blackmail rap. Either somebody's out to get you and they're pushing Bundy into a corner until he does the job for them—"

"Nobody's out to get me."

"Except the Senator, ducks," Jill said.

"—or else somebody really is blackmailing Bundy and using your name as a cover. But that wouldn't work on a smart old bird like the Senator unless he could be shown that Jack Morley had access to whatever info was being held over his head."

"Access to it?" Jack blurted. "I *found* it."

"Found what?"

"I can't tell you," Jack said. "Believe me, it's not that I don't trust you. It's me I don't trust. Letting go with a secret the first time is the hardest. After that it gets easier all the time—for a lush. I just better keep my fat mouth shut, that's all."

Again I let that ride. After all, Jack knew himself better than I knew him. And whatever it was he'd learned about Senator Bundy obviously was eating at not only the Senator but Jack too.

"Okay," I said. "You stumbled onto something that's got Bundy all hot and bothered. Along comes somebody else who knows what you found and maybe how and where you found it. He figures it can make him rich, courtesy of Senator Bundy, but he also figures it can make him dead, again courtesy of Senator Bundy, so he decides to use your name when he hits the Senator with it. Would you say that's about the situation?"

"Yeah, that's about it."

"Who's the guy?" I asked. "Can you at least tell me that?"

Jack said he could not tell me that.

I blew up. "For crying out loud, do you want to get off the hook or don't you? What kind of a miracle worker do you think I am?"

"Several people I know of could be pulling this," Jack said with enough Pernod in him by this time to have calmed down. "But if I told you who, that would be the same as telling you what they've got on the Senator. That's not your concern. Your concern is convincing the Senator I'm not the guy blackmailing him."

"Thanks for letting me know what my concern is." I got up angrily and took two steps away from the table. Then I turned around and came back. "If a client held out on me like that, I'd kick him out of my office."

"Okay, okay," Jack said wearily. "I get the message. I'll pay your round-trip fare to Geneva. Sorry to have bothered you."

"You're no client," I said.

It took a few seconds for Jack to get that. "You mean you'll do it?"

I nodded. "I'll give it a try."

"Thank God," Jill Williams said. "You see, Mr. Drum, Jack never did get around to telling you the most urgent fact of all."

"Which is?"

She glanced at Jack, who shrugged. "Jack's received a phone call. The caller said that unless he stopped extorting money from Senator Bundy he would be killed."

I looked at Jack too. Maybe that would have been the most urgent fact of all to my old friend Jack Morley, Assistant Chief of Protocol, Department of State. But it probably didn't amount to a hill of beans to the unkempt and Pernod-soaked Jack Morley sitting on the terrace of the Café Rotonde.

Two

At noon the next day I parked my rented Volkswagen on Avenue Georges Cinq a couple of blocks in from Fouquet's red awning. Traffic was streaming past heading for the Champs Elysées, like an army of mechanized lemmings hell-bent on drowning itself in the ocean of pleasure between the Rond Pont and the Arc de Triomphe. I had read in the *Paris Trib* that Senator Bundy was holding forth at a press conference in his suite at the Hotel Georges Cinq before driving out to NATO and explaining to the generals there how the cold war ought to be fought.

He had a sixth floor corner suite, which I reached just as the press conference was breaking up. The double doors burst open and Senator Bundy hurtled through as if he'd been shot from a gun. Clay Bundy was in his sixties, but gave the impression of a man half his age. He always moved like that, in sudden, dynamic spurts. He still had his hair and it was still black. His face was almost unlined. Only the bloodhound dewlaps on either side of his pugnacious jaw betrayed his age. In fact, in Washington he was often referred to as Bloodhound Bundy—but not to his face. By reputation he was an arrogant snob with a terrible temper.

Half a dozen reporters clustered around him coming along the hall, like a school of pilot fish with a shark that could have swallowed them all without showing a tooth. He was fielding their questions, in French and English, with an almost disdainful expertise. Force de frappe, he said, and Polaris submarine and Port Area Command and airlift a whole goddamn division inside of three days and le grand Charles and that's really it, boys, I've got a busy schedule, terminé, terminé.

By then he was close to me and I said quickly and close

to his ear: "Senator, what about the Morley situation?"

He didn't even break stride. We all reached the elevator and stopped. When it arrived, the half-dozen reporters waited for Bundy to plunge inside. He didn't. He said: "Go ahead, boys. That really is it." The reporters filed into the elevator obediently. Senator Clay Bundy latched onto my elbow. "Not you, fellow. You stick around."

The elevator went down. "Say it again," the Senator told me.

I said it again: "Senator, what about the Morley situation?"

"What are you doing here? You're no reporter. Your name is Drummond or something like that. You're a private cop back in Washington."

"Drum," I said.

"That's right, Drum." The way it came out, he was congratulating me for knowing my own name. But he said: "There is no Morley situation."

"I heard different. Jack Morley?"

"I never heard of any Jack Morley."

"You think he's blackmailing you. You're wrong."

The elevator returned, and a liveried flunky came swinging out with the gate. I went in past him. "All right," I said. "Sorry to have bothered you. I guess there must be two senior Senators from California, both chairman of the same committee. I guess I got the wrong one. I'll say hello to Jack Morley for you anyway."

The gate clanked shut. The flunky waited. "You better hold it, son," Senator Bundy said in a flat voice. "I have a call to make. I can meet you in fifteen minutes at Fouquet's. Just ask for my table."

"I'll be there."

"You'd better be there."

The flunky took me down, and I walked the two blocks over to Fouquet's.

Senator Bundy's table was outside, on the Georges Cinq side of Fouquet's. From it I had a fine view of the Arc de Triomphe and, closer up, the nubile coeds in their yellow smocks hawking English-language newspapers. The Senator joined me there in exactly fifteen minutes. He sat down and ordered an Americano. I was working on a Pernod.

"Don't ask me why they call it an Americano," he said. "It's campari, sweet vermouth and soda. We don't drink it in the States."

"They drink it in Argentina," I said. "Italian immigrants."

He was impressed. "South America. I'll be damned. What else do you know, son?"

"That Morley isn't blackmailing you."

Senator Bundy took a long swallow of his Americano, that looked—and probably tasted—like red mouthwash.

The waiter came with a menu for each of us. Mine had illegible purple squiggles on it that looked as if they had been made by a flock of psychotic chickens whose claws had been dipped in purple ink. Senator Bundy seemed to have no trouble with his. He glared at the waiter and said: "I'll start with the moules marinière, and I mean marinière not à la crème. With that, half a bottle of Pouilly, 1959. The fumé, not the fuissé. Afterwards, the steak au poivre, rare. And I mean very rare. Some braised celery with it, and nothing else. Well, maybe a tossed salad, with oil and vinegar but don't drown it. And rub the bowl lightly with garlic first. And, let me see, a Château Lafite Rothschild, 1947."

"We don't have a forty-seven," said the waiter. He was sweating.

"They don't have a forty-seven," Senator Bundy told me sneeringly. "Got a forty-nine?" he barked at the waiter.

"Yes, sir," the waiter said, relieved. He looked at me uneasily.

"Make it the same." The waiter departed.

Senator Bundy turned his glare on me. "Well, if Michelin gives them a two-star rating, I expect service."

"What would you do if they got three stars, hold a gun on the chef to see he didn't make any mistakes?"

Bundy shrugged my little joke aside. "Speaking of mistakes, son, you made the big one of your life by tying up with Morley." He had dropped his deep voice to a conversational tone. After his almost ferocious assault on the waiter, he seemed to be whispering. "When I get through with Jack Morley he'll look like he fell off the Eiffel Tower and hit every goddamn girder coming down."

"Senator," I said, "if Morley were blackmailing you, don't you think he'd have made the usual provisions for his safety?"

"Meaning if anything happened to him, the dirt gets delivered where it could do the most damage? Is that where you come in?"

"If that's where I came in, I wouldn't be here now. I told you Morley wasn't blackmailing you."

The Senator's thick white eyebrows climbed toward his dark hair. I decided the color of his hair had come out of a bottle. "You can't be serious. I know for a fact he is."

"With what?" I asked quickly.

Up went the Senator's eyebrows again. "You mean you actually don't know?"

"All I know is that Morley discovered something which could have you over a barrel, but good, and somebody else who Morley won't identify got wind of it too and they're hitting you with it in Jack Morley's name. He's got nothing to do with it."

The waiter came with the half-bottle of Pouilly and the mussels. He poured a little of the Loire Valley white wine for Senator Bundy's approval and stepped back apprehensively. Bundy looked at the glass suspiciously. He held it up and studied it. He turned it in his fingers slowly. Then he brought it to his nose and sniffed. Then he lowered it to his mouth and took a delicate, microscopic sip. His face had taken on the expression of a mathematician wrestling with a problem that might or might not refute Einstein's Unified Field Theory.

"It's the fumé," he said grudgingly, and the waiter poured for us, served the mussels and retreated hastily. Senator Bundy called him back. "It ought to have been a shade cooler. Next time see that it is."

The waiter retreated again, nodding.

Senator Bundy's angry voice returned to normal. He seemed to be a guy who got emotional over all the wrong things. "The funny thing is," he told me conversationally, "I believe you're being honest. I still think Morley's the man. I just think you don't know it, that's all."

I took a sip of the fumé. It tasted like white wine. But the yellow and orange mussels, steamed in wine, were delicious.

"Well then, look," I said, "if Morley is your pigeon, and you lean on him, he'd have had enough sense to see you get reamed with what he's got on you afterwards. And if he's innocent and you lean on him, that still leaves a blackmailer you don't know. Make sense?"

The Senator was busy extracting the succulent mussels from their partially open shells. He used a light pincer-action with an empty shell to do it, and he seemed to be enjoying himself.

"Yes, it makes sense," he said after a while. "I'm damned if I do and damned if I don't."

"No. Just if you do."

"What do you suggest?"

"Tell me the grift and hire me to find the real blackmailer for you."

Senator Bundy laughed. "Morley's already hired you, hasn't he? Working around Washington, didn't you ever hear of a conflict of interests?"

"Morley didn't hire me. We're old friends."

"If you mean tell you why I'm being blackmailed, that's out."

I shrugged. "I kind of thought it would be."

The waiter came with the Lafite Rothschild. He left it on a wicker basket on the table. Bundy beckoned him. "Open it now. A Bordeaux's supposed to breathe before you drink it." The waiter opened the bottle, wiped the rim carefully with a white towel, sniffed the cork and went away.

"But I could still find the real blackmailer for you," I suggested. "The one who's using Morley's name."

"What if you find out it is Morley?"

"I'd tell you," I said. I meant it.

Senator Bundy poked among the mussel shells on his plate and discovered he'd eaten all there was to be eaten. He sighed, shoved the plate a precise inch away and busied himself reading the label on the Lafite Rothschild.

"Old Blair Hartsell used to tell me about you," he said, his nose still a couple of inches from the label. "He said you were the best private cop in Washington, and coming from a sharp old coot like Senator Hartsell that's as good a rec-

107

ommendation as you're likely to get."

I said nothing.

The waiter brought over our steaks, partially grilled. He lit an alcohol lamp and heated some butter over it in a big chafing dish. He added a healthy slug of Otard cognac to the melted butter, tipped the chafing dish expertly until blue flames danced over it, then dropped the steaks there. Senator Bundy watched the whole operation as if it were a religious rite.

"I've been in Paris two weeks," he said. "There's a Frenchman named Père Massicot who runs a stall in the Flea Market. That's, I think the term is, the drop. I've paid Massicot and his brother two installments of ten thousand dollars each. The stakes have gone up: the final payment, due at the end of the week, is a hundred thousand."

"Do you have it?"

"I can get it. But what's to guarantee they'll stop?"

"Not a thing. There never is."

The waiter served our steaks and poured a generous slug of the aged Bordeaux wine in a big snifter glass for Senator Bundy to taste. Bundy glanced contemptuously at the glass and dropped its contents down the hatch in a single indifferent gulp. I began to relax. I decided that meant I was in.

"I forgot to mention," the Senator said, "that Père Massicot's brother is in the hospital."

"You put him there?"

"This steak is superb," the Senator said, chewing a mouthful. "You don't expect me to answer that, do you? But figuratively speaking I can say that the younger Massicot brother—ah, fell off the Eiffel Tower. He was in a lot of pain, Drum, and he was scared clean out of his béret, and before they took him to the hospital he admitted he was working as Jack Morley's agent. You still want the job?"

"Yeah. I still want it."

"The concierge at the Georges Cinq will have a retainer for you later this afternoon. You also can get in touch with me any time, day or night, at this number." The Senator scribbled something on a scrap of paper. "They'll always know where to reach me."

Our salads came. Senator Bundy thought his was out of this world.

Three

As far as I know, they don't sell fleas at the Paris Flea Market. They don't sell old dinosaur bones either. But they handle just about everything in between. It wasn't an unlikely place for a blackmailer's drop at all.

To get there, you take any metro to a correspondance for the Port de Clignancourt line, and then take that line to its end. This puts you on the outskirts of Paris at the Clignancourt gate, and that is where the Marché aux Puces, or Flea Market, is located.

I left the metro less than an hour after Senator Bundy had hired me. The sky was dark with the threat of summer rain. Wave after wave of tourists, disgorged by the subway, were advancing on the stands, tents and stalls of the Flea Market, like assault troops launching an attack they could not possibly win. Nobody ever got a bargain at the Flea Market.

Père Massicot owned Stall 51 in an alley that specialized in old coins, none of them rare, and old paintings, none of them valuable. Massicot himself specialized in converting old coins into sets of buttons. He had two display cases full of them, each set of buttons attached to a loop of wire, outside his gloomy stall. The no-front stall itself was about twenty feet deep and only half that wide. It was cluttered with other display cases containing buttons, coins, medallions and cheap jewelry. Odd pieces of armor festooned the walls—here a set of greaves, there a plumed helmet, over there a breastplate or a sword.

Unless Père Massicot was a truculent-looking kid of about twenty in a pair of blue jeans and a turtleneck shirt, or a cute little French dish not a hell of a lot older, he wasn't holding down the fort.

The cute little French dish, who couldn't have been more than five-three or -four in her high-heeled pumps, was mad. It was really something to see. She could crowd more anger into a single gesture than most people managed in a lifetime of frustration. "Père Massicot," she said in French, "you will find him for me now." She set hands on hips, cocked her pretty head to one side and leaned a stubborn little chin toward the kid in the turtleneck.

He lit a cigarette and casually blew smoke in her face. "I told you before. Again I will tell you. He is not here. Perhaps he will not be here at all today."

"This time I will wait."

"Wait elsewhere."

He picked up a blitz cloth and began to polish some coins. His eyes were roving the girl, though, slowly and with frank appraisal. She was wearing a blue suit cut close to her figure. Her brown hair was short-cropped and slanted down in bangs over one eye. The way she was dressed and the cut of her hair, along with her size, should have made her look boyish, but she looked about as boyish as the Venus de Milo. She was small but built to scale. Her breasts were high and rounded under the snug jacket, she did not have what are euphemistically called tennis hips, and her legs were superb. She had the biggest, brownest eyes I had ever seen.

"Perhaps after all you can wait here," the boy said, finishing his appraisal. He glanced without interest at me. I dropped my gaze to a display case of coins. "And then, this evening, I could take you to where Père Massicot lives."

"Will he be there?"

The boy laughed, making the sound a lewd suggestion. "Who can say?" he said. "But I will be there. Père Massicot is my grandfather."

"Where is he now?"

Père Massicot's grandson shrugged. "Out. He may come later with a bottle of wine and some bread and cheese, or he may not come at all if it rains. This is just a sideline with my grandfather, a plaything for Saturday, Sunday and Monday. What's your name?"

"And the rest of the week, what does Père Massicot do?"

"Me, I never asked him," the boy said indifferently.

"I'll tell you then. He is a blackmailer."

"Père Massicot?" the boy said. "You're crazy. A blackmailer!"

"Yes, a blackmailer."

The boy giggled and blew smoke in her face again. He had narrow, close-set, mean-looking eyes, sallow cheeks and a receding chin.

"Don't do that again," the girl advised him. "I don't like it."

"Oo, la, la," the boy grinned. "She has a temper. I approve of that."

"I hardly expected a child like you to know your grandfather was a blackmailer."

He giggled again and blew smoke in her face again.

Her head jerked up and her brown eyes were blazing.

She removed one hand, with a small purse dangling at the wrist, from the lovely amphora shape of her hip, plucked the cigarette from between his lips, dropped it and stepped on it.

"Oo, la, la," he repeated. "She is a spitfire." He grabbed her hand and yanked her toward him. His eyes looked excited. She shook loose and swung her small purse against the side of his head. His eyes rolled and he staggered back against a display case. That surprised me. She hadn't taken much of a swing with the purse and it didn't look that heavy.

But hitting him made the catch open, and out of the small patent leather purse popped a small, snub-nosed, gun-metal-blue automatic. She tried to clutch at it in midair. She missed. It hit the floor and skittered to a stop at my feet.

Deciding that a talk with a gun-toting girl who thought Père Massicot was a blackmailer was a good idea, I retrieved the automatic and dropped it in my jacket pocket.

"Give it to me," the girl said.

"Is it loaded?" I asked in French.

"But of course. Why carry a gun with no bullets?"

"I'll hold onto it."

A voice behind me said: "Rain. All summer long on Monday it rains. They should open the Flea Market on Saturday and Sunday only; it would be sufficient."

I turned around. An old man stood in the entrance to the stall. His white hair was wet with rain, and I saw tourists fleeing from the downpour along the alley behind him. The old man was carelessly dressed in a rumpled gray double-breasted jacket and a pair of dark pin-stripe pants. He had a long thin loaf of bread tucked under one arm, a wheel of cheese in his right hand and a bottle of wine in his left. The bottle was corked but neither sealed nor labeled—vin ordinaire, usually Algerian, that you could buy in any local bistro. The old man had sleepy-looking, hooded eyes and an enormous Adam's apple.

"What happened to you, Pierre?" he asked.

The boy was leaning against the display case, taking long, slow, deep breaths. He straightened up with an effort and went back to polishing coins. "Nothing. It is nothing, grandfather."

"Père Massicot?" I asked.

"Oui. I am called that. Monsieur wishes?"

"Jack Morley sent me."

The girl's eyes widened at the mention of Jack's name. She stared with longing at my pocket, where her little automatic was.

The old man cried: "What? You come here? You dare to come here after what happened to my brother? I told Monsieur Morley it was terminated, absolutely terminated. I did not expect beatings. I did not expect attempted murder. Absolutely it is terminated. I wash my hands of it."

He lunged past me and sat down on the only chair in the place. It had battered wooden arms and a faded and frayed red plush seat.

"When did you tell Morley?" I asked.

"Last week. After what happened to my brother. Go away."

"You told him in person?" The old man's outrage seemed genuine enough. I didn't think he was lying. I wondered if Jack Morley had changed more than I had realized. Maybe Senator Bundy was right about him and I was wrong.

"But no, of course not," Père Massicot said.

"Then how did you tell him?"

Père Massicot opened a clasp knife and cut himself a wedge of cheese. He took a bite of that and cut off a chunk of bread and bit into that too. Crumbs flew from his lips. "A glass," he told his grandson. He had set the wine bottle on top of one of the display cases. He smiled a crafty smile at me and said, "I contacted Monsieur Morley in the usual way."

"Which is?"

"If you were his friend, you would know."

Then it hit me: Senator Bundy still had a payoff to make, the big one. Nobody had called him off.

"That wasn't so dumb of you," I said. "Telling Morley you were all through but not bothering to mention it to the Senator. A hundred thou—"

"That is enough, monsieur. Until now you were speaking in generalities. Are you quite insane? We are not alone here."

I got the impression, though, that the girl had suddenly become more interested in me than she was in either Père Massicot or his grandson.

Pierre brought a smeared glass to the old man, who gestured at the wine bottle. Pierre pulled the cork and poured the glass full.

"You'd better see me alone then," I told Père Massicot.

"You are threatening me, monsieur?" The old man's dry chuckle was two generations removed from his grandson's nervous giggle but still reminded me of it. "I told you my role in this affair was terminated."

"I'm threatening you if you neglected to terminate it with the Senator," I said. "You'll see me."

Père Massicot stared at me for a long moment. He took another bite of cheese. He raised the smeared tumbler and took three long swallows and said, "Ahh."

Then he said: "You will tell Monsieur Morley for me—" and his voice broke. His hooded eyes blinked. He glanced curiously at the wine glass.

"You will tell Monsieur Morley—" he began again, and stopped once more because his voice broke a second time. He blinked again and dropped the tumbler in his lap, splashing wine. He half rose from the chair and then slumped back into it.

Very calmly and in a faint voice he informed his grandson: "Pierre, I have been poisoned, you had better summon a doctor."

He clutched his throat. He leaned forward with his head between his knees and made retching sounds. Then he fell forward, on his side, drawing his knees up. I crouched over him and dug my index and middle finger into his scrawny wrist. They caught three faint and raggedy pulse beats, then nothing, then a single flutter, then nothing again.

Pierre was heading out into the rain. I didn't stop him. His grandfather was dead, but let a doctor tell him that.

"Has he really been poisoned?" the girl asked me.

I sniffed at the wine without touching the bottle. Even for Algerian vin rouge it had a faintly bitter smell.

"He's been poisoned all right," I said.

"And is he badly sick?"

"He's dead."

Her reaction was to cry a single anguished "Mon Dieu!" before rushing outside and running down the alley as fast as her trim legs could carry her.

"You forgot your gun," I said to no one in particular, and went after her.

Four

By then the rain had chased most of the denizens of the Flea Market indoors. A fat woman carrying an inverted galvanized metal washbasin over her head watched me hurtle by. A tourist with a movie camera poked his head out of a stall to immortalize Chester Drum hurtling along the alley. I splashed through a puddle and saw the girl a hundred feet ahead, ducking into an intersecting alley.

I followed her. She was still a hundred feet ahead, but no longer running. She didn't look back, not for several seconds, and then suddenly she did, and then she was running again. I broke into a trot. She turned another corner and I turned it after her into an empty alley.

There were stalls on either side. She had to be in one of them, waiting until I rushed past. I didn't bother to look. Finding her would have been a cinch, but I wanted to more than find her. I wanted to learn where she was going.

"Hey, wait!" I shouted, waving an arm and splashing down the alley. After a while I ducked into a stall where they sold antiques. Two faces, glued together at the lips, rose into view behind a big, gaily colored carrousel horse. They came apart about a half inch. The female face pouted. The male face gazed at me until I shook my head. They joined at the lips again and sank behind the carrousel horse.

In a little while the girl came by. Rain had plastered her hair tight against her head. She was walking fast. She had a smug smile on her pretty face. After all, she'd given me the slip.

I went outside after her, and this time she did not look back at all.

She was seated at a table in a bistro called the Red Flea at the edge of the market. The place was large, dingy and crowded. It had a central bar with a big zinc counter and off in one corner a bandstand where a three-piece combo of accordion, bass and drums was working not very strenuously at a medley of songs about Paris. A gypsy woman wearing a bright red floor-length skirt, a white blouse and a blue and gold vest was patrolling the tables hoping to pick up a few francs by telling a fortune or two.

I got a table a quarter of the way around the bar from where the girl was sitting. I could just see the back of her head and smoke rising from the cigarette she was smoking. She lit three more cigarettes in the time it took me to drink a couple of Pernods.

The gypsy came over. "Monsieur has an interesting face and gray eyes that would hide secrets from all but the most gifted of Romany's children," she said. "And also I believe the small scar on your right cheek was put there by a knife. Am I right?"

"Right as rain," I said. She smiled, showing three gold teeth, though the idiomatic expression, translated literally into French, must have meant nothing to her.

"To read the palm of one with those eyes and that scar would be a delight, monsieur."

I gave her ten francs and she sat down across from me, taking my hand in hers and running a grubby index finger lightly over the palm.

"A handsome face and a hard hand," she said approvingly. "Monsieur might treat women harshly but never with scorn. Am I right?"

I smiled. She smiled also. "Monsieur does not wish his fortune told. He wants information. What is it?"

"That girl—small and pretty with short hair and big brown eyes. You know her?"

The gypsy woman looked directly into my eyes. Her own

Stephen Marlowe

eyes were a startlingly pale blue against her dark and swarthy skin.

"Yesterday I read her palm," she said uneasily. "She comes from the south and believes in the arts of Romany."

"Where in the south?"

"Col de Larche. It is a village in the Alpes Maritimes."

"Who is she?"

"Upstairs there are rooms for rent. The little one has been staying here two nights with a man called Gaston Guilbert. Very big, very young and with a fierce temper. Monsieur is advised to look elsewhere for a woman."

"What's her name?"

"I have heard Gaston Guilbert call her Dominique."

I hadn't seen any wedding ring on Dominique's finger. "Are they lovers?"

The gypsy woman shrugged. "There will be but one love in Dominique's life. It is not yet but soon, according to the evidence of her palm. Monsieur is advised to flee. It will be a short love and tragic."

"No offense," I said, "but I prefer information to prophecy. Can you tell me anything else about them?"

"The future moves back through the present and becomes the past. To a woman of Romany information and prophecy are the same."

I glanced past the big gold loop earring dangling from the gypsy's left ear. Dominique seemed in no hurry to leave.

"Okay, let's have it your way."

"Ah, monsieur is American. The accent. I should have realized. But of course, no wonder you do not believe. America, it is so young and still so brash." The gypsy shrugged again. "Alors, Dominique, I did not tell her all that was to be read from her hand."

"Why not?"

118

The pale blue eyes were as flat and depthless as opaque glass. "Why should I terrorize the little one? Of what use to inform her the line of love and the line of life intersect briefly and then end abruptly in death?" Her thin lips drew down in pity but then parted to show me the gold teeth again. "As for what is written on monsieur's own hand . . ."

She spread the fingers of my hand on the table between us. Her own fingers rasped like a cat's tongue. She bent her head over my hand and mumbled to herself. Then she looked up, directly into my eyes again, and her own eyes were wide.

"But of what interest are the mouthings of a woman of Romany to one who does not believe? I will return monsieur's money if he wishes."

"No, forget it." I smiled a little, enjoying her smooth, professional technique. I expected her to ask for another ten or twenty francs to tell a fortune she found difficult.

Instead she got up and said very softly: "I advise monsieur to leave here at once."

Her fingertips rasped against my palm as she withdrew her hand. She was shaking.

But instead of leaving I went over to Dominique's table. She was drinking a café espresso and drumming her fingers impatiently on the table top. The combo had begun a new medley of tunes. It meant nothing to Dominique until they broke into "Valentine," and then she stopped drumming her fingers, turned toward them with a wide smile of delight on her pretty face, and saw me.

The smile faded from her lips but lingered in those big brown eyes. "It is my mother's favorite song," Dominique said. I could sense that she was waiting to regain her composure; coming up behind her like that I had startled her.

"I thought you might want your gun back, Dominique," I said.

That triggered a series of questions in rapid French. "Who are you? Why did you follow me? How is it that you know my name?"

I sat down in a chair that was angled toward Dominique's. She turned to face me directly, canted her head to one side and stroked the damp side curls of hair in front of her ears. Her eyes sparkled with eager expectancy, as though she had no doubt that I would answer all her questions and that my answers would delight her as much as "Valentine" had.

"Why are you looking at me like that?" she said.

She'd taken the words right out of my mouth, but I hadn't been aware of looking at her in any particular way.

"Like what?" I asked.

She flashed the same smile she had flashed at the musicians. "Oh, as if I am a gift tied with a big red ribbon and you are about to open it."

I laughed and she said, "You're still looking at me like that."

"Doesn't everybody?" I said lightly. I think, even then at the beginning, we both felt the quick and very strong attraction between us. Dominique was trying to make light of it, as I was.

"You are funny," she said. "How are you called?"

"What if I told you my name was Jack Morley?" I asked her. "I bet that wouldn't be funny."

She looked at me gravely. "Why did you say that? You are not Monsieur Morley. I know him." She added: "I wish I didn't. Truly, who are you?"

"Well, I'm a friend of Jack's. Actually he's a pretty nice

guy. My name's Chet Drum. What have you got against him?"

She gave me a dry-ice look. "You call a blackmailer a 'nice guy'?"

I sighed. If enough people told me that Jack was a blackmailer I might have to consider the possibility that he was. "Who's he supposed to be blackmailing?"

"But surely you know, if you visited Père Massicot."

"No. Tell me."

She didn't say anything right away.

"I wasn't the one who went calling on Massicot with a gun—a few minutes before he was poisoned. What was that all about?"

"Mon Dieu, I would not have used the gun. Only to threaten him. Only to learn where I could find this Jack Morley, this so-called agent of the American government."

"He does work for the government."

"Yes?" she said quickly. "And you can tell me where to find him?"

"You still haven't told me who you think he's blackmailing," I reminded her.

"If you truly do not know and if as you say he is your friend, why would you believe me?"

"No reason. Try me," I suggested.

She considered that with a pout, a frown of concentration and a shrug. "A few weeks back this Jack Morley came to Col de Larche. That is my village. He remained there two weeks, in the hotel managed by my mother and father."

"Doing what?"

"He claimed to be looking for a dead man."

I remembered Jack's job as a field investigator for Graves Registration. "He find him?"

"But of course not," she said indignantly. "I assure you

121

it was only a sham. After two weeks he left."

"You wouldn't happen to know the name of the dead man he was looking for?" I asked.

"He made no secret of it. An American flyer, in an airplane called I think a Mustang, was shot down near Col de Larche by the Germans during the war. That was a long time ago, before I was born, but it was a very big event in my village as Col de Larche is off the main roads and saw very little action."

"What was the American flyer's name, Dominique?"

"A very rare and strange American name with 'junior' after it." She frowned again. "Wait, it will come to me."

I waited. She said doubtfully: "A name like Bundle?" She shook her head. "No, that isn't it. But a name of baptism like earth or soil in your language? It was a very rare name of baptism, much like that, but I—"

"Clay Bundy, Junior," I said suddenly.

"Yes, that's it!" she exclaimed. "Didn't I tell you it was a rare name?"

"Not rare enough," I said in English, and she looked at me blankly.

"Well," I asked her, "if he didn't find any trace of Bundy, what did he find?"

She leaned forward. "Monsieur? I cannot hear you. The music."

The three-piece combo was now playing loud Dixieland jazz.

I said, "If he didn't find Bundy, what did he find?"

She hesitated a moment. "I'm not sure I know exactly. I'm even less sure I should tell you."

A trumpet had joined the accordion, bass and drums. The horn blared raucously.

"What do you think he found?"

She shook her head. "I'm sorry. I cannot hear you." She smiled. "Perhaps it is just as well."

I signaled for the waiter. "I'll take you somewhere where it's quiet."

Her brown eyes narrowed slightly. "That won't be necessary. We can talk in my room upstairs."

I paid her check and mine, and we threaded our way among the crowded tables, past the bar and to a doorway at the rear of the room. That led to a steep stairway, dimly lit by a bulb at the landing. I went up behind Dominique, intrigued by the movement of her hips.

She reached the landing and turned left down a narrow hallway. At the third door she stopped and got a key from her purse. She dropped it, mumbling something under her breath, and we both crouched for it. Her hand closed on the key. My hand closed on her hand. Our faces were about an inch apart. Her breath caught, and then we both were standing again. I released her hand. She unlocked the door.

I followed her into pitch darkness. "The light," she said, turning and groping for a switch on the wall. Our bodies made brief contact and my shoulder jarred the door shut.

Suddenly there was a click. Bright light flooded the room, starkly revealing a single bare window, two beds, a dresser, a chipped sink and a bidet. The faded, floral patterned wallpaper was peeling.

A man wearing slacks and an undershirt got off one of the beds. Dominique moved away from me quickly, toward the dresser and the mirror over it and her own nervous reflection in the mirror. She was holding the automatic that I had picked up at Père Massicot's Flea Market stall.

"Massicot is dead. Poisoned," she told the man in the undershirt. "And this one, he is a friend of Jack Morley. He can tell us where to find Monsieur Morley."

The man in the undershirt, who was very big but also quick on his feet, smiled, came toward me and told Dominique: "You will lock the door."

Five

There was a moment when I might have taken the automatic from her. I still stood with my back to the door, and she had to come past me to lock it. But I let her come. I even stepped aside and raised a be-my-guest palm toward the door and smiled a little. She locked us in and returned sideways past me, not quite scuttling, to her station at the dresser. She looked at the big man and me in the mirror and nibbled at her lower lip when the big man said, in response to my smile, "You think it funny, what M. Morley does?"

"Depends on what he's been up to. Enlighten me," I said in English.

"You are his friend," the big man answered in the same language. "Dominique says so. Will you deny it?"

"Nope. I'm his friend all right. So what?"

"Then," Dominique said, "you will tell us where he is."

The big man half-turned toward her. "Dominique, you will let me attend to this."

"But surely if he can tell us where Jack Mor—"

"I will attend to this," the big man said more sharply. Dominique pouted and subsided into sullen silence. But she kept looking at the big man as though she expected him to hit someone, no doubt me. I took a good look at him. He was young, no older than Dominique, with angry eyes and petulant lips that had done their share of sneering. He had a thick neck and powerful, sloping shoulders, and his bare arms were muscular. I could sense he was taking my measure too, and hoped he had reached the same conclusion I had reached: if we tangled, both of us were going to get hurt.

He said, in a more reasonable tone of voice: "There is a limit beyond which our father cannot pay. M. Morley, who has seen the way we live in Col de Larche, should appreciate this. That limit has been reached. For this reason my sister and I came to Paris, to inform M. Morley. If you will be good enough to inform him for us, we can return to Col de Larche at once. You will do this?"

I laughed.

"You know for a fact that he won't stop?" The big man clenched his fists. "One cannot draw blood from a stone, I warn you."

"Gaston," Dominique said in a small and not very hopeful voice.

"Jack Morley can't stop what he hasn't started," I said, wondering if I believed my own words.

"You deny he is blackmailing our father?"

"He isn't blackmailing anybody. Go back to Col de Larche. Tell your father that."

"You are mistaken," Gaston Guilbert said. "Or else you are a liar."

I shook my head. "Morley isn't blackmailing anybody."

"Then why do you laugh?" Dominique asked me.

"It's your brother," I said, and watched Gaston Guilbert's face darken with angry blood. "I walk into this thing blind, or almost blind, and practically the first thing he does is tell me your old man is being blackmailed. You don't know a damn thing about me. What's to stop me from hopping a train to Col de Larche, digging for some dirt and putting the bite on the old man too?"

"But yes, you can always try that," Gaston Guilbert sneered. "You can walk into Col de Larche, monsieur, as your friend Morley did. But this time I know better. This time you they will carry out."

Dominique broke the tension between us by saying: "You already know why he is being blackmailed. You must."

"I know that two people are being blackmailed," I said frankly, "and one of them lives in Col de Larche and the other is the father of an American flyer who apparently crashed and died there during the war, and both of them are convinced Morley's putting the bite on them. Only they're both wrong."

"You expect us to believe this is all you know?" Gaston Guilbert asked.

"Well, not quite. I also know that Père Massicot, who was collecting in Morley's name, got himself poisoned. Are you sure the only reason you came to Paris was to tell Morley—"

That was as far as I got, because you don't keep flapping your gums when a guy the size of Gaston Guilbert takes a wild swing in the general direction of your head. I went in under it, heard Dominique cry out in only mild dismay and had time to tell myself I should have known it would wind up like this the minute I saw Gaston climb truculently off the bed, and then his big arm wrapped itself around my neck and drew me toward a meeting with the left fist and let go so that I could wallop the locked door with my spine and sit down at its base, staring up at Gaston Guilbert and the mayhem in his eyes.

"Oh Gaston," Dominique wailed in French, "you will kill him!"

Gaston neither kicked me while I was down nor let me get to my feet in my own time. Instead he grabbed my left arm, hauled me upright, cried, "Cochon, to accuse me of this," and swung his left again.

The cochon who had accused him of that caught the hook with an open right palm and countered with a fair left of his own which sent Gaston hurtling back to the bidet, where the backs of his knees caught, flipping him onto the bed. He sprang up and caught a right flush on his mouth and landed on the bed again and sprang up again. Only this time the footboard splintered and the bed gave way. That distracted me, and the next thing I knew I had slugged the door a second time with my back, which hurt considerably more than the bed had hurt Gaston, though this time instead of hauling me to my feet he tried to kick me in the head.

He was barefoot. I caught his heel with my left hand and his big toe with my right, and heaved. He lurched backward toward the dresser, Dominique leaping out of his way just in time, the automatic forgotten in her hand. He hit the dresser, the dresser hit the wall and the big mirror came down, not in one piece.

Somebody pounded at the door just as Gaston came for me again. I crossed my right and popped a knuckle when it connected with the hinge of his jaw. I felt that one clear to the shoulder and stepped back, panting. If Gaston could absorb that and come back for more, I was in trouble. I couldn't throw them any harder and would be a one-handed fighter anyway for the duration.

But Gaston settled slowly on his knees and then, with a sigh, slowly forward on his hands and face.

The door was opened with a passkey. A fat, frumpy concierge stood in the doorway, fingering the mustache that

127

grew on her upper lip. Dominique, with her legs planted wide, stood straddling her brother. It looked exactly as if she had slugged him with the automatic still gripped tightly in her right fist.

That seemed as good an exit-cue as I was likely to get. The concierge's eyes were already roving the room: the collapsed bed, the damaged dresser, the broken mirror. She'd have the flics on their way as soon as she could mustache up to a phone, and I had business elsewhere.

I shouldered past her and said: "Go easy on them, they had a lover's quarrel."

Downstairs the gypsy woman gave me a sad, sage look and nodded her head slowly.

Six

"He *hired* you?" Jack Morley asked in disbelief. "Bundy?"

"Sure. To find out who was blackmailing him."

"But that's wonderful," Jill Williams said. "You must have convinced him Jack's innocent."

I shook my head. We were sitting far back under the green awning in front of the Rotonde. It was twilight, just twenty-four hours since I'd met Jack, and raining very hard now. Except for the lottery vendor in her booth, we had the Rotonde terrace all to ourselves. Clots of traffic spurted like arterial blood every time the light changed at the intersection of Raspail and Montparnasse. Water from a leak in the awning splashed on a table closer to the street.

"I didn't convince anyone," I said. "Bundy's just keeping all bets covered."

"Oh," Jack said, crestfallen. "Then he still thinks I'm the guilty party."

"Well, he's not entirely convinced now. The name Massicot mean anything to you?"

Jack scowled over his Pernod. It was his fourth, and he was holding them well. "No. Should it?"

"Massicot owned a stall at the Flea Market. He was bagman for whoever was blackmailing the Senator in your name."

"Will the real Jack Morley please stand up?" Jack said with a smile.

I told him: "Massicot was murdered this afternoon. Poisoned."

"God," Jack said, and then I told him what had happened at the Flea Market and afterwards.

Jack reassumed his light tone when I finished. "As you can see, I don't take any half-way measures. Now there are two people think I'm blackmailing them."

"Do you know this Raoul Guilbert up in Col de Larche?"

The little piétons sign flashed amber on the traffic light and Jack watched a few pedestrians scurrying across Boulevard Montparnasse through the rain. He lit a cigarette. He'd had enough Pernod to make his hands steady. "Yeah," he said. "I know him."

"Jack," I said, "you went up there on government business didn't you?"

"That's right," Jack admitted. He still wasn't looking at me.

"What kind of business?"

"I told you yesterday. For the Adjutant General. To close the books on men missing in action since the war."

"You mean, to establish the fact they'd died?"

"Yeah." I think he knew what I'd ask next. He didn't like it. He gulped the rest of his Pernod.

129

"And you went up to Col de Larche to close the books on Clay Bundy Jr.?"

"You guessed it," Jack said reluctantly.

"I didn't guess anything. Dominique Guilbert told me. What did you find in Col de Larche?"

"Proof that he died."

"What kind of proof?"

"Enough, after over twenty years. A few scraps of the Mustang he'd been flying. A chunk of fifty-caliber machine gun—including the serial number. It was Bundy's plane. Now he's officially dead."

"That's no reason to blackmail the Senator," I said mildly.

"Tell that to whoever's doing it. The Senator's son is officially dead. I filed my report."

"How come you went looking for Clay Bundy Jr.—after all these years?"

"The usual reason. Suddenly his name popped up with a Cong. Inq. stamped next to it. That's a Congressional Inquiry."

"Does the congressman have a name?"

Jack laughed harshly. "Well, it sure as hell isn't Clay Bundy."

"Why not? What's so odd about a father wanting to learn what happened to his own son?"

"The Senator was here in France right after the war. Forty-six or -seven, I think. He found out all he had to know then. They had a funeral for Clay Bundy Jr. in California. A big, California-type funeral, but with no corpse, of course. It must have been a little eerie."

"If it wasn't Bundy who put through the inquiry, then who was it?"

"We batted that around in the office for a while before I

left. Nobody could even guess. But Bundy's got plenty of political enemies." Jack looked at me suddenly, as if aware he'd said the wrong thing. He took a nervous nibble at his lower lip.

"Why enemies?" I asked. "What could they hope to gain?"

"Search me," Jack said.

"I think Clay Bundy Jr.'s still alive. I think you know he's still alive. That's why the Senator thinks you're blackmailing him, isn't it?"

"I told you the case is officially closed."

"I know what you told me. You heard what I said."

"Chet, maybe you better go back to Geneva."

"Somebody killed Massicot today, and he died thinking he was your bagman. Do I have to draw a map?"

"I can take care of myself," Jack said. "I'm calling you off the case as of now."

"You can't call me off. I'm working for Senator Bundy."

"Christ, you're a real buddy," Jack said.

"He wants to help you, ducks," Jill told him gently. "Why don't you let him?"

Jack dry washed his face with both hands. His fingers rasped against the beard-stubble on his jaw. It was a tired, defeated gesture.

"Who are you protecting?" I asked. "Clay Bundy Jr.?"

"He's dead. I told you he was dead."

"But supposing he was alive," Jill said, still gently.

"Leave me alone. Both of you, can't you get the hell off my back? I'm not putting the bite on Senator Bundy. I'm not putting it on Raoul Guilbert. I'm not blackmailing anybody."

"We know that," Jill said, but I wondered if I did. Dominique Guilbert had seemed so gravely certain. "Still and all, Jack, Mr. Drum only wants—"

"Garçon," Jack called, interrupting her. "Another Pernod. Make it a double."

Jill waved the waiter off. "That can wait. When did you eat last?"

"This morning. Breakfast. I'm not hungry."

"Two croissants and a pot of coffee," Jill said, dismissing Jack's breakfast. "We'd best put some food in you before doing anything else, ducks."

Jack stared at her gratefully. She took his hand in both of hers. Despite his protestations that he wasn't hungry, for the moment at least Jack liked the idea of being cosseted. "You and that Devon appetite of yours," he said with a faint grin. "There's no reason you have to starve."

"I don't intend to." Jill glanced at me, waiting for me to carry the ball. She knew the beard-stubbled, Pernod-drinking Jack Morley better than I did. She was hoping some babying might get him to open up.

"I know a joint off the Rue des Grand Augustin," I said brightly, "that serves the best paella in the world."

"Did you say paella?" Jack asked. "I love paella."

"In Paris?" Jill asked.

"I love it anywhere."

"I mean, what's paella doing in Paris?"

Jack laughed. "Leave it to Chet. If he says it's good paella, all of a sudden I'm hungry."

At least for the time being we were friends again. I paid our check and we got into a cab and drove to the Catalán.

Like so many State Department people, or ex-State Department people, Jack was a bullfighting buff. The very Spanish atmosphere of the Catalán, the gypsies stamping their hard heels on the resounding floor of the small, raised stage, the saffron-flavored paella we were eating and washing down with iced sangria—all got Jack to talking about the bullfights he had seen. We didn't try to change the subject, though it wasn't what we wanted to hear. I had the feeling, and Jill must have had it intuitively too, that the important thing was to keep Jack talking and feeling at ease.

". . . not flamboyant like a matador from Sevilla," he was saying, after we had drained our second pitcher of sangria and finished the last succulent chunks of chicken, lobster and shrimp in the paella pan. "No, a matador from Ronda, or one who fights as if he's from Ronda, performs with an aloof, cool disdain that really grabs you by the throat. I remember Manolete once, with a really brave bull, the kind that charges like it's on railroad tracks, and when it was all over he didn't make one of those big, flourishing gestures the Sevillanos are so good at, he just stood there, close to the bull he had killed, with his shoulders slumped and his head down, and there wasn't a sound in the plaza, and there, with that one simple gesture, with his shadow long on the sand, he was united in the death he had given the bull and the bull had almost given him. God," said Jack staring at the pitcher of sangria, "it was really something." He looked up a little uneasily. "I hope this doesn't sound corny to both of you."

"It sounds beautiful," said Jill, who had never seen a bullfight.

"I got me a theory," Jack went on. "Not just matadors, but everybody's either a Sevillano or a Rondeño. There's so damn much of the empty gesture in diplomatic work, maybe that's why my former colleagues in State all kind of took to their opposite, the Ronda style of bullfighting. Take Chet here—he's a Rondeño if ever I saw one. Me, I guess I'm from Sevilla. It's the gesture, the damn bloody bigger-than-life gesture that finally gets me, and I sort of lose sight of what it's all about. Even going on a rotten, if necessary, bender. Not only do I have to feel sorry for myself and really wallow in it, but I have to drag my friends into it too."

"That's what friends are for," Jill said.

"I bet you'd just crawl into a corner with a jug, Chet," Jack told me.

"I don't know," I said, remembering a couple of memorable benders which had been, as Jack had put it, rotten, if necessary.

"You know what there is about bullfighting that really gets an aficionado? It's the closeness to death. If you want to see how men behave a hairsbreadth from death, see a bullfight. But see a Rondeño if you can. There's nothing flamboyant or corny about dying."

Jack rambled on some more, mixing tauromachia and philosophy. He suggested a third pitcher of sangria, and we drank that, and by the time we finished it was late. The gypsies had done their final stamping, a flamenco singer had wailed his last keening lament to a lost love in Andalusia, and the waiters were standing around, shifting from tired foot to tired foot and hoping we'd call it a night.

"You know why I've been foaming at the mouth like this all night?" Jack asked. "Because after what you went through today I know I ought to tell you what happened up there in Col de Larche, and I know I'm going to, but I just have to work up to it, that's all."

I made no comment. Jack shrugged self-consciously and said nothing else for a while. Our waiter ducked in at the lull with the check.

"Think it stopped raining?" Jack asked. "I can use some air."

Outside, the rain had slackened off. It was hardly more

than a heavy mist that put halos on the street lamps and a shine on the ancient cobbles of the narrow St. Germain streets. We walked down to the river arm-in-arm, with Jill in the middle, and all at once as we came out on the Quai de la Tournelle there was Notre Dame with its flying buttresses floodlit and the mist shrouding the two square towers.

"Oh God, it's beautiful," Jill said, and by then she was walking with a bouncing step not only because Paris is the most beautiful city in the world, especially at night and especially in the rain, but because she was beginning to get the idea that her man would be all right.

"Let's go down and walk along the river," Jack said, indicating a ramp that descended from the parapet.

"I'm beginning to feel a little superfluous," I told him.

Jill squeezed my arm to deny that, but Jack laughed and said: "Well, I've got to admit it crossed my mind to do some old-fashioned smooching with my Devonshire lass under a bridge down there."

"Silly," Jill said, but I could tell she was pleased.

We were standing at the top of the ramp. I disengaged my arm from Jill's and for no reason at all thought of Dominique Guilbert. I lit a cigarette.

"Listen," Jack said. "What I started to say in the Catalán. I'm going to tell you all of it. I've got to. I was wrong yesterday."

Jill leaned up and kissed him. "Jack, that's wonderful."

"Or maybe a bit selfish," Jack said. "Once I dump it in his lap, the problem belongs to Chet too. That'll be a relief." He gave us his shy, self-conscious smile and patted Jill's firmly rounded posterior. "But if it kept this long, I guess it can keep till tomorrow. We've got a date under a bridge."

"Oh, you," Jill said, but she was still pleased.

Maybe I should have insisted on hearing it there and then, but my original motive for coming to Paris was to help Jack, and at the moment Jill's eager willingness would do him a hell of a lot more good than my professional ear. Anyhow, it was late, I'd had a long day and there was no reason it couldn't keep till morning.

"Breakfast at the Raspail Vert?" I suggested.

"You're on. Eight-thirty, okay?"

I said eight-thirty would be fine.

With their arms around one another's waists and their hips bumping, they started down the ramp. I flipped my cigarette over the parapet, looked across the dark water of the river at Notre Dame, felt the special kind of loneliness you feel only in Paris at night in the rain, informed myself silently that I needed a woman but felt too jaded to go through the motions of picking one up at a late café tonight, turned, started walking along the Quai with my head down and my hands jammed into my pockets, excused myself as I almost bumped the middle one of three figures coming toward me, and crossed the street, in no great hurry.

Just as I reached the sidewalk on the other side I heard Jill's scream of terror.

I turned fast and ran back across the street. All I could see was the parapet, supporting a row of bookstalls that had been padlocked for the night. The sidewalk was deserted. It crossed my mind that the three figures I had encountered were no longer in sight and that the only way they could have disappeared so quickly was if they had gone down the ramp. I started down, still running, and heard Jill's second scream ending on a choked whimper.

At the bottom of the ramp I looked to the right along the

cobbled walkway that skirted the river's edge and saw nothing. I looked left and half the distance to the soaring arches of the Pont Neuf saw a group of figures struggling. One of them broke away. It was Jill, and another figure started after her and thought better of it and went back. Another form broke away and took two or three steps after Jill and then was hit, not very hard, from behind, and fell down. He got to his feet and was hit, not very hard again, and went down a second time and got up. By then Jill had reached me and I was close enough to see that the man who had fallen twice and got up twice was Jack.

"Don't stop," I told Jill. "The cops. Get the cops."

She kept going, her mouth wide in a rictus of fear.

Jack's three assailants saw me coming. One of them hit Jack with a blackjack, swinging it deftly, most of the motion in his wrist, and Jack put a hand to his ear, almost casually, like someone a little hard of hearing who hasn't quite heard what you have said, and took three small staggering steps to the river's edge and went over. The three figures ran away from me, toward the dark arches of the Pont Neuf and then under them, their footfalls echoing on the cobblestones. I peered over the side into the river and couldn't see Jack. Yanking my shoes and jacket off, I jumped in.

I surfaced, treading water, and looked around. Though there is no tidewater as far up the Seine as Paris, the river smelled brackish. I treaded water in a circle and when I had spun around a second time saw something floating about ten yards out toward the Ile de la Cité. It was Jack, and he was floating on his face with his head in the water.

It took only a few seconds to reach him. He was heavy, despite the buoyancy of the water, and completely inert. Struggling with him, I got him over on his back, passed my left arm under his left arm, cupped his chin with my hand

and side stroked back toward the bank.

The wall was too high. I couldn't bring him out of the water without help. Still holding him with his head clear of the surface, I found a handhold on a block of stone slippery with algae. The water lapped gently against the wall, rocking us both there, making my hand slide along and then off the algae-covered stone. I found a new grip, clung there until the little wavelets loosened my fingers, and repeated it all over again. Jack weighed a ton. He never moved, except for the motion the water imparted to his body. I began to get cold. I took a mouthful of water, reached for a higher grip on the stone and stared up into the powerful beam of a flashlight.

It slipped off my face and onto Jack's body, and then I could see Jill with a flic on either side of her silhouetted against the night like bats in their big black capes. They told me to let go of Jack. At first I didn't, and finally I did, because from above, with one of them supine and leaning far down while the other held his legs, they could manage to bring Jack up and out of the water. I let them do it and clambered up after him. He was stretched out on the cobblestones, on his back. Jill was sitting near his head, stroking his wet hair, crying softly. One of the flics was kneeling opposite her. The other just stood there.

"What's the matter with you?" I demanded in French. "Turn him over, he needs artificial respiration."

"Please, monsieur," said the kneeling flic.

"What the hell's the matter with you?"

I grabbed hold of Jack's arm to turn him over myself.

"Monsieur," said the kneeling flic in a firmer voice, and I looked at him. He was shaking his head slowly. "This man, his skull is crushed, in the region of the temple. I must tell you he is dead."

I stood up. Jill buried her face against my chest. "Damn it," she said, "damn it, damn it. They coshed him, and he hardly struggled, except trying to protect me, it was like he knew he was going to die and he took it like one of his god-damn Rondeños."

Seven

Death, even violent death, in a city the size of Paris will not make the headlines unless you are a bigshot or have met your end under circumstances more sensational than having your skull split open in the late hours by three unknown as-sailants. Usually a small paragraph buried in the back of the morning papers would have been all Jack merited in the way of a public epitaph, not that it mattered one way or the other to Jack.

But several things made the story news, and Jack got page one below the fold in the Paris paper I read over my coffee and croissants the next morning. Jack had most re-cently been an obscure U.S. government civil servant, but once he'd held down the number two spot in the State De-partment protocol section. Also, geography gave the story a certain grim appeal: in better weather than last night's, the Seine bank opposite Notre Dame is a favorite haunt of Pari-sian lovers. It was like murder on the bank of the Tidal Basin in Washington or in Central Park in New York before Central Park became off-limits after dark to anyone but the foolhardy.

The story also had Jack in the company of his British paramour, and the French, convinced like everyone else that the grass is greener on the other side, will tell you that the Anglo-Saxon male may be a chilly lover but that his

139

sister makes the most expert, willing and versatile of bed companions. There was mention, too, of an international private detective with a controversial reputation who had been grilled by the metropolitan police and had failed to enlighten them on anything but his past associations with the deceased. An early arrest, the police indicated after having paradoxically admitted that they had no leads, was expected.

I tucked the paper under my arm and drove the rented VW through rush hour traffic to the Georges Cinq. Senator Bundy was having breakfast in the interior courtyard with a couple of two-star generals from NATO. They left about a quarter to ten, looking angry, bewildered and defeated, the way only military men can look when they have just been told by a ranking member of Congress how to perform their duties.

Tossing the paper on the table, I said, "Seen it?"

Senator Bundy nodded. "I'm sorry about your friend. I guess I had him wrong."

"Père Massicot didn't make the papers," I said coldly, "but you can stop worrying about making that last payment."

The Senator said that I had better explain that, and I explained it. Then I said, with a smile that didn't match the bright sunlight streaming in through the glass roof of the courtyard, "Did you have them both killed?"

Senator Bundy broke a croissant, dipped half of it in his coffee cup, nibbled at the moist end, set it down, dabbed at his lips with a stiffly starched linen napkin and said, "I hear you haven't picked up your retainer yet. You can pick it up and get the hell out of Paris."

"Before or after I tell the flics you thought Jack Morley was blackmailing you?"

Senator Bundy sipped at his café au lait and looked at me over the rim of the cup. It was probably a look like that that had given the two major generals their early morning blues. "How much?" he asked.

"How much what?"

"It says in the paper you had no professional connection with Morley. Naturally you wanted to see me first, to let me buy your silence. How much?" Controlled cynical anger made a razor slash of his thin lips. His beefy face was pale.

"Let's talk about Clay Bundy," I said, and he looked up, not getting it until I tossed another word into the silence. I said: "Junior."

"My son is dead. He was killed in the war. His P-43 went down in the Alps."

"Then why were you paying off Massicot?"

"That's none of your affair any longer. You came here trying to protect Jack Morley, and I gave you the chance. You did a great job. You're all finished here now."

There was nothing I could say to the first part of that, and I didn't need his harsh sarcasm to remind me I had been within earshot when Jack Morley was beaten to death.

"But if, somehow, he really hadn't died," I said.

"Hadn't died? Morley? I don't get you."

"Not Morley. Clay Bundy Junior."

"My boy is dead. Morley established that."

"How?"

"The way they do those things. The files are open to the right people in Washington. I'm sure you could get access to them."

"And read that Jack Morley found a chunk of fifty-caliber machine gun with the right serial number on it?"

"Well, what did you expect after more than twenty years?"

141

"What did you expect when you went to Col de Larche after the war?"

He set his cup down hard, rattling the saucer. "Listen, mister. I'm going to say this only once. I went to Col de Larche because they had my boy down as missing in action, and that's worse than learning he was dead because you don't know for sure. I went there. He crashed all right. He was killed. Then somebody opened the whole business up again, and Morley was sent to Col de Larche and he found out the same thing I did. Clay Bundy Junior died in 1944, and he died a hero. That's it, mister. I don't know what motivation you'd have for trying to besmirch the reputation of a dead man, but I'll tell you this: if I were you I'd stop trying. His mother back in the States is not a well woman and that's all she'd need, to have the papers making a circus out of this. I won't have it, mister. I'd break you first. You know how much effort it would take? A couple of phone calls, and they'd pick up your paper in Washington and you'd be looking for a job in One Potato, Idaho, as a night watchman. Don't make me do it. I could break you like a twig."

"Is that the way you put it to Morley?"

"I never laid eyes on Morley."

"Who opened your son's case up again?"

But he shook his head. "You can pick up your check any time today. I'm giving instructions for it to be destroyed to-night if you don't claim it. Now get out of here or I'll have you thrown out."

His angry eyes shifted just enough to take in a pair of barely post-college types sitting at a nearby table in the courtyard. Apparently they were the lads who would do the throwing. They wore identical pale blue seersucker suits, identical crew-cuts and identical looks of what they thought passed for inscrutability as they sat sipping coffee and giving me the hard once-over out of narrowed eyes. Then their eyes shifted away from mine, as the Senator's had, and they were watching the maître d' approach from the far end of the courtyard. He was wearing a tailcoat and a smile that managed to be midway between obsequious and supercilious as he led his patron, who was a woman, at a brisk march among the tables. She was close behind him, her face hidden by his shoulder, and I didn't recognize her until he did a sharp right turn down an aisle among the tables while she kept coming straight toward us. For a couple of seconds it was funny, the maître d' still marching briskly and smiling professionally, unaware that his patron had walked off at a tangent.

The patron was Jill Williams, and she was turned out in a wheat-colored suit with a dark silk scarf at her throat, and as she neared us it stopped being funny. The maître d' realized his mistake and paused in mid-stride. The two seersucker suits started to get up but sat down again because Jill waved her right hand at them. Then she recognized me and almost said my name but said, instead, "Senator Bundy?"

He just looked at her. In her right hand she was holding a big Colt .45 automatic that must have belonged to Jack Morley. A .45 is no woman's weapon.

"You'd better put that down, young lady," he told her slowly. His voice was steady and his eyes were like flint. You had to give him that. "Put it down and then we'll talk."

"There's nothing to talk about. I came here to kill you."

The maître d' heard her, and saw what was in her hand. His face turned white and he clutched the back of a chair for support.

She said it again, elaborating to screw up her own

courage: "I'm going to kill you because you killed Jack Morley."

He never lost his poise. "Then you'd be making a tragic and irremediable mistake. I had nothing to do with Morley's death."

Her voice took on an almost childlike quality. "You did so. You're a liar."

I said, slowly: "Jill, look at me. Jack was my friend. I'm going to get up and you're going to put that gun in my hand." She shook her head. "Right now," I said.

I stood. "Keep away," she said. "You keep out of this." She was still pointing the .45 at Senator Bundy. I needed three steps to reach her outstretched hand. When I had taken two of them, one of the seersucker suits decided to play hero.

"I'm aiming a gun at you under the table," he told Jill. "I can't possibly miss. I'm going to count three. If you don't drop your gun, I'll shoot. One."

Everything had happened so quickly that I hadn't realized until then that the .45 in Jill's hand wasn't cocked. I saw her finger tighten on the trigger and then, when that didn't change the status quo, she yanked back on the slide. At least she tried to. By then I was between her and the seersucker suit and she was discovering that a woman does not have the strength to cock a .45 and keep it aimed at the same time. Plenty of men don't either.

"Two," seersucker suit announced.

I grabbed for the gun in Jill's hand and got it. She stumbled away from me, crying out. The seersucker suit who had given the ultimatum got up fast, jerked her hand behind her back and raised it between her shoulder blades in a hammer lock. She whimpered. "It's all right now, Senator," he said, breathing hard. "Nothing to worry about." He raised her arm higher and she whimpered again. "You there," he told the maître d' imperiously in French. "Call the police."

I did some fast thinking. They could hit Jill with an assault rap if they wanted to, but the Senator could do without that kind of publicity. "Hold it," I said, pulling the butt-plate clear of the .45 far enough to see that the clip was fully loaded. I slammed it back with the palm of my hand, contemptuously, and said: "Well, well, well. She was bluffing all along. Not even loaded, how do you like that?"

They all looked at me.

"Let go of her," the Senator said at last.

Seersucker suit was surprised enough to lever Jill's arm a little higher.

I reversed the .45 in my hand, holding it by the barrel, "Do that again," I said, "and you'll be down on all fours under the table looking for your teeth."

He released her. She sat down at an empty table, folded her arms on the tablecloth and buried her face in them, like a kid during rest period in a classroom. She made snuffling noises.

"Wasn't loaded, huh?" the other seersucker suit asked.

"That's right."

"How about that?" he said.

Senator Bundy should have been rattled, but his hand was rock-steady as he raised the cup to his lips and finished his tepid coffee. "I take it you know this woman?" he asked me.

"She was a good friend of Jack Morley's. I don't have to tell you she's been through plenty. She was there last night when he got it."

"I had nothing to do with Morley's death. Can you convince her of that?"

145

"I don't know it for a fact myself."

Senator Bundy smiled faintly. "You're a hard son of a bitch to get along with," he observed without malice.

"But I can convince her that coming at you with a gun, even an unloaded gun, won't get her anywhere."

The smile broadened. At that moment I almost liked Senator Bundy. "And a loaded one?"

"Leave her to me," I urged. "It's for your own benefit. You can lean on her, sure, but tell me, you want the kind of press that will earn you?"

"I don't. Of course not."

"Then let me walk out of here with her. Can you handle the maître?"

The question seemed to surprise him. Probably he was convinced he could handle anyone. Maybe he could. "All right." He nodded slowly. "I guess I ought to have my head examined, though."

Jill came with me to the archway at the end of the courtyard. She walked heavily, and I could smell the anise on her breath. As we were leaving, Senator Bundy said something in French that made the maître d' laugh nervously.

Jill Williams had kept house with Jack in a small hotel a block from the Odeon. It is on a small street that even the Parisian taxi drivers have difficulty locating, and it is the only hotel in Paris where you can get a good, clean room for ten francs a night, service and tax compris. Those who know of it are reluctant to spread the word. Why spoil a good thing?

I parked the VW facing the curb near the Odeon and walked across the square with Jill and down the narrow street in the direction of Boulevard St. Germain. The street is exactly one block long and the hotel holds down number one. If you can find it the next time you are in Paris, more power to you.

I took Jill upstairs. She had packed all of Jack's things in a battered old Gladstone and an imitation leather two-suiter. "It's all he had," she said. "Everything. It really isn't much, is it?"

She expected no answer, and I gave her none. Sometimes, after the sudden death of a loved one, you can't stand to be where you lived together and you just run away, but sometimes you keep the personal effects, almost like a fetish, and the place where you lived together becomes a shrine. It was too soon to tell what Jill would do.

"I would have shot him," she said. "I hope you understand that."

No comment.

"I may try it again."

"No you won't," I said.

She kicked at the Gladstone bag. "But I might."

"You don't know for sure Bundy had anything to do with it. And even if you did—"

"Those are words, just words. They won't bring him back."

"Nothing will bring him back, Jill. He's dead."

She sat down on the Gladstone bag, covered her face with her hands and started to cry. I let her alone and then, after a while, lit a cigarette and gave it to her.

"I'm afraid," she said. "I'm so afraid. I don't want to stay here and I don't want to go away. I have no reason to stay and nowhere to go."

"No relatives back in England?"

"No one. I was a dancer in Pigalle. About five years too old, but it was all right for a while because the French like English showgirls. I had lost my job, and it would have been

147

difficult to get another one, and then Jack came along. He was good for me, and I for him. We needed each other." She made a face and blew her nose. "Two crutches supporting each other. Maybe an outsider would have found it pathetic. We didn't. He was so good to me. He was everything. And I—without him I'm nothing."

"Cut it out," I said.

"I'm nothing. I'm too old to start a new life."

"How old are you?"

"Twenty-eight."

"Yeah, that's ancient, all right," I said.

"I found the gun while packing his things. I drank Pernod, and I looked at it, and that was the only way I could get myself to leave. With a gun. To kill Senator Bundy. Does that make sense to you? Any sense at all? Am I sick?"

"Everything makes sense when someone you love dies," I said, more sententiously than I had intended. "Or nothing makes sense. Stop tearing yourself down."

"I just want to sit here and do nothing. I can't face the street again. I can't do anything. I'm numb."

I looked at her, pathetic and vulnerable, sitting on the suitcase packed with her lover's possessions. "In that case," I said, "we're going to take a walk. Come on."

"But I just told you—"

"That's why. Go powder your nose."

"You don't have to feel you're responsible—"

"Who told you you have a monopoly on grief?" I said harshly. "Jack was my friend too, and I walked away from there a minute before they killed him. Let's go."

I left the car where it was, near the Odeon, and walked Jill's feet off. It was one of those days made to order for the director general of tourism. Yesterday's rain had washed the air clear and the sky was that almost unbelievable blue that Utrillo tried to paint. It was warm but not hot, like May in Washington. The dog days come to Paris, if at all, in August. Cleverly, that is when the Parisians surrender their city to the tourists and leave for the seashore.

We walked down St. Germain to the river and crossed on foot to the vast open space of the Place de La Concorde. I told Jill the existentialist joke about the driver who went round and round the great square, trapped because all the exit-streets had mysteriously disappeared, until a flic waved him down and informed him that he must leave at once or be hauled off to the local lockup. When the driver protested that there was no way out and he seemed doomed to spend the rest of his life circling the Place de La Concorde, the flic looked him squarely in the eye and said, "But of course, that is precisely why you must leave." The joke is better told in French and best told when you are ensnarled in Paris traffic, but Jill smiled tentatively and even laughed a little.

She took my arm when we entered the Garden of the Tuileries and walked in the deep shade of the avenues of plane and chestnut trees. Behind the massive, U-shaped Palace of the Louvre, we zeroed in on the best view Paris has to offer, and possibly the best city view in the world, the one where you sight through the small arch of the Arc de Triomphe du Carrousel, back across the Tuileries and the Place de La Concorde, and up the Champs Elysées to the enormous Arc de Triomphe of the Etoile hanging against that blue Paris sky. The view is no accident, and it explains why they paid Baron Haussmann all that dough to redesign Paris.

We took a fiacre to the Bois and had a picnic there. I

found myself talking about what it was like to grow up on the wrong side of the tracks in Baltimore during the Depression, and about my one and only marriage, which hadn't worked out. When I got to the part where I learned my wife was a murderer we were lying side by side on the grass, full of bread and cheese and much red wine, and Jill turned her head impulsively to brush her lips against my cheek. Suddenly, maybe because I had been talking too much about myself and finding that some of it hurt, I found myself wanting her. Our eyes were close. Hers were shining. We got up in a hurry, awkwardly, and brushed the grass off our clothing and took the fiacre back to town and started walking again.

Twilight hung over the rooftops of St. Germain. Jill had kicked off her shoes and stood at the window of her hotel room smoking a cigarette.

"Tired?" I asked.

"No. It's funny but I'm not. We walked miles."

"Paris," I said. "Quite a town. A walking town."

I came up behind her to look out the window.

"I needed today," she said. "My God, how I needed it." She let her head fall back against my shoulder. Her hair smelled of perfume and the Bois. When I drew back she asked lightly, "Is it the Chester Drum cure for disconsolate females?"

"Or for lonely private detectives."

"What are you going to do?"

"I don't know." But of course I did.

"No. Please tell me."

"Go to Col de Larche, I guess."

"I knew you would. Being you, you'd have to. But I wanted to hear you say it."

We said no more for a while. Dusk washed the colors from the shopfronts across the street.

"You don't have to worry about me any longer," she said finally. "I won't try anything foolish again."

"I know that."

"All I had to do was get through today."

In a sense she was right but in another sense she was whistling in the dark, and we both knew it. With Jack's death, an abyss had opened up under her life. She had nowhere to go and no one to take her there.

"That isn't true," she said all of a sudden. "I'm scared. Everywhere I look there's nothing. I'm so scared." She let her head fall back against my shoulder again, and this time I didn't move. "Hold me."

Her dancer's waist was supple under my hands. Her hips swelled out from it, rounded and firm. She turned quickly, to face me, and my hands slid around her body and down a little. Her hands went around my neck. Barefoot, she wasn't as tall as I had thought. She got up on tiptoe and pulled my head down, and I kissed her.

When her lips began to tremble under my mouth she parted them, and the kiss got wild. I kept telling myself, while we were locked together, that this was wrong, it was all wrong, it was because her past was dead and her future unknown and she wanted to cling to the present, which was all she had, and whatever I did, if I did anything but break it up and get the hell out of there, would be taking advantage of her. But my hands were ranging all over her, the firmness of haunch, the long smoothness of back, the sweet soft roundness of breast. She drew back and bumped the windowsill, and unbuttoned the wheat-colored jacket and shucked it and her white blouse too. I looked at her eyes, that were heavy-lidded now, and her lips, that were swollen,

151

Stephen Marlowe

and she saw the desire in my eyes, and then she came against me again and she felt my desire. "Love me," she said against my mouth. "Love me, love me."

She sat on the edge of the bed, her hands behind her back, fumbling, and there was that slight and awaited and somehow sad but exciting fraction of an inch sag as hook and eye were parted, and she lay back on the bed.

I stood over her. "Jill," I said. "Jill, listen to me. I'm going away. In the morning. I'm going alone. I won't be coming back."

"I know that. I know it."

I said nothing else.

She looked up. It was almost dark in the room, and her teeth and the whites of her eyes gleamed. "But you want me?"

I just nodded. In another moment I'd get out of there. What else could I do?

"You told me something before," she said. "You told me I didn't have a monopoly on grief. You were right."

I just stood there.

"Well, goddamn it, I'm not asking you to feel sorry for me now. What the hell makes you think *you* have a monopoly on desire?"

I looked down at her, and suddenly everything changed. She was right, as earlier I had been right.

"Go on, then, if you want. Get out of here."

But instead I went to her.

Eight

Out of Lyon the road runs flat, but you can see mountains in the distance. They are all around you, thrusting high and

152

white against the sky, by the time you reach Grenoble. For a while after that the road up into the High Alps twists and climbs, but it is a good road. Then you reach Gap, and after that the road is very bad, narrow and pot-holed, clinging to cliffs and plunging into valleys and widening into remote Alpine villages; a few dun-colored, pitted stucco buildings, a church, a herd of cattle or sheep grazing in an unexpected meadow, and the road is off again, switching back, chasing itself higher into the mountains, until beyond Lauzet you are above timberline, and even in midsummer in the sun it is cool, and wherever there is shadow, snow clings to the rocks and ledges.

Col de Larche is a mountain pass and a village a few kilometers from the Italian border and little more than a hundred kilometers north of the Riviera at Cannes. It is eight thousand feet above sea level, and the scenery is awesome. Tourists come, and stay a while to gape at the mountains and stare down into the dizzying depths of the valleys before driving east into Italy or south through the Maritime Alps to the watering places of the Côte d'Azur. If they stay overnight, they put up at the Grand Hotel des Alpes. The choice of lodgings is obligatory: there is no other hotel in Col de Larche.

I wasn't wild about that as I reached the Col late Wednesday afternoon. Dominique Guilbert's family owned the hotel, and the one and only time I'd met her brother Gaston she'd held a gun on me and Gaston had come off second best in our brawl. I expected a reception somewhat less than enthusiastic.

The Grand Hotel des Alpes was a long, low building. Its overlapping wood plank walls, painted a bright red, looked like the lapstreak hull of a fast cabin cruiser. I parked the

VW in front among a dozen cars, none with French plates, and went inside.

I saw Dominique right away. She stood behind the reception desk at the far end of the lobby, looking up at a tall and gangling American tourist with those big brown eyes of hers. I was struck again by her total absorption with the task at hand. The American was registering a minor complaint of some kind, and her pert face was a study in sympathy and concern.

". . . sure would like to ride the wachamacallit—the téléférique—before I leave Col de Larche," the American was saying. "I hear the view's real special, and me being a camera bug and all."

"But I am sure you can understand, Monsieur Kidder, how difficult it would be to run the téléférique for one person only. Should others wish to ride to the top, then of course. How long will you stay with us?"

"Depends on the weather," Kidder said, "and if I can take this altitude okay. Great Barrington, Mass., ain't any eight thousand feet above sea level."

"Well, I hope something can be arranged before you go."

Dominique smiled, hopefully and optimistically, and Kidder started past me, saw my crew-cut and said, "American?"

"You guessed it."

"Kidder's my name. Great Barrington, Mass. Traveling alone?"

He had a long, sad face with large-lobed ears, a long nose that had been broken and set crookedly and small, earnest eyes behind shell-rimmed glasses. I told him my name and said I was traveling alone.

"Well say, join me in a drink? They got a pretty good American bar here. But better watch yourself, on account of at this altitude a drink will really sock you."

"I'll remember that," I said, "and I'll take you up on that drink after I check in."

Kidder gangled off across the lobby, and at the sound of my voice Dominique looked up quickly from the ledger she had been studying. "You," she said, her face all round ohs of surprise, the brown eyes wide, the red lips pursed. "Why do you come to my village?"

I set my B-4 bag down. "Well, to start with I'd like a room."

"Perhaps we are full."

I glanced past Dominique's head at the keyboard. At least half the pegs had keys on them. "It doesn't look like it."

"No," she admitted. "But it would be better if you went away. My brother, when he sees you—"

I grinned. "Remind me to duck."

Dominique didn't think that was funny. Maybe it wasn't. She handed a carte de séjour across the counter, and I filled it out with the aid of my passport. She was leaning across the counter on her elbows reading upside-down what I had written on the police card when I came to the line for occupation. American passports don't require that information any more. I could have filled in anything from aardvark breeder to zither player, but I wanted a re-action and wrote the truth.

"You are a detective?" Dominique asked me.

"It's one way of making a buck."

"Of making . . . ? Oh, I see. A private detective? And you are presently engaged?"

"More or less," I said, which was stretching the truth a little.

"You are working for this Jack Morley? But why?"

"Morley's dead. He was murdered in Paris Monday night."

Dominique's reaction was one of incredulity. "Mon Dieu, what are you telling me?"

"First Père Massicot at the Flea Market and then Jack Morley. It looks like your father's run clean out of black-mailers."

Dominique plucked the carte de séjour off the counter. Her face was pale. "You think that is funny?"

"It wasn't meant to be. Do you?"

Dominique tore my carte de séjour in half, and then in half again. "I regret that we cannot accommodate you without a reservation, Monsieur Drum. South of here, in Larche itself, you may have better luck."

Just then a woman emerged from a doorway behind the counter. She was tall. Her gleaming black hair was streaked with gray and worn in straight bangs across her forehead. I put her age at a well-preserved thirty-eight or forty, though the bangs made her look younger. Her leggy, somewhat angular figure could have held its own with anything short of Dominique's sleek and well-rounded perfection. She wore dark glasses with broad side bows and a black dress with short sleeves that were met high on her arms by a pair of the longest white gloves I had ever seen. The overall impression was this: had Charles Addams employed good-looking models a little past their prime, she would have been one of them.

She looked at me and at the torn carte de séjour on the counter, and asked Dominique in French, "There is a problem?"

"No problem, Maman. I was only telling Monsieur Drum that we regret we cannot accommodate him without a reservation."

156

"But surely you are aware we have—"

"Monsieur Drum, he is a friend of the American Jack Morley who came to Col de Larche during the spring."

Their French was rapid, but I could follow it. Madame Guilbert parted her lips on the left side to show half a set of good white teeth. The right side of her mouth remained immobile. It was an odd and disconcerting smile, with only half her face in the act and the other half frozen. Then I saw the tracery of tiny white scars on her jaw, right cheek and temple, and I realized her face had been through massive plastic surgery.

"Monsieur," she asked, "do you speak French? Unfortunately, unlike my daughter, I have no English."

"A little."

"My daughter has made a mistake. We have a room for you, a fine room with a view of the mountains. It will be sixty francs a day, service and tax included, on the demipension. That is satisfactory?"

I said it was more than satisfactory. Dominique looked very unhappy while I filled out a new carte de séjour. She took her mother to the far end of the counter, where they spoke in whispers with their heads close together. They were arguing. I got the idea I was the subject under discussion. Madame Guilbert ended it with an, "Absolutely yes," and Dominique sulked in my direction.

"I will show Monsieur his room."

"Okay."

There was no elevator. She led me to the stairs, mad enough to flounce, and I watched the intriguing motion of her hips. I turned for a final look at the counter from the foot of the stairs, but her mother had disappeared.

Amos Kidder, of Great Barrington, Mass., was drinking

a scotch and water in the small American bar of the hotel. He raised his glass in my direction. "Johnnie Walker Black, and they use it for bar scotch," he said. "Howdya like that? Ever been to Scotland?"

"Few years ago."

"Can't find a decent scotch in the whole country, on account of all the best brands go to the States or here to France. 'Le whisky' is the drink these days over here, they tell me. Is that yellow stuff any good?"

He meant the Pernod I was drinking.

Before I could answer, he went on: "At first I thought it was that there absinthe that's illegal. But I heard you call it Pernod. You know, absinthe makes the heart grow fonder. Hah, hah, hah."

I managed to wince only a little, but if Amos Kidder was the type that ran off at the mouth that suited me fine. It was why I'd picked up his option on a drink. I was hoping he could tell a fellow American something about the setup here in Col de Larche.

"Been here long?"

"Got in last night. Just wandering around the Continent for a bit. My first time over, yes sir. You only live once, so I just up and closed the hardware store for the summer and said to hell with it, a man needs a vacation. Eight weeks in all, and I figure Great Barrington can get along without me that long. What's your line?"

"I'm a private detective."

"Say now, is that so? A private eye, huh? I never met a real live shamus before. Hah, hah, hah." He winked at me. Cutting the volume of his voice down, though the only other occupant of the bar, the white-jacketed old man who had served our drinks, was at the other end polishing glasses, he asked: "Are you on a case or something?"

"No, same as you. Vacation."

"Oh, confidential, huh?" he said out of the corner of his mouth. "Well, I ain't one to pry. 'I was sitting there over a drink when she walks into the bar with a mouth like a knife wound and gives me the thousand-buck hello.' "

"What did you say?"

"Hah, hah, hah. Comes from a TV private eye show. I watch them. I'm a great admirer of private eye shows. That's some line, huh? A dame with a mouth like a knife wound. What they say, expressive. It must be some life you lead." His long face got very serious. "Say, I always wondered. Do you mind being called shamus?"

"No, I'm used to it," I said gravely.

He thumped my back. "Have another drink, shamus? Ain't much else to do around here at night, unless you're one of those young fellows that likes to dance. They got one of those places where they spin records in a glass cage, I forget wachamacallit."

"A discothèque?"

"Say, that's right. A discothèque. That sexy kid works behind the desk, she's the boss' daughter, was there last night dancing up a storm. She's got a build on her, that one does. She was really dancing up a storm."

"I didn't know she was the proprietor's daughter."

"Oh yeah, it's a family operation all the way, just like the White Pillars Inn back in Great Barrington. Mr. and Mrs. Guilbert, now, they don't speak a word of English, but the kids have gone modern on them, and Gaston and that there Dominique that's stacked, they speak English real good. The old lady runs the joint though. She really wears the pants around here. She cracks the whip, you watch that old man of hers jump."

"Really?"

"Yeah, I seen it. Say, you met her, the old lady that has the lopsided smile? Plastic surgery. I can always tell. I had a brother-in-law of mine that got his face all cut up in a car accident. He had plastic surgery. It leaves those little white scars if you look real careful. Anyhow, I seen Madame Guilbert reading the riot act to her old man last night. In the dining room. I wouldn't want to mess with her, no sir."

"What were they arguing about?"

"Search me. My French, like they say, leaves a little to be desired. But I heard them mention the kid's name a few times."

"Dominique?"

"Uh-uh. The boy. Gaston. He must be some kind of a regular French j.d. the way they were carrying on about him. I got the idea he was down in Cannes, in some kind of trouble, and Madame Guilbert didn't like it. Mon-sewer Guilbert kept on saying there wasn't a damn thing they could do about it, but Madame Guilbert said there was. You could see her standing there and yammering away, real soft, in that throaty voice of hers, and he took it and damn near—howdya say?—genuflected. Well, hah, hah, hah, she's bigger'n he is. Maybe he's scared of her. He's a real little guy, that's probably how come that stacked daughter of theirs, Dominique is so tiny. It's funny, him being a hero of the Resistance and all, the way he stands there and takes what his wife dishes out. Well, I seen too much of that and I figure it's why I never married."

"I didn't know he was a hero of the Resistance. That's interesting."

"Ain't it though? But I guess you got to take that with a grain of salt. The way they tell it, one out of every two froggies was either a bigshot in the Maquis or else Charles de Gaulle wouldn't make a move without him. I guess it upsets them, looking back on how they just rolled over and played dead for old Adolf Shickelgruber, so they all claim they fought in the Underground."

I perked up my ears at that. Coming from Amos Kidder, it was an unexpectedly astute comment on the French. I began to think Kidder was something more than a wet-behind-the-ears American tourist, the kind you meet in droves during the summer from Trondheim to Taormina. If anything, he had troweled it on too thick. Also, for someone who'd arrived in Col de Larche last night, he seemed to know a lot about the Guilberts. I raised my second Pernod and looked him in the eye suddenly. He hadn't expected that. His eyes, behind the shell-rimmed glasses, were green and yellow-flecked, curiously flat, like pictures of eyes, but bright with a cold intelligence. Then he became aware of my stare. He cleared his throat and blinked, and I seemed to be looking at someone else's eyes, bland, vacuous and insensitive. It was a pretty impressive trick. I wondered if I'd ever see Amos Kidder with his guard down again.

Nine

The discothèque, as the French have developed it, is a cross between an uptown nightclub and a neighborhood juke joint.

It sports a large dance floor, button-sized tables, drinks somewhat but not outrageously overpriced and a disc jockey high up on one wall in a glass cage. In aloof isolation, the disc jockey plays no requests; it is his business to guess the mood of the crowd and spin appropriate platters. The earliest discothèques, which first saw the dark of night under the stars on the Côte d'Azur, were outdoors, the jockey's cage mounted on a tower and the dancing done al fresco.

The discothèque du Col in Col de Larche, thanks to the cold of the high altitude nights, was indoors. I got there after nine that night, feeling restless, edgy and slightly light-headed with the altitude. I had seen Amos Kidder at dinner, but we'd only nodded to each other across the almost empty room. I had not seen Dominique, nor had her brother Gaston made an appearance at the family hotel. I decided the night life of Col de Larche, if any, would center around the discothèque.

Ordering le whisky avec siphon at a solo table under the jockey's cage, I scanned the room. It was crowded, mostly with local types dressed for the Riviera and to hell with Col de Larche's forty-degree nights. That meant tight tapered ducks or jeans, usually white, for both sexes, belted low at the navel or below, and shirts knotted at the waist to show plenty of bare and sun-tanned midriff. It was a young crowd. The boys wore their hair a little too long and the girls a little too short. That and the standard uniform made the boys look slightly effete and the girls slightly tomboyish.

There was no mistaking Dominique's sex though. I spotted her after a while dancing slowly backwards in my direction to the beat of a cha-cha-cha. Her head was canted to one side so I could see her face in profile. She was in the arms of a tall, thin kid who was staring down at the top of her head with a look of intense concentration on his face. Dominique moved sinuously, as though every bone in her body had a few extra joints. She was as supple as garden hose on a hot day. Her white ducks began a couple of inches below the abrupt flare of her hips. Those hips were really something to see in motion. It wasn't anything so blatantly obvious as a bump-and-grind routine. It was a controlled surging flow, absolutely attuned to the cha-cha-cha rhythm, uncontrived and somehow dreamlike, that made you think this was what Latin dancing was all about. At the same time there was an innocent gamin quality to the way Dominique danced, but instead of detracting from the sex appeal of those fluid hips, it increased it. Dominique made every good dancer in the discothèque that night, and there were plenty of them, look like a marionette on jerky wires.

The tall boy danced her back to her table, where she was sitting with two other girls, did a stiff bow and went away. I got up and drifted in that direction while the jockey was changing platters. I was out of uniform. My seersucker suit made me stand out a mile off, like a kid in blue jeans at the senior prom. I saw the look of refusal building on her pretty face as I approached, but she was my only entrée into the life of Col de Larche, and in the life of the village, if anywhere, could be found the reason for Jack Morley's death.

"Saw you out there," I said. "I bet you could make even me look like Gene Kelly on one of his good days." I was smiling my best stag-line smile and not thinking it would do me any good.

The ice in Dominique's gin-and-tonic clinked against her teeth as she finished it and looked up at me. There was a gin-and-tonic in front of each of her friends too, and half a dozen little pink chits on the table with their edges torn. If each of them stood for a round of paid drinks, then, even though a French gin-and-tonic contains about a thimbleful of gin, Dominique and her friends had got an early start on the evening.

She licked her lips, and I realized the look of refusal hadn't been that at all. Despite the fluid grace of her dancing, Dominique was nervous and tense. I got the notion that if I'd cat footed up behind her, she'd have let out a

163

scream on her way up to hitting the ceiling.

My opening gambit drew nothing but a faint social smile from Dominique and frank stares of curiosity from her friends. A tango had commenced. Beyond the table I could see the tall boy wandering shyly back in Dominique's direction. She saw him, and relief flitted across her face. She got up. The tall boy started to grin gratefully. He reached out for her and wound up holding air. I had taken Dominique's hand and was steering her toward the dance floor. It is very easy to be a boor when you are interested in something other than the social amenities.

"Was this Gene Kelly a football player? Or perhaps a wrestler?"

"Huh?" I had forgotten my allusion to the dancer.

"Then would you please stop holding my hand so hard?"

"Afraid you'd go away," I said brightly.

"I'll dance with you. I won't make a scene." Dominique's hand was cold. I eased the pressure on it. "Besides, it may even be interesting. That suit of yours. The stripes, they are very American. I never danced with a zebra before."

"The zebra, close relative of the horse," I recited, "lives on the African veld. Its striped hide blends perfectly with the local flora. It is unknown in America except in zoos."

Dominique looked up at me and abruptly smiled. She was still tense about something, because her lips were trembling a little, but the smile was honest. "A tasty morsel," she picked up for me, "it is much favored by lions and leopards when they cannot find giraffes." My hand touched her bare midriff and hers the back of my neck. "Mon Dieu, but you are tall as a giraffe."

She was small, trim and excitingly pliant in my arms. The top of her poodle-cut hair didn't quite reach my shoulder. She had a way of dancing with her head canted to one side and thrown back, so she could look up into your eyes. We began to glide across the floor to the alternatingly slow and fast beat of the tango. With its long, insinuating steps it is a dance of leg contact rather than body contact and very pleasant work with Dominique as your partner. Pretty soon I forgot why I was dancing with her. We said nothing else until the music stopped. I don't have a pair of left feet, but I'm usually one of those guys who has got to hear every beat, especially in a tricky number like the tango, and translate it to my legs. With Dominique in my arms I just danced and the hell with it, and we were good enough to clear the floor in the area of the jockey's cage. Also, something flowed between us and fused. This is hard to explain. It doesn't happen often and it sounds corny when you try to tell it. It had happened to me only twice before in my life, and the first time I married her and the second time I should have. It happened again with Dominique, quickly, without warning, like an electric circuit completed, and until that moment I had thought myself too jaded to feel it that suddenly and that completely again. Maybe I was one of the lucky ones. Maybe.

The music stopped. We stood there, still holding on. I heard feet shuffling. The buzz of conversation. The clink of glasses. It was all disjointed, unreal and miles away. I was holding Dominique in my arms.

"Hello," I said in a tentative, funny voice.

"Hello."

"Music's stopped." My voice still sounded funny.

"They're staring."

"I don't care. Do you?"

"I don't care either. Do you?"

"I just asked you that."

"Mon Dieu," Dominique asked, knowing the answer, "did it happen to you too?"

Then something intruded. I was aware of an anxious face behind Dominique. It was the old man who had served drinks at the Grand Hotel des Alpes bar.

"Monsieur Gaston phoned," he said. "From Cannes."

"Yes?" It took a few seconds for Dominique to refocus.

"He has been hurt. He did not wish Madame to know. He asked for you."

"Hurt? He is badly hurt?"

The old man shrugged. "He was able to telephone. Not the girl. Not the poule." He mouthed the last word with scorn. A poule is a prostitute.

"The fool. Oh, the fool. Where is he?"

"The usual place when he is in Cannes. The Martinez."

The tall boy who had danced with Dominique earlier came up. "Henri," she asked him, "you have your car? I must go to Cannes. At once."

"My father has it. He has gone overnight to Briançon."

"I have a car," I said. "At the hotel."

Dominique stared at me blankly. "You? But why would you—"

"I could drive you to Cannes."

"You?" she said again, using the formal vous. "But Gaston, he would be furious."

"He wants you. I can take you there."

She thought only a moment. "Very well."

Ten minutes later we were driving south through the night on the high mountain road down to the Cóte d'Azur.

Ten

Before midnight we were on the Boulevard de la Croisette, the main drag of the poshest resort in France and maybe in the world. Floodlamps strung in palm trees on the mall in the middle of the broad boulevard gave it an indoor look, like a Technicolor movie set of life on the Riviera. Late traffic streamed slowly in both directions along the Croisette. The sea-front promenade was crowded with late strollers.

"There is the Carlton," Dominique said, indicating a big hotel on our left. "It is soon now, the Martinez. You can see it ahead, where the boulevard curves."

I had tried to pump her on the way down, but she'd had very little to say. Her brother Gaston was involved with a poule named Gina, their relationship had become more than professional and Gina's pimp had been threatening Gaston for months.

"That's all?" I had asked.

"All? He is crazy with jealousy, like most pimps when their women become involved emotionally with another man."

"Didn't Gaston realize that would happen?"

"He realized it," Dominique had said. "But you have not seen Gina."

Now in Cannes I pulled the VW up the Hotel Martinez's circular driveway. It was a huge yellow stone building, brightly lit, with tiers of terraces. I gave the doorman my key.

"You are staying at the hotel?"

"Visiting a friend."

"Ça va bien. Ask at the car desk when you are ready to leave."

The lobby was crowded, despite the hour. A man in evening clothes, an American, was asking the concierge whether the action was faster at the public or private casino. Dominique, looking very small and anxious, got her brother's room number.

"Chet," she said, "will you wait for me?"

"I'd rather go up with you."

"I'm sorry. You know I am grateful. But Gaston must not see you now. You understand?"

"We driving back tonight?"

"I do not know. That depends. You will wait here?"

I could have argued with her but decided against it. "In the bar. Give me a call after you find out how he is."

"Yes."

She squeezed my hand and headed for the bank of elevators.

I was sipping moodily at my third cognac when a woman's voice blared over the P.A. speaker above the bar. "Au téléphone, Monsieur Drum. Monsieur Drum, au téléphone."

A boy in the green Martinez monkey suit led me to a booth.

"Dominique?"

"Yes."

"How is he?"

"He was attacked. By thugs." She sounded breathless and concerned. "A doctor has seen him. He is sleeping now, under sedation. Two of his ribs were broken. It would be unwise for him to drive back alone, the doctor said. I will drive him back tomorrow."

"There anything I can do?"

"I don't think so. You have done enough already. Will

you drive back tonight?"

"I'm not sure yet," I said, a little curtly.

There was a pause. "Chet, are you angry with me?"

"No," I said, automatically. Then I thought about it and realized I'd spoken the truth.

"Will I—see you again? In Col de Larche?"

"Want to?"

"But yes. Oh yes, I want to. I wish, I wish you were with me now."

"That can be arranged."

"No. I will sleep in Gaston's room."

"Then I'll see you in Col de Larche."

"Because you want to also, or on business?"

"I don't know," I said frankly. "Probably a little of each. Good night, Dominique."

"Bonne nuit."

I got my chance at the bartender a little after one-thirty. The crowd had thinned out and we were alone at one end of the bar on opposite sides of the hardwood.

"What does a guy do who just popped into Cannes and he's lonely?"

The bartender looked me over. He was a fat man with a red face and a big mustache. "Along the Croisette, at any of the cafés, one can find the women of the night at this hour." He winked. "Beezniz girls, as they call themselves in your language."

"An American I met in Menton mentioned a girl named Gina."

"Ah, Gina." The bartender rolled his eyes and kissed pudgy fingertips. Then he glanced at my somewhat rumpled seersucker. "But Gina is very expensive. Five hundred francs for the night. She does not accept less. She does not work more than once in a night. And if she does not like you, the answer is no."

Five hundred francs is a hundred dollars. "I guess I can afford it once," I said. "How do I get in touch with her?"

"It may be that she already has selected her friend for the night. It is late."

"I'll take the chance."

He looked at me, and at the ten-franc note I placed on the bar.

"Le Festival. A bistro on the Croisette, in the same block as the Carlton. If Gina is still unoccupied, you will find her there."

"How do I know her?"

The bartender smiled. He looked like he was about to swallow his mustache. "Monsieur, I assure you, you will have no difficulty recognizing Gina."

Le Festival was an open-fronted bistro with a terrace outside and colored glass and bamboo decor inside. I scanned the terrace. There were a few beezniz girls sitting alone and sulking in the shank of the night, but none of them seemed the sort to make the Martinez bartender swallow his mustache. They appraised me with bright, avaricious eyes. I walked past them. One of them looked up at me boldly and touched my hand. "All alone on a night such as this, cheri?" she asked. I shook my head and went inside.

A few couples were sitting over their nightcaps at small glass and bamboo tables. A black pianist, his shirtsleeves rolled up and his face shiny with sweat, was belting out Dixieland jazz. Two middle-aged Englishmen, dressed too warmly in tweeds for the Riviera night, their faces that peculiar shade of magenta that only the English seem to get from over-exposure to the southern sun, sat staring lecherously at a girl who held down a table near the piano. Standing, she would be tall, taller than Jill Williams. She wore her black hair piled high on the crown of her head and long in back, falling below her shoulder blades. Her face was gaunt and deeply tanned, a fashion model's face with high cheekbones and thin lips that managed to look cruel and passionate at the same time. She wore a yellow dress, cut low in front, and no fashion model ever sported the cleavage she displayed. I decided, with no coaxing from anyone, that this was Gina.

I selected a table near hers and sat facing the piano. That put Gina in my line of vision a shade to the left of straight ahead. By the time I ordered and got my gin-and-tonic she was giving me the slow, careful once-over. I ignored that for a while, finished my drink and a cigarette and then looked in her direction as if her scrutiny had caught my eye. Her eyelids lowered demurely. I waited until she looked up again, and then I smiled what I hoped was a shy and properly hopeful smile. Gina cocked an eyebrow and appraised me appraising her. Five seconds passed. Her lips, still looking cruel and passionate, parted in a faint, moist smile.

I called the waiter. "Another gin-and-tonic," I said, indicating Gina's table with a nod, "over there. And whatever mademoiselle is drinking."

He glanced at Gina quickly. Her head bobbed a fraction of an inch. He held back my chair for me and I drifted over to her and smiled, warmly now, and sat down.

"It will be a Black Velvet," she said in English somewhat more accented than Dominique's, "what I am drinking. Very expensive, but I like it."

"That's okay. I'm a millionaire—for one night."

Gina grinned. "But that is exactly how I like my million-

171

aires—for one night. And you know what a Black Velvet is?"

"Champagne and Guinness stout. Sounds awful and looks worse, but it's not bad. It's a great hair of the dog."

"Hair of the dog?"

"For a hangover."

"Maybe I will have a hangover in the morning."

"Maybe."

"You have come to Cannes on holiday?"

"I don't believe in holidays," I said.

"No? Then what do you believe in?"

"The roundness of the earth, the certainty of death, and beautiful women who drink Black Velvet in the middle of the night."

Gina laughed. It was throaty laughter, and not at all forced. She was relaxing. She had decided that her first impression was right: I could be her friend for the night.

Our drinks came. We clinked glasses and our hands touched.

"Salut."

"Salut."

"Where are you staying?"

"The Martinez." I had taken a room before walking to Le Festival.

"Ça va. The night concierge is an old friend. And my flat, it is being painted."

"Another drink here?"

"Only if you wish it also. It is growing late."

"Then let's go see your old friend at the Martinez," I said. I could have interrogated Gina there at Le Festival, but at the first indication of it she might have clammed up, figuring she owed me nothing. In my room, with my five hundred francs in her little envelope purse, things would be different.

★ ★ ★ ★ ★

Gina placed her purse on the vanity table of my room in the Martinez. She sat down and combed her long black hair, her eyes never leaving my face in the mirror. The movements of her arms were slow and sensuous. Her eyes were languid, but when she spoke it was in a matter-of-fact voice. "First it is necessary that you pay me."

She put the five hundred francs in her purse. I was standing behind her. Still seated at the vanity table, she reached back for my hand and placed it on her shoulder. I drew back. Gina was one hell of an exciting woman and I didn't want to get anything started. Right now the advantage was mine, but with a little fun and games she might have me eating off the palm of her hand.

"You are annoyed because I asked for the money first?" she said softly. "But I promise, I will seem a beezniz girl no longer. Come."

She headed for the bed. I stood where I was. I didn't trust myself to approach a large horizontal surface with Gina.

"You are shy? Perhaps this is your first time with a beezniz girl?" She gave me a knowing smile. "But of course it must be. You are not one to have to pay for a night of love. Un-zip me, please. You must learn, bébé, that a beezniz girl is the same as a mistress or a wife, with only one difference. Can you guess what the difference is?"

"No, tell me," I said, liking this beezniz girl-cum-philosopher and wishing I didn't.

"The difference is that, for her favors, a mistress or a wife demands constant payment, while a beezniz girl asks payment only for—services rendered. So you see, we are really much more just." She sat on the edge of the bed with her back to me and looked over her shoulder coyly. "And now, don't be a naughty boy who stands so far from me that I must shout to make myself heard. I like you, bébe. Come here and permit me to do something about it."

"Thanks," I said, "but I didn't bring you here to do anything about it."

The coy look froze meretriciously on her face. Her eyes narrowed. A beezniz girl never knows what she is letting herself in for until the boudoir moment of truth. "Understand that I am straight," she said. "Straight only, with perhaps one or two interesting variations for friends I like."

"I drove down through the Maritime Alps last night," I said.

"Oh, is that your problem? You are tired? You would perhaps like a small nap first, here on the bed with me? There is no hurry. Why didn't you say so?"

"I drove down from Col de Larche," I said.

That got no comment from Gina.

"With Dominique Guilbert."

"That is of no interest, what you tell me," Gina said coldly.

"Gaston Guilbert's sister? She got a call that Gaston was hurt."

"Gaston? Hurt? What are you saying?"

"The way I heard it, your pimp paid some thugs to give him a beating."

"That is ridiculous," Gina gasped.

"I heard Gaston is one of those friends you have a couple of interesting variations for, and your man got jealous."

Concern and anger fought a skirmish on Gina's tanned face. "It is a lie, what you heard."

"Then tell me the truth yourself."

"Gaston, he is badly hurt?"

"They busted some ribs."

Gina stretched out diagonally across the bed to reach the telephone on the night table. She spoke a number quickly and waited with the receiver in her hand, muttering angrily to herself. Then in explosive bursts of French:

"And would I phone in the middle of the night if it were not important? . . . Yes, but yes . . . At Le Festival . . . About Gaston Guilbert . . . Comment? . . . Merde alors, you try and stop me. I see anyone I wish, anyone . . . No, not tonight. He is not with me tonight. He has been hurt, beaten up, possibly by professionals. I have been told that you . . . Cochon, let me finish, it is of no consequence who told me . . . That it was you who had Gaston beaten up. I—"

The receiver, which had been making faint rattling sounds against Gina's ear, now made loud rattling sounds. She listened, taking the receiver a couple of inches away from her ear, and shrugged at me. Finally she said: "I am glad, for your sake. I understand, yes. But you must understand that your jealousy . . ."

She returned the receiver to its cradle. She'd been hung up on. "Can you tell me why I need him?" she asked me. "My pimp?" She used the word and explained the relationship with surprising matter-of-factness. "He is not faithful to me, I know this. He takes my money. He beats me. Can you explain it?" She expected no answer; I was a convenient sounding board. "Because I am like the others. Because every poule I ever knew has her man. Because this makes life seem real and of importance to us. Because we need someone to feel about."

She was still lying diagonally across the bed. Kicking off her shoes, she turned over on her back. The yellow skirt rode up her thighs. "But this is not what you wanted to hear. I will admit that Etienne was jealous of Gaston Guilbert. It even occurred to me that what you said might have been the truth. Etienne denies it."

"You believe him?"

"But yes. I can always tell when he is lying. He was telling the truth."

"Well," I said, "there goes a five-hundred-franc theory shot to hell."

"Not necessarily. And as for the money—"

"What do you mean, not necessarily?"

"As you are aware, I am expensive." Gina ran her hands down her thighs and flashed a smile at me. "As you are not yet aware, I give more than value for value. Alors, not only could Gaston not always afford me, but he wished to buy me presents, expensive presents. In the spring, he commenced to gamble. He could not gamble at the municipal casino, as they would not extend him credit. He could not gamble at the private casino for the same reason. But there he encountered a man, a Spanish loyalist exile named Rosales, who owns an establishment where it is permitted to gamble on credit. Gaston admitted to me he was heavily in debt to this Rosales. I assume he has been unable to pay. And it is known to me that Rosales will have a man who cannot meet his debts beaten."

"You think Gaston's in trouble with the Spaniard?"

"It must be so."

"Where can I find Rosales?"

"You have only to lose at the private casino, to lose heavily and to be refused credit while at the same time showing a desire to continue playing, and you will be contacted. The Spaniard has his contacts among the croupiers."

"Sounds easy enough. Maybe those five hundred francs are still working for me after all."

Gina gave me a peevish look. "This has nothing to do

with the five hundred francs. I like Gaston and hope that you can help him. I also like you. The five hundred francs are another matter entirely."

To prove it, Gina raised a sleek leg, rolled down a sheer nylon and studied the leg as if she had never seen it before.

It is very hard to tell a beautiful dish to stop. Try it some time. Instead, I changed the subject quickly. "How much of Gaston's paper does the Spaniard have?"

"Paper?" Gina removed the other nylon.

"How much does he owe him?"

"Oh. I don't know. A lot." Gina sat up, raised her hands behind her back and unhooked the yellow dress.

"Cut it out," I said. "I'm going to the casino right now."

The dress was off. That left Gina in black bra and panties. There was no sign that the deep tan ended anywhere.

She was lovely and knew it and looked at me and knew I knew it.

"There is no hurry. The casino remains open until seven. And the Spaniard's contacts are cooperative at any time." Gina laughed delightedly. "Oh, you should see your face. And I, I have a reputation to maintain. I always give value for value. Always."

"Not this time," I heard myself saying. I was heading for the door, feeling ambivalent about it, but heading there. "I've got work to do."

"Wait. You are going to the casino? That makes you le type sportif, n'est-ce pas? Then make a wager here first, with me. One bet only. For five hundred francs."

I was at the door, with my back to the room.

"I will wager five hundred francs," Gina said, "that if you turn around and if I remove one more item you will not leave for the casino until I permit it."

"No bet. You'd win hands down." That wasn't merely a sop to Gina's pride: I meant it.

I turned the door knob and opened the door.

Dominique was standing just outside it, her face three inches from my face, one hand raised to knock.

I had an instant to wonder where they hid the button that you pressed when you wanted a hole to open in the floor that you could fall into and pull in on top of you, and then Dominique was saying:

"I called the reception desk, hoping you had stayed, and they gave me your room number."

"That's nice," I said.

"You look strange."

"Me? Do I? Guess I'm sleepy. I was just going to sleep, as a matter-of-fact."

"But you were just opening the door to go out."

"Me? I was answering your knock."

"I did not have a chance to knock."

"I could have sworn you knocked," I said.

"I wanted to talk to you." Dominique looked past my shoulder, that was blocking the doorway. She couldn't see anything of importance, because a long foyer led from the door to the room, but she must have been wondering how come I was so gauche as not to invite her in.

"To talk to me? Swell! Then why don't we take a walk?" I suggested brightly. "I was just about to take my constitutional, as a matter of fact."

Now it was Dominique who looked strange. "But you have said you were just about to go to sleep."

"Who, me?"

"Besides, I at least am tired. I do not wish to walk." She looked past my shoulder again, suggestively. "Nor do I wish to stand here in the hall," she added a little coldly. "In fact,

I would love to sit down."

"Room's a mess," I said, smiling idiotically. I was waiting for the faint pad of Gina's feet. She could hear us at the door of course, and I was trying to give her enough time to tiptoe barefoot to the bathroom and shut herself in.

I did not hear the faint pad of Gina's feet. She'd had plenty of time, and I realized she was punishing me for refusing to collect what I had paid for. Gina was one poule in a million, but that wasn't going to do me any good now.

"Then let me straighten it for you. While we talk."

"I couldn't—"

Behind me, in the room, the telephone rang.

I looked at Dominique. I felt as if I should have been sweating. I wasn't. My mouth was very dry.

"Aren't you going to answer it?" The phone rang again.

"Got to be a wrong number," I said, and meant it. "Nobody knows I'm here."

"I know you are. And Gaston does. Gaston awoke, and we talked. He told me what happened to him. Gamblers. He is deeply in debt. I told him you had driven me here. At first he was furious, but I explained that somehow I knew I could trust you and perhaps you could—"

The phone rang once more.

"That has to be Gaston. He hated the idea of me coming to you alone, in the middle of the night. In fact he said he would phone."

"Oh," I said. "Then that explains it."

"Well then, answer it," Dominique said in a very cold voice.

The Martinez house phone was not automatic. Apparently it rang whenever the switchboard operator thought it ought to ring. She thought it ought to ring, once again, precisely when Dominique said the word answer.

That did it. Dominique began to move past me. I could either stop her bodily or let her enter the room and see Gina. Stopping her bodily was out of the question, but so was letting her enter the room and see Gina. It was a perfect setup to make a laboratory rat neurotic. I stood there for an instant, feeling like a laboratory rat, and then followed Dominique along the foyer. When I could see the foot of the bed coming into view ominously over her poodle-cut hair I said quickly: "Listen, I contacted Gina. As a matter of fact she's right—"

Dominique stopped in her tracks at the doorway between foyer and bedroom. I bumped her and took a look where she was looking. Gina had pulled the cover up to her waist. What I saw was a lot of tanned skin, Gina's black hair spread on the pillow, Gina's red lips smiling sleepily, Gina's bare arms stretching, and the black silk bra.

"So I see," said Dominique through clenched teeth. Her brown eyes had narrowed. "And no doubt you have spent the night questioning her." She hauled off and slugged me a pretty good slap across the chops and got out of there. The door slammed behind her.

Gina was laughing silently into the pillow, her shoulders shaking.

I picked up the phone and listened.

"Oui, s'il vous plâit?" said the switchboard operator.

"Well what do you know," I said to Gina's back, "he went and hung up on me."

Eleven

I was playing vingt-et-un at the casino, and winning.

Vingt-et-un is twenty-one, or blackjack, a very simple

game in which to let yourself get taken to the cleaners if that's what you have in mind. That was why, after buying five hundred francs worth of chips, I had sat down at the vingt-et-un table. At craps or roulette, a lucky streak could earn a pile even for someone who has a hard time seeing the spots or counting to thirty-six. But at vingt-et-un, where the object is to get as near to twenty-one as possible without going over it, all you had to do was buy one card too many and lose. Of course, you couldn't make it too obvious. To satisfy the dealer that I was merely the worst chowderhead of a vingt-et-un player, I would occasionally stop on the short side of twenty-one. Such as with a fifteen, which the dealer should have had no difficulty in beating.

Anyhow, that was the theory. But if I stopped at fifteen, the dinner-jacketed dealer would invariably make his mandatory draw to sixteen and wind up with a six or more on the last card and pay the table.

I had been playing for an hour, standing at the high table and trying my best to lose. I looked at my watch. It was after five. I looked at the pile of chips in front of me. It added up to more than five thousand francs, which is a thousand bucks. I looked at my first two cards. A ten and a five. If I drew one, the odds were fair I'd wind up with a good hand under twenty-one. If I drew two, I'd probably go out. I waited for the dealer to reach me. The man on my left, who had been losing steadily, busted twenty-one and turned his cards over in disgust.

"Card," I said, tossing a fifty-franc chip on the green felt.

By the house rules, you got two hole cards and the rest, if any, face up. I was dealt a deuce. Added to my ten and five, that gave me a seventeen. Playing to win, I would have stopped.

"Card," I said again, parting with another fifty-franc chip. Maybe, I thought, my luck was turning.

The dealer supplied an ace. That gave me eighteen on four cards—again, a splendid place to stop.

Anything over a three and I'd be an automatic loser.

"Card," I said, happily contributing another fifty francs to the casino.

The dealer, dead-pan, turned up a three.

That gave me exactly twenty-one on five cards. And, according to the house rules, twenty-one or less on five cards paid double.

The dealer stopped at nineteen, and I raked in my chips. Everyone else lost. Scooping the used cards up with his wand and flipping them into the discard slot, the dealer broke a fresh deck.

"I guess that cleans me out," the man next to me, who was American, said. He was a plump, balding man in a rumpled chino suit. "The missus is gonna skin me alive. Five hundred bucks. There goes our trip to the Balearics." He wandered disconsolately toward the bar.

The way I was going, I might break the bank before I started losing. The bald man had given me an idea. I played one more hand, winning on seventeen when the dealer drew a face card to his fifteen, and turned my chips into the cashier. My take was five thousand, eight hundred francs— eleven hundred and sixty bucks. It didn't seem the best way to get invited to the Spaniard's private game.

I found the bald man at the bar. He was drinking what looked like plain water.

"Plain water," he told me. "Jesus H. Christ, I don't even have the dough for a drink. You quitting?"

"A winner," I said. "Let me buy you one."

He had a scotch, I had a cognac, and we started talking.

His name was Hollister, his wife hated gambling, and she was still going to skin him alive.

"Ask them for credit, why don't you?" I suggested.

"I already did, but I'm just a tourist and they don't know me from a hole in the ground. No soap."

"That's too bad," I said.

"You're telling me."

"A guy down on his luck, one more stack and he's liable to earn himself a pile. I've seen it happen a hundred times."

"Yeah." Hollister bit off some scotch.

"I'm surprised you didn't take them up on the Spaniard."

"What? How's that?"

"The Spaniard."

"What the hell Spaniard you talking about?"

I told him about the Spaniard's private game and acted surprised that the cashier or someone hadn't invited him to it.

We had another round of drinks. Hollister's eyes were bloodshot. "You mean, just tell them I want to play with the Spaniard?"

"No, you've got to play it cagy. Ask for credit again. Tell them you're pretty desperate."

"I am pretty desperate."

Hollister dropped his option on the Spaniard and began to tell me about his eleven-country tour of Europe with the missus. "Of course, that's counting Luxembourg and Monaco." He shook his head. "This here's the first time I laid hands on a card. Emily gimme the warning before we left. 'You wanna gamble, gamble. You wanna tour Europe, tour Europe.' She'll skin me alive."

After our third round of drinks, he smiled a slack-lipped

smile and said, "Stick around, I'll be right back." He set out, listing slightly, for the row of cashiers' windows on the far side of the tables.

He was back in five minutes, grinning from ear to ear. "It's all set."

"What is?"

"The Spaniard, thanks to you. I'm in. They got a car that leaves every fifteen minutes, right in front of the casino. A Bentley." He glanced at his watch. "I better get moving."

"Mind if I tag along?"

"Why the hell should I mind? Your idea in the first place. Come on."

I felt pretty good. Not only had I found my way to the Spaniard's lair, but I'd taken the casino for over eleven hundred bucks.

There were five of us in the Bentley, not counting the chauffeur. It was a limousine. Hollister and I held down the jump seats. Behind us were a sleek-haired, well-manicured Italian who looked like a gigolo, a Texan wearing a modified ten-gallon hat and a string tie, and a little old woman, nationality unknown, who had a halo of blue-grey hair and looked like everybody's idea of grandmother.

The Bentley purred up into the hills above the Middle Corniche, taking the curves like mercury sliding in a dish. It was daylight. Far out in the curve of the bay, a big white cruise ship rode at anchor. An early morning launch was trailing its wake out toward the mother ship.

We pulled up at a massive iron gate set in a high stone wall. After a while the leaves of the gate swung in. We drove through and they clanked shut behind us. "Get a load of that," Hollister said. There wasn't a soul in sight. The gate had opened electronically.

A crushed-shell driveway speared straight ahead between sentinel rows of palm trees, and then I saw the villa nestled far back in its own private park. It had a red tile roof, five terraces that I could see and not quite as many wide French doors as the palace at Versailles. Gaston Guilbert had chosen a luxurious joint in which to lose his dough. If there were enough like him, I thought, maybe that was why the joint was luxurious.

A handsome woman of thirty-five greeted us in an interior courtyard. She looked like the madam of a sporting house, the kind that unfortunately went out of business soon after the turn of the century. She seemed to know the Italian gigolo type, and had a special smile for him. To the rest of us she was coolly courteous. We had drinks in the courtyard, on the house. I ordered a tall glass of orange juice, sans alcohol.

"You will go through there," said the handsome woman when we had finished our drinks. She indicated an archway on the left of the courtyard. "To arrange for your loans. It will be quite painless," she added with a little laugh. She had spoken in French and then repeated it all in flawless English.

The old dame, the gigolo and the Texan went on through. I approached the archway with Hollister.

"A moment, gentlemen."

I stopped in mid-stride.

The woman beamed at Hollister. "You may go, monsieur."

Hollister looked at me uncertainly.

Her hand plucked at my sleeve. "You and I, monsieur, we will use the other archway."

185

There was an identical archway on the far side of the courtyard.

Hollister waited. "How come?" I asked.

She shrugged. "Monsieur, I only work here."

"It okay?" Hollister asked me.

"Sure. Go on in there and break the bank."

We shook hands, and Hollister went away.

I jerked a thumb toward the other archway. "Any special reason?"

"What reason could there be, monsieur?"

I'd told Hollister it was okay, but I was less than delighted with having been singled out. Suddenly, maybe because I needed a good night's sleep and was edgy, I wished I had my gun. But the Magnum .44 was back in Col de Larche in the bottom of my B-4 bag.

"Monsieur?"

We went across the courtyard together. Birds chirped. Something made ripples in a lily-pond to our right. The waiter who had served our drinks was cleaning up, whistling a paso doble between his teeth. We passed under the archway. The woman took my arm abruptly, as if we were entering a ballroom and would be announced by a flunky after giving him our card.

I heard a faint whisper of sound to my right and behind me. I started to turn, but the woman clutched my arm.

The stone archway, or something just as heavy, fell on the top of my head.

Twelve

A dog was barking in an echo chamber.

A man's oily voice said in Spanish, "Be still, Franco.

186

Perhaps he is a friend. Perhaps."

The dog made a slurping growl. I felt my head, fingering a bump a phrenologist could have written a book about, if there were still any phrenologists and if they wrote books. My hair was matted with blood, sticky and almost dry. That meant I'd been out more than a little while. It didn't mean, necessarily, that I was badly hurt. Scalp wounds bleed like mad. At least this one had stopped.

I opened an eye and looked along a terra cotta tile floor to the forepaws of a Doberman. It was a big male, black and brindle, and it sat tensely back on its haunches about three feet from my face. Dobermans are one-man dogs and better for police work than German shepherds. For the opposite of police work, too.

My head began to ache. I sat up because I knew I would have to sooner or later, and that made my head worse. The Doberman's slurping growl greeted my movement. He looked ready to spring.

"Have patience, Franco," the oily voice said in Spanish. I hoped it belonged to someone who would be pleased that I could talk the lingo. I can get along in French when I have to, but I can think in Spanish. I've knocked around Latin America a lot.

I stood up, reeled and took hold of a wall for support. The oily voice belonged to a very fat man with a few quivering chins too many. He sat behind a tile table decorated with a mosaic of a bullfighter doing the pass of death with his muleta.

He was spooning gazpacho from an enormous tureen to his fleshy lips. There was a soup bowl on the table, empty, which he had bypassed. There also was a stack of francs which I decided was the money I'd won at the casino.

"Sit down," the fat man said in English, and I made it to

187

the table and slumped in the chair across from him.

"You can speak Spanish," I suggested.

The fat man smiled and said, "With much pleasure, then."

I looked around. The dining room was small, with just the table and chairs and a long lowboy against one wall. All four walls were decorated with bullfight posters.

"As you notice, we are quite alone," the fat man said. "But I feel secure, and I feel you can understand why," he went on in his oily voice. "At a word from me, Franco would tear your throat out. Wouldn't you, Franco? Eh, eh, perritito?"

He tickled Franco behind the clipped left ear with a fat finger. Franco obediently produced the slurping growl.

The fat man ladled gazpacho from the tureen into the soup bowl. "There is nothing like gazpacho to make a man feel better," he told me. I sipped at the cold olive oil, vinegar and tomato base soup. It was delicious.

"And now, as to why you have come to the Villa Lagartijo, my friend?" He picked up the stack of francs and let it fall open on the table. "Did you wish to arrange a loan so you could play at my tables?" He laughed. "Using these five thousand francs as security, no doubt?"

I was wondering when he would stop the polite and patient approach in that fine Castilian accent of his. I wanted to get down to business. "Five thousand, eight hundred francs, to be exact," I said. "When do I get them back, Señor Rosales?"

He laughed again, phlegmily, and ignored my financial request. "Ah, then you know my name. That relieves me. You might have blundered into the Bentley by mistake and, as you have experienced, my underlings are very careful."

"Yeah, I know your name. I don't know how you spotted me."

Señor Rosales reached into a pocket of his white linen jacket and drew out four glossy black and white photographs. He tossed them across the table, and I was staring at snapshots of Hollister, the Texan, the gigolo and the grandmother.

"Neat," I said. "You had them mugged at the casino."

"Ironically, insofar as you are concerned, with an American invention. A hidden Polaroid Land Camera, using very fast film. This way we always know what our guests look like before they arrive at Villa Lagartijo. Ours, you see, is an illegal enterprise and though the proper palms have been greased and we have little to fear from the police, there is always the chance that a gunman will come here and attempt to—ah, liquidate our assets. Under such circumstances, we would naturally be unable to register a complaint with the authorities."

"What's to stop your hypothetical gunman from coming in in the approved fashion?"

"Nothing. Nothing at all. But our reputation is such that he would be foolish to try. Indeed," said Señor Rosales with a moon-faced smile, "I am enhancing our reputation by talking to you. Let the good word spread. Well, as I was saying, our reputation is such that the number of welched loans obtained here at the Villa Lagartijo is minuscule. In fact, or so my auditor tells me, we have a better rate of return than Credit Lyonnais." Credit Lyonnais is the largest bank in France. I was impressed. Señor Rosales had wanted me to be impressed. He was a man who liked to talk about his line of work. As he had said, such talk, freely circulated, helped build his reputation. That suited me fine. If he got used to the idea of me asking questions, I'd get around to the ones I'd really come here to ask.

"That," he was saying, "is because Credit Lyonnais must resort to legal methods to assure the return of its capital, whereas our collection agents employ a more physical approach. Fortunately, with a nod to our reputation, that is rarely necessary."

"What if a tourist gets a loan from you, loses it back here at the villa and then skips the country on the next plane?"

"Our collection agents, I assure you, are not limited to France or even the Continent. That is another reason for the photographs. And, of course, a prospective borrower must show his passport. Once, I do recall, one of our clients did precisely what you suggested. One of our North American agents showed him the error of his ways in, I believe, Kansas City."

"I know a guy who welched and he's right here in France," I said.

Señor Rosales laughed phlegmily again. He looked relieved. "Ah, so that's it. I was wondering when you would get down to the purpose of your visit here. Who is the man that you represent?"

"I don't represent anybody."

"Do me the favor of being honest, my friend. Though I have been told I am not the most taciturn person in the world, my time *is* valuable. And you'll admit I showed a certain amount of patience answering your questions when it should have been the other way around."

"A guy named Gaston Guilbert," I said. "Your collection agents gave him a beating. Last night. Here in Cannes."

"Naturally I deny everything. But assuming there was such a person as Gaston Guilbert, and assuming he was in debt to me, and assuming he had been administered a professional beating last night, can I also then assume you are here to arrange a schedule of payments that will be mutually satisfactory?"

"No," I said.

The fat man was surprised. His hand tightened on Franco's collar. The dog growled. "Then why have you come here?"

"To find out how much Guilbert owes you."

"And why—if there is a Guilbert and if he owes me anything—should I tell you?"

"No reason at all, from your point of view."

"And from yours?"

"You asked me to be honest with you. Here goes. A friend of mine was killed in Paris. I'm trying to find his murderer."

Señor Rosales didn't bat an eyelash. "And this friend's name?"

"Jack Morley. Mean anything to you?"

"No. Frankly, I'm relieved. I would hate to think any of my agents had become—sloppy." Señor Rosales finished the last of the gazpacho in the tureen. "Gaston Guilbert's original debt was for six hundred thousand francs."

I whistled. Six hundred thousand francs is a hundred and twenty thousand bucks. "Didn't you demand security?"

"The debt was accumulated gradually, during the spring. His father owns property. I took a chance. Guilbert, after all and as he is learning, had more to lose than I."

"You said the original debt. He reduced it by how much?"

At first I thought the fat man wasn't going to answer. But for some reason he chuckled and said: "By seventy five thousand francs."

"Paid how?"

"Why, in person."

191

"No, I mean what kind of money?"

"Dollars. Fifteen thousand American dollars, in hand."

Senator Bundy's first two payments, made to Père Massicot and ostensibly for ultimate delivery to Jack Morley, totaled twenty thousand bucks. I wondered what kind of coincidence, if it was a coincidence, I had stumbled onto.

"What's a collection agent's take in France?" I asked the fat man suddenly.

"I beg your pardon?"

"I mean, is there a standard commission? What do your agents get, for example?"

Señor Rosales looked at me. Again I thought he would refuse to answer. There was no reason he should answer me at all. But he said, chuckling again, "Twenty-five percent would be a good average."

The coincidence was still building. But it hit a snag on what was to have been Senator Bundy's final payment—the big one, the hundred thousand bucks. Take a quarter of that away, and what was left wouldn't pay off Gaston Guilbert's debt. I had the notion, though, that something was missing in my arithmetic.

"The name Père Massicot mean anything to you?" I asked Señor Rosales.

"No. You think it should?"

"I don't know," I admitted. Then I asked, on impulse: "One more name. Kidder. Amos Kidder. An American."

"I never heard of him," Señor Rosales said.

He stood up, ponderously. I hadn't realized how tall he was. He was an enormous man who must have weighed three hundred pounds. "You are finished?" he asked.

"It's all I can think of now."

"If you go out that door—" he indicated the only door in

192

the room "—and follow the hallway to its end, that will bring you in sight of the central patio. You can return to Cannes in the Bentley."

"You mean, that's all?"

"I mean, you are free to go. Does that surprise you, or the fact that I answered your questions? But you have harmed me in no way and, in your own way, you have been diverting. You showed a certain amount of bravery coming here, after all, and getting up off the floor to ask your questions. That is a rare commodity I have always admired. When I was young, shortly after Joselito was killed by a bull in Talavera de la Reina and Belmonte went into his first retirement, thus ending the golden age of bullfighting, I wished to be a matador. It was, along with money, my ruling passion.

"But you have only to look at me. Though I was not fat then, still I was far too tall for a torero. It was out of the question and, in any event, shortly afterwards I had to flee Spain. Bravery and money." He sighed. "There is not enough of the one in the world and I fear too much of the other is spent unwisely. If you have shown me a little of the one, that is almost enough for me and I thank you."

"Speaking of money," I said.

We both looked at the pile of francs on the table. I hadn't picked up Senator Bundy's retainer, nobody had paid me to come to the south of France and I'm no millionaire.

Señor Rosales laughed his phlegmy laugh. "Qué lástima," he said. "What a pity that in my old age a show of bravery is no longer quite enough to satisfy me. I told you my time was valuable. You have paid for it with your five thousand, eight hundred francs. Muy buenas. A very good day to you señor, and I hope you find your friend's killer."

I didn't argue with him on any count.

Thirteen

When I reached Col de Larche late Thursday afternoon, it was raining. Low clouds roiled down like smoke from the surrounding peaks. The parking lot of the Grand Hotel des Alpes was a quagmire.

I sat in the VW a while, smoking a cigarette and hoping the rain would slacken off long enough for me to make a dash for the building. The rain came down like water pouring through a break in Boulder Dam. I gave it fifteen minutes and another cigarette, and the only change was that it grew darker outside though it was only five o'clock on my watch. Then I said, out loud, "The hell with it," and was about to open the door and make my run when two figures came out of the hotel.

They were a man and a woman, both tall, and they were running. The man carried a little black bag that looked like a doctor's bag and the woman carried a big black umbrella. They came splashing through the mud in my direction. I rubbed a clear space on the side window of the VW, which had misted over with my breathing, and watched them. I had never seen the man before. When I recognized the woman as Dominique and Gaston's mother, I rolled the window down a couple of inches. At first I thought the man must be her husband, Monsieur Guilbert, but then I remembered what Amos Kidder had told me over our drinks. Guilbert was a little man, far smaller than his wife.

I watched them reach a Renault Floride parked about a car's width from the VW. Madame Guilbert held the umbrella high while the man fumbled at the door of the Floride. He opened it a few inches and turned toward her. He seemed to be looking straight at me, but with the rain, the

194

dimness and the misted-over window he couldn't see me.

"Gaston, he will be all right?"

"Ribs heal quickly. Aside from that, nothing."

"You are certain?"

He placed a hand on her arm. "Nicole, stop worrying."

They were very close together. Suddenly she went into his arms. The umbrella partially hid their kiss.

"Charles," she murmured.

"Chérie."

I was a reluctant Peeping Tom, but if I got out of the VW now they would see me. I stayed where I was.

"Remain a while, Nicole," he said after another kiss. "In the car."

"I cannot."

"They won't miss you."

"Well, only a little while. Oh, Mon Dieu, Charles, Charles."

They got into the Floride and shut the door with a soft click. For a few seconds I could see them, two dim figures on the front seat. Then the figures came together and became one figure, and after that the windows of the Floride misted over faster than the VW windows had.

Five minutes passed while they played their parking lot love scene. The rain had slackened off. I wanted to get out of there but couldn't, not before the woman did. I would have settled for another cigarette, but didn't dare light a match. I began to wonder if Nicole Guilbert's extracurricular philandering had anything to do with the life and death of Jack Morley. Come off it, I told myself. That's what the French call an idée fixe.

Another figure separated itself from the façade of the hotel. It was a small man, stocky, his figure crouched over as if the rain weighed him down. He peered anxiously around the parking lot and then made straight for the Floride. Monsieur Guilbert? At least as to size he fit Amos Kidder's description.

He squared his shoulders and raised his head as he approached the Floride and my car. The rain was coming down harder again. His dark suit was soaking wet. For an instant he seemed to be staring straight at me through the oval I had cleared on the window of the VW. There was a look of intense agony on his face.

He turned, slogged through the mud to the Floride and jerked the door open. I winced.

"Pigs," he said, his voice strident and unsteady. "You are both pigs."

Nicole Guilbert got out of the car. She began to open her umbrella, saying nothing, but the man took it out of her hands and hurled it away with a savage gesture. The other man, the one called Charles, remained in the car.

"And now?" the umbrella-hurling man said.

"What do you want me to say?" Nicole Guilbert asked calmly. "Surely this comes as no surprise to you. Have the decency to be civilized about it."

"Decency? You can talk of that? Civilized?"

"Raoul. You are shouting."

He slapped her face. He had to reach up to do it because she was a full head taller.

The man called Charles got out of the car. "That's enough, Raoul. Don't touch her again or I'll—"

"You'll what?" Raoul demanded.

"Just don't touch her. Only that."

Raoul laughed all of a sudden. It was a choking sound. "I will not contest a divorce," he said.

"This is no time to speak of a divorce," Charles said uneasily.

"I don't want a divorce," Nicole Guilbert said. "You know that. Tu es fou."

"You call me mad?" Raoul Guilbert said. "Naturally you do not wish a divorce. You are not one to bite the hand that feeds you."

"Yes? And what would that hand feed me with—were I to contact a certain American?"

Raoul Guilbert laughed again, the sound ending on the same note of desperation. "Go on then, I dare you."

"Stop it, both of you," Charles said. "Since it is evident you are bound to each other—"

"I hate him!"

"—have the good sense not to destroy each other. I am going, Nicole. Will you be all right?"

"Yes, yes, I won't strike her again," Raoul said, suddenly weary.

Charles got into the Floride and started the engine. He rolled down the window. "Adieu, Nicole."

"Adieu, Charles."

The husband and wife stood there, only a little way apart, and watched the sleek car leave.

"I did not mean that about a divorce," Raoul said. He retrieved the umbrella, shook mud from it and opened it.

"I did not mean that about the—American."

"And the children. At least for them we must maintain appearances."

"Has it ever been otherwise?"

They went, side by side, into the hotel. A moment later, a 2CV that had been parked at the far end of the lot started up with a clashing of gears and went slipping and lurching off through the mud. I hadn't been the only Peeping Tom in the hotel parking lot.

197

★ ★ ★ ★ ★

I waited in the bar until eight, hoping to find Amos Kidder before dinner. But at the reception desk, wearing her long white gloves and looking poised despite what had happened that afternoon, Nicole Guilbert told me she thought Kidder had gone to the Riviera for the day.

The dining room was empty except for an Italian family and three Germans drinking beer. It was still raining.

Dominique, wearing a black dress, a frilly white half-apron and a little white cap perched on her poodle-cut hair, was waiting table.

She stood stiffly at my side after I had read the menu. "Monsieur wishes?"

"How's your brother?"

"The pâté maison is a speciality. I recommend it. Et après—"

"Come off it, Dominique."

"Or perhaps a salade Niçoise to start, and afterwards—"

"Use your head, Dominique. The only place I could talk to her was in my room."

"What monsieur does is of no interest to me. If you have not decided, I can return in a few moments."

"Climbing into the sack was strictly Gina's idea."

She blushed slightly. "We also have, to start, saucisse and moules ravigote. But the moules, for them you would have to wait perhaps twenty minutes."

"I'll have the pâté," I said.

"Very well."

"And I didn't climb in with her."

"Has monsieur decided on what he will have afterwards?"

"The baked Virginia ham with candied sweet potatoes, the pecan pie and iced coffee."

"We do not have any of that. Those are American dishes. We have entrecôte, gigot, caneton a l'orange—but for that one must wait half an hour—or the salade Niçoise, larger of course, as an entrée."

"I'll have calamares en su tinta, flan and a bottle of Federico Paternina Banda Azul."

Dominique didn't quite stamp her foot. "I never heard of any of that. Stop it."

"That was Spanish for squid in its own ink, caramel custard and a Spanish wine sort of like Bordeaux," I said, somewhat lamely. Dominique looked upset.

"Then I suggest that you go to Spain. Or at least stop making fun of me."

"Okay," I said, ready to give up. "I'll have the entrecôte, rare, a salad and a half-bottle of Nuit St. Georges."

"Very well." She scribbled on her pad. Her lips moved slightly, and I thought she was on the verge of tears. A great little old peacemaker, you are, I told myself. I was more than a little angry with myself: I couldn't sort out my feelings about Dominique, and I wanted to.

When she looked up from her pad I saw that she hadn't been on the verge of tears. She was trying her best not to smile.

"You—didn't?" she said.

"Who, me? Didn't what?" I asked innocently.

"You know. With Gina?"

"I already told you, but you didn't believe me."

Dominique's big brown eyes crinkled almost shut, and finally she showed me that radiant smile of hers. Her laughter filled the dining room. The Italian family and the Germans looked up.

"Oh, you should have seen the expression on your face when you opened the door of your room in the Martinez and I was standing there."

Making up with her made me feel even better than I had expected. A girl I knew, a kind of intellectual type, once told me I was the last of the romantics, if you could get through my thick hide, or maybe a sentimental existentialist—whatever the hell that means. Anyhow, I was suddenly feeling great.

"About the wine?"

"Yes?"

"If you can join me in some after you feed the troops over there, how's about making it a whole bottle?"

"Mais oui, monsieur. A votre service."

Dominique skipped away from the table, grinning.

A couple of hours later, having helped me kill not one but two bottles of the château-bottled Burgundy, Dominique was making like an interior decorator with a prospective client.

"And over here," she said enthusiastically, "over here during the slack season we will break through the wall and add an entire wing to the hotel. For a nightclub. Maman regrets that our guests must spend their francs at the discothèque. In that way you would say she is very French, is it not so?"

"It all sounds pretty ambitious," I said. Aside from the nightclub, Dominique had mentioned a proposed extension to the dining room, a chalet-style balcony that would girdle the hotel building on the second floor and a heated outdoor swimming pool. "It also sounds expensive. Where's Maman going to get the dough?"

Dominique looked up at me. She was still wearing the black waitress dress, though she had shucked the white apron and frilly white cap. "Oh, I did not mean all at once. This year, the nightclub. Next year, who knows? You should have seen the hotel when I was a little girl. It was only a small pension, with beds for perhaps fifteen. Everything you see here Maman has accomplished."

"Did she always own it?"

"It was in the family, yes."

"And your mother kept plowing the profits back in?"

I had to explain what that meant.

"Precisely," Dominique said. We were standing in the deserted lobby of the hotel. It was done in a sort of rustic modern motif, and in very good taste. There was a lot of exposed wood that looked like teak. A lawyer I know, a sailboat bug who came into some money, got himself a custom-built twelve meter sloop. He was chest-thumping proud of everything from the scarlet Genoa sail to the two heads, one fore and one aft, but what really got him going was the deck and the wood fittings. They were all teak, and they put his sloop into the luxury yacht class.

"Teak?" I asked Dominique, indicating a long, low cocktail table.

"Yes, all of it. Maman saw it on exhibit in Copenhagen and had to have it." Again Dominique looked up at me, gravely, out of those big brown eyes. "You are thinking it is very expensive?"

I admitted that was what I was thinking. "Not only that, but if your father's being blackmailed where's he going to get the money for that and the nightclub?"

Dominique shrugged. "When it comes to business matters, I am an utter idiot. I do not know. Perhaps this year there will be no nightclub after all." She glanced at me uneasily. "As for the blackmail, I know nothing about that whatever."

"You knew enough about it to look up Père Massicot in the Flea Market."

"That was by—accident."

"What kind of accident?"

She wouldn't meet my eyes. "You are asking too many questions. I hardly know you, even though . . ." Her voice trailed off.

"Even though what?"

"Nothing."

But I could feel it too, that electric tension building between us as it had at the discothèque. Just looking at Dominique was enough to make my pulse pound. What it would lead to I didn't know, but at the moment I was after information.

"A tall guy," I said. "Named Charles. He's the family doctor, I guess. What else can you tell me about him?"

That question didn't seem to bother Dominique. "Charles Auber. He is both a physician and the mayor of Col de Larche. And also he is Maman's oldest friend."

But not Raoul Guilbert's friend, I thought, remembering the parking lot love scene. Still, if there was a skeleton in the family closet, they had rattled its bones in his presence. What was it Nicole had threatened? She'd go to a certain American if Raoul gave her a hard time. To Senator Bundy? But why?

"Was he mayor when the American pilot crashed here during the war?"

"Yes. I think so. He has been mayor a long time." Dominique turned away from me. "But I told you you are asking too many questions. I wish you would stop."

"You don't have to be afraid of me, Dominique."

She faced me again. Our eyes met, and her lips parted in a gamin's small, wistful smile. "Afraid of you? It isn't that."

"Then what?"

"Please. It is late."

"No. Come on."

We were still looking at each other. I couldn't draw my gaze away.

Dominique sighed. "Mon Dieu, but I am not afraid of you. I am afraid of how I could—feel about you."

Maybe that was no more than a pretty good exit line for a girl who wanted to change the subject and knew you found her attractive. Or maybe Dominique meant what she said. I was still confused by what had happened between us so quickly. Maybe Dominique shared my confusion.

Anyhow, she walked away from me across the lobby. I followed her and placed a hand on her shoulder and felt it stiffen under my touch.

"It is late and I am talking too much. Please leave me alone. Please, Chet."

But she stood stiffly, not moving. I looked down at the tiny hairs, that were almost golden, on the nape of her neck. I wanted to kiss her there.

"I wish we had met some other way," she said softly. "Can you understand that?"

"I'm glad we met. However we met." The words sounded foolish and inadequate. I felt like an awkward kid.

She turned suddenly and came into my arms. She was shaking a little. I kissed her eyes, that were shut, and tasted salt on my lips. Then she strained upwards on tiptoe, tilting her head in that funny way of hers, and I kissed her, and then she drew away from me and took a breath and flowed back, and then I really kissed her. It was like doing something well enough all your life and then discovering the real way, the only way to do it, that you never dreamed existed, and when it was over she turned and fled to the stairs, running, and I just stood there, still tasting her, and for some reason thought of the gypsy in the Flea Market and how she had read Dominique's hand, not liking what she saw there, and she would not read mine.

Fourteen

The Hotel De Ville, or City Hall, in Col de Larche was a big gray stone building about two hundred meters up the road from the hotel in the direction of the Italian frontier. The post and telegraph office held down the ground floor. Upstairs they had Col de Larche's few municipal bureaus and a half dozen or so rooms rented to the business and professional types who filled the community's needs. It was the only office building in the village.

I walked there early the next morning and climbed the stairs to the second floor. The interior of the Hotel de Ville had a musty smell and it was dim because most of the heavy wood shutters hadn't been opened yet to the bright sunlight. There was nobody in the mayor's reception room and no lock on the door to his inner sanctum. I poked my nose in there, out of habit, and saw the shuttered window, a few old chairs, a wall of books and a desk that must have seen service around the time Louis Napoleon had dreams of glory. Back in the small reception room, I sat down, lit my first cigarette of the day, got up again, threw the shutters open, found a copy of *Paris-Match* waiting in dog-eared isolation on a low table and thumbed through it sitting on the low windowsill.

After a few minutes the door opened and Nicole's lover came in. He was wearing a gray suit and had dark smudges under his eyes. I got up, and we smiled at each other the way strangers will when they meet in an office owned by one of them. He looked faintly surprised and said in French, "This is the office of the mayor."

"I know, and you must be the mayor," I said in English. "Do I call you Monsieur Auber or Docteur Auber?"

His smile broadened. "That depends on why you have

come to see me, Mr. Drum," he replied, in English this time. "You wonder how I know your name?" He chuckled. "That should be easy for you to figure out—since you are a detective."

At first I didn't get it, then I did. "Sure. My carte de séjour. I guess a guy named Kidder is the only other American in town, and you must have met him."

"I have had that pleasure."

We shook hands and both sat down. He offered me a Gauloise and I showed him the lit cigarette in my hand. He offered me a dubonnet, which I accepted. It wasn't yet ten in the morning, but the French don't drink by the clock. We toasted silently and sipped from our stem glasses. The aperitif wine had a cloying taste.

Charles Auber was a patient specimen, tall and thin but not too thin, whom women would probably find attractive. He was forty-eight or fifty and had no wrinkles on his face except around the eyes, and neither a paunch nor a Charles de Gaulle stoop. I sat there saying nothing, like a man in a railroad station waiting room who didn't care that his train was late. Patient types are hard to interrogate, especially patient politicians or patient doctors, and Auber was both. I wanted to let his curiosity grow, even if he wound up thinking me a damn fool in the process.

"Nice wine," I said at last.

"For the morning only."

"Americans usually drink by the clock," I said, and gave him the sort of inane grin Amos Kidder would have been proud of.

"Yes, and they wind up with harder livers than we French, because once they start it is difficult to stop them."

He offered his blue pack of Gauloise again, and this time I accepted one, which he lit with a criquet, and we talked banally for a while about the merits of black French tobacco as opposed to the paler American breed. By then Auber's smile and pleasant manners were a little forced.

"You will be here long?"

"I just wanted to chat a while. You want to know the natives, see the headman, I always say." I laughed fatuously.

"Yes, of course. The headman." He didn't quite scowl. "But I meant, how long will you stay in Col de Larche?"

"Oh, I don't know," I said offhandedly.

"Is it a holiday? Have you been in France before?"

"A few times. But it's no holiday. I always keep my grind to the nose-stone. Ha-ha-ha." I found myself imitating Amos Kidder with considerable success, and that less than delighted me.

"Grind to the nose-stone? Yes, of course. I see. Then why are you here?"

"Business," I said.

He waited politely. It took considerable effort, but he managed it.

"I still don't know whether to call you Monsieur Auber or Docteur Auber," I said.

"I already told you that depends on—"

"It depends on whether you were in Col de Larche when an American named Clay Bundy Jr. crashed during the war, and whether he came down alive, and whether, as a doctor, you treated him," I said, my voice suddenly sharp.

Auber looked at me, making a fresh appraisal, as though I had just walked into the room. Nothing but the newly-kindled curiosity showed on his face.

"I was here," he said calmly. "I assure you that Bundy died in the flaming wreckage of his pursuit plane."

"I was under the impression he parachuted."

"Then you were under a mistaken impression. He tried

to bring his crippled aircraft down in one piece. He failed. His father was here, and confirmed that fact to his own satisfaction. So, far more recently, was an employee of the American Army, a civilian named Mr. Morley. The Air Force was a branch of the Army at that time, you see."

"I know Morley was here. He took a secret back to Paris with him and wound up in the Seine with his skull split open."

That seemed to come as a surprise to Auber. He frowned at me and spent some time lighting another cigarette to mask his reaction. "Just what sort of detective are you? With the Army? CID, I believe it is called?"

"I'm not with the Army."

"And you believe there is a connection between Morley's trip here and his subsequent murder in Paris?"

"I'm sure of it," I said.

Auber showed me the palms of his hands. "I don't understand how that could be. The young American flyer died. That is a certainty."

"Then prove it to me. Is he buried here?"

"Naturally the Senator and Mr. Morley asked that question before you. The answer is no. He was cremated."

"You mean in the wreckage of the plane?"

Auber considered for a moment, then shook his head. "I wish I could say that that were so. Or perhaps I wish I could tell you what I believe in your language is called a white lie. I told you one before. But then—" Auber shrugged "—unlike the Senator and Mr. Morley, and I believe as you Americans say, you come on slowly. The lie, the simple lie instead of the more complicated and painful fact, would not satisfy you. Because, naturally, you could check what I tell you against what the Senator learned when he came here shortly after the war to discover what had happened to his missing son. Alors, my friend, but facts are sometimes painful."

"Why are these particular facts painful?" I asked.

He answered with an abrupt question of his own, and it surprised me. "Have you met Madame Nicole Guilbert?" His voice savored her name.

"Yeah, I've met her."

"And noticed the long gloves she always wears?"

I said that I had noticed them.

Auber grinned. "Then for the moment you may call me docteur. Because when the American pilot crash-landed his aircraft near this village, I had not one patient but two. The first was the American. He had third-degree burns over seventy percent of his body. He was obviously dying, though he managed to live for three days. There was no morphine at that time in what then was Vichy France. I could do little to stop the pain. We hid him at the Grand Hotel des Alpes until his death. My second patient was Nicole Guilbert."

I waited. His voice had gone husky with emotion. He was either telling the truth or enough of the truth to make him remember something he still found painful. He went on: "Nicole reached the plane moments after it crashed. She dragged him from it. Both her arms were severely burned to the elbow, and one side of her face also. For her face, as perhaps you have observed, she has had plastic surgery. But her arms are still deeply scarred. She refuses to take the time or incur the expense. She will not spend the Senator's money on something as vain as cosmetic surgery for her arms. To her the hotel is everything. That and her children. But I—"

"Did you say the Senator's money?"

"When he learned what Nicole Guilbert tried to do for his son, naturally he was grateful. From time to time he sends money. She would not accept it, except for the hotel. At any rate, Nicole was in grave danger when she took the dying pilot in. There were spies everywhere in Vichy France and she could expect no help from her young husband. At that time he was fighting with the Maquis and she believed he was dead."

A sheen of sweat was covering Auber's forehead. He lit another cigarette; he had been chain-smoking. His damp fingers darkened the paper. "I helped her destroy the body. It seemed the safest course to take. Had she been denounced for harboring the American, she might have been shot."

"How did you destroy it?"

"He was not a big man. He seemed even smaller in death. We burned the body. In the hotel furnace. Completely. Then the ashes were scattered. Clay Bundy Jr. ceased to exist."

"Well," I said after a silence, "that's one way it could have happened."

"One way?" Auber asked angrily. "What do you mean? That I lied to you?"

"Senator Bundy was being blackmailed. He thought by Jack Morley. Show me the part of your story a blackmailer could have held over the Senator's head."

"I know nothing about that." Auber fussed with some papers on his desk, waiting for me to leave.

"You said Clay Bundy Jr. was not a big man. Would he have been about Raoul Guilbert's size?"

Auber looked up from his papers. He cleared his throat. "Yes. I suppose so."

"You said seventy percent of his body received third degree burns in the fire when he crash-landed. What about his face?"

209

"Naturally his face also. Of course."

"So that, had he survived, his face would have been restored by plastic surgery—just like Nicole's?"

"He did not survive, Mr. Drum."

I ignored that for the moment. "And Raoul Guilbert, the original Raoul Guilbert—wasn't it thought he had been killed fighting for the Maquis?"

"The villagers believed that for a time. They were mistaken. It was wartime, there were no lines of communication with the Maquis irregulars—"

"Then you see what I'm getting at, don't you? Suppose Guilbert really had been killed fighting for the Maquis. Suppose the pilot Bundy survived his crash-landing and went into hiding at the Grand Hotel des Alpes. Suppose he fell in love with Nicole. Then along comes the liberation and of course he's got to get in touch with his Air Corps unit because there's still a war to fight against Japan. But he doesn't. For him the war's over, he's in love with a young and beautiful widow, he wants to start a new life for himself here in France. That would make him a deserter."

"I must admire your imagination, Mr. Drum," Auber said sarcastically. "That is the most fantastic story I've ever heard."

"It gets even better," I told him modestly. "Suppose Bundy has plenty of time, in hiding, not only to go French but to learn—being coached by Nicole, who'd be an expert—the habits, mannerisms and past history of her dead husband, Raoul Guilbert. Then, after the liberation, Guilbert apparently returns from the dead. But it isn't Guilbert of course. It's Clay Bundy Jr., and even Raoul Guilbert's kids, who would have been infants then, don't know the difference. Suppose the Raoul Guilbert living here in Col de Larche right now as Nicole's husband is really

Bundy. And suppose, somehow, that Jack Morley found him out. By the time Morley got here, Bundy had gone French for twenty years. He was a father and a husband, a respected member of the community. He'd led a good life and by then what had happened in 1945 was ancient history. If you were Morley, what would you have done?"

"I cannot answer a hypothetical question concerned with a series of events which could not possibly have occurred," Auber told me coldly.

"Or, if you were the Senator? Maybe he found out the same thing, right after the war. I know the old man and you don't. He'd have been hell on wheels as a father—which could help explain why his son was so eager to start a new life when he got the chance. For all I know he hated the old man's guts. It wouldn't be hard. And naturally no aspiring politician whose son was a wartime deserter would get very far on the political scene back in the States. Maybe what the Senator's been paying Nicole Guilbert all these years is hush money."

Auber said nothing. I stood up and went to the window. A cart rolled by on the cobblestones, pulled by a team of oxen. It swayed under its load of hay. I looked down at it, wondering how much of what I said I believed and how much was just to see Auber's reaction. I turned after a while to face his tense silence, and then he started talking.

"You are forgetting several things. In the first place, I saw the body burn. I helped burn it. There can be no doubt of that."

"Not if you're telling the truth there can't."

Though his face became mottled with angry blood, he held his temper in check. "And why would I lie?"

"Gaston and Dominique," I said. "Maybe they don't know Bundy's been masquerading as their father or that they've been deceived by him and their mother all their lives. It could come as quite a shock."

"And you think I'm protecting them?"

I nodded. "Protecting them—to protect Nicole."

"Nicole?" His eyes were wary.

"Nicole," I said flatly.

He clenched his fists on the desk top and stared down at them. "You could make yourself unpopular here in Col de Larche," he said.

"If I wanted to win popularity contests I'd get into some other line of work. You said I was forgetting several things, M. Auber. You mentioned one. What else is there?"

"Raoul Guilbert. He does not speak a word of English."

"Cut it out," I said. "I wouldn't speak a word of English either if I were taking the place of a Frenchman born and raised in these mountains."

"And his appearance? Even with a face made over by plastic surgery, do you think Bundy would look like Raoul Guilbert? The villagers, wouldn't they know the difference?"

That part had been bugging me all along. "You've got me there," I admitted, expecting to see a smug smile or at least an expression of relief on Auber's face. But instead he looked worried.

"Ironically enough, in that you are mistaken. Raoul Guilbert, you see, does not look like Raoul Guilbert."

I just stared at him blankly.

"Have you met him?"

"No. I saw him once or twice, from a distance."

"Had you met him you would have observed on his face the same small white scars that, I suppose, you have seen on Nicole's face."

"Are you trying to tell me he helped get Bundy out of the burning plane too?"

"But no. He was not in these mountains at that time. In 1944 Raoul Guilbert participated in a Maquis raid on a Nazi ammunition depot near Orleans. He was severely burned about the face and neck. He came home swathed in bandages, like a mummy. Years of plastic surgery gave him the face he now has." Auber managed to dredge up a smile. "You see the irony? As far as his appearance is concerned, Raoul Guilbert could be Raoul Guilbert, Clay Bundy Jr.— or anyone."

"Who did the work?" I asked. "There wouldn't be a plastic surgeon here in Col de Larche."

"Ah, my friend, but there is. Though I rarely practice it, I was trained as a plastic surgeon in Paris. I made over Raoul Guilbert's ruined face, as I made over Nicole's."

There was nothing more he could tell me. If I believed his story, Raoul Guilbert was Raoul Guilbert and I had come no closer to discovering what Jack had found in Col de Larche or why Senator Bundy had been blackmailed. If I didn't believe it, I still had no proof that Clay Bundy Jr. had taken over a dead man's life. And even if I could get the proof, just what the hell would I do about it? Bundy—if it was Bundy—had been guilty of desertion twenty years ago, and there is no statute of limitations on desertion during wartime. But since then he'd led a decent life, if a quiet one. Who was I to blow the whistle on him? And wouldn't Jack Morley have felt the same way, except that Jack was burdened with his duty as a government investigator? Maybe that was what had been eating at him in Paris.

Auber opened the door for me. "Believe me, monsieur," he said, "Raoul Guilbert is Raoul Guilbert."

You and Gertrude Stein, I thought, and got out of there. I had nothing but a hunch to refute his parting words, and his recounting of the past had been painful to him. The

213

only thing I knew for sure was where the money for the hotel came from. I was almost sorry I had bothered Auber. Almost.

Fifteen

Dominique, wearing tight white jeans and a crew-necked Basque blouse, was tiptoeing across the hotel lobby. When she saw me, she raised a finger to her lips and squinted her eyes almost shut in an exaggerated request for silence. She was stalking something and, being Dominique, was stalking it with an intensity that would have seemed ridiculous in anyone else. In Dominique it seemed perfectly natural.

Then I saw what she was stalking. It was a small, scrawny black cat with a pipe-stem neck and mange scars all over. Every now and then the cat would pause and survey Dominique out of unblinking yellow eyes, and Dominique would stand statue-still for the feline once-over before cat and girl would continue on their way. Dominique waggled her fingers behind her back as a sign that I should join the parade.

We marched across the lobby and through the kitchen and out the kitchen door. The mangy cat sat down in the kitchen yard and began to lick itself.

"Minou," Dominique whispered.

"Minou?" I repeated.

"Shh! The cat. She dropped a litter of kittens, hiding them somewhere. I wish to find them. Poor Minou! It is her fourth litter in a single year. Look at her. She looks so silly. I don't know what the Toms see in her."

Minou advanced through the high grass of the kitchen yard, in no great hurry. We followed her to a weathered, gray outbuilding. It was an old barn with sagging roof and walls. Minou slipped in under a rotted plank in the wide double door. Dominique withdrew the large wooden bolt, cautioned for silence again and went inside with me a step behind her. There was a faint, dry smell of hay in the barn. Sunlight penetrated a few holes in the roof, spotlighting the bare earth floor here and there. I didn't see the cat right away and neither did Dominique. She was peering around anxiously. Finally she called out coaxingly in a soft, sweet voice: "Minou, Minou, Minou," and I saw a black feline head appear over the side of a crate near the hayloft ladder. I took Dominique's arm and pointed. Minou awaited our approach warily. We crouched over the crate, our heads close together, and peered in. Black Minou purred and blinked, deciding we were friends. Six mouse-sized kittens, three striped and three black and white spotted, were in the crate with her.

Dominique laughed softly and made cooing sounds as she picked up one of the tiny creatures and set it on her palm. It made a thin, piping noise until Dominique stroked it gently with two fingertips, barely touching the striped coat.

"Look," she said, "look, the eyes aren't even open yet." She replaced the kitten in the box and stroked Minou's head. She pouted. "Maman will let us keep no more than two. But they are all so cute. Maman will make me decide. She will say it is good for me. She believes I am too senti-mental. But how can I? How can I decide which kittens are going to die?"

We stood up. Dominique's big brown eyes were trou-bled, but her lips were almost smiling. She touched my hand and looked up at me. "How can I?"

"Don't," I said. "Decide which ones are going to live."

Dominique really smiled then. "And I thought we French had the most practical minds in the world."

"No. Only the most attractive women."

"Oh, that is what you call a 'line'." She shrugged. "Do you always say exactly the right thing?"

I just shook my head and stared at her. The appeal of her beauty, there in the interior of the barn, with darkness all around but shafts of sunlight piercing the broken roof, with her face still flushed from the excitement of finding the kittens, with her eyes glowing, was enormous. And for the first time I could understand that strange beauty of hers. It was uniquely French and hard to pin down. Piaf's sad-happy voice has something of its quality—Piaf, who could be a world-weary prostitute and an eager street urchin in the same song. Dominique was like that—the Earth Mother scaled down to size and the gamin grown up. It would be as easy to fall in love with her, I thought, as rolling out of bed. Or rolling into bed. Maybe I was half in love with her already.

"Why do you look at me like that?" She spoke those words slowly, her head cocked to one side, the gamin grin ready to break out again. She knew damn well why.

"Trying to decide," I said.

"To decide what?"

"If I should fall in love with you."

Out flashed that grin, "And do you always decide beforehand?"

"Never."

"Good. Neither do I. Chet?" The grin vanished. She looked timid.

"Umm?"

"If you should decide?"

"Umm?"

Back came the grin. "I am way ahead of you."

There was no stopping us then. She surged into my arms. Her eyes were huge and dark. She murmured, "Mon Dieu, Mon Dieu, Mon Dieu," against my mouth. I kissed her hard, too hard I thought at first, almost bruisingly. But her head went back, her body arched and her lips responded, moist and swollen. Our hands went wild. Her breath came in hot, frantic little gasps. She purred like Minou purring over her kittens.

"Dominique."

Neither one of us had heard the footsteps.

She sprang away from me, her eyes going wide as she stared over my shoulder. I turned, barely in time to sidestep her brother Gaston's first wild lunge. Behind him stood their mother Nicole, one white-gloved hand raised like a traffic cop. "Gaston, don't . . . please . . ."

But he came for me again, serving up another wild swing. I ducked under it, my shoulder jarring his ribs, and he screamed. I held on, both arms around his waist and my chin on his right shoulder. If he got loose and did some more swinging, he might wind up driving one of his broken ribs through a lung. If he kept struggling to break up the clinch, the same thing might happen.

"You dumb bastard," I said, "do you want to kill yourself?"

Who he wanted to kill became clear when he squirmed, butted my jaw with his shoulder and brought a knee up toward my groin. I turned a leg sideways and caught it on the outside of my thigh, but he didn't have to know that. Then I groaned, convincingly I hoped, let go of him, lurched backwards a few steps, doubled over and sat down hard.

He advanced with mincing steps, like a football place kicker who had lost his stride. What he had in mind to kick was my head. I rolled away from it and scrambled to my feet, deciding whatever damage he did to himself was preferable to his using my head for a football.

Dominique and Nicole swarmed between us, the daughter facing Gaston and the mother facing me.

"Stop it, stop it, are you an animal?" Dominique cried in French.

"If he lays a hand on you again he'll wish he were dead."

"Fool," Dominique said, "you think I didn't want him to?"

Gaston's head jerked back, as if it had been struck. "And you call me an animal?"

She slapped him. His face went white. A sound that was half laughter and half a sob escaped his lips. Then he turned, looking at none of us, and left the barn.

There was a long silence. Finally Dominique told her mother, brightly, "Minou. Her kittens. We found them."

Nicole was looking at me coldly, but her words were for Dominique. "Of course, that is what you were doing here," she said. "Looking for the kittens. Go inside now. Your father wishes to speak with you. With all of us."

Dominique nodded vigorously. She said nothing. She went outside after her brother.

"You must not mind Gaston," Nicole Guilbert told me calmly. "He has a violent temper and he has always fancied himself as Dominique's—protector."

She was speaking French. "Sure," I said in English, "what's a little kick in the head among friends?"

"You must realize—" she began, in English this time, and then abruptly stopped talking.

"Well, well, well," I said. "That couldn't be English. How the hell could it be? You don't speak a word of English. I guess it must be franglais. What about good old

218

Raoul? I bet he's a pretty good guy with the franglais too."

She shrugged. "Later. You will see later. You will understand. After our little family conference."

She left me alone in the barn with Minou and her kittens. The French, I thought, I'll never understand them. Does anyone?

Sixteen

They came trooping into my room after lunch, all four of them, even Dominique, looking grave and dedicated like acolytes with a votive offering.

Mother and daughter sat on the edge of the bed. Gaston remained standing with his back to the door. Raoul Guilbert sat on the one chair in the room. His plastic job wasn't as good as Nicole's, or maybe the damage to his face had been worse. There was an artificial look to his features, like a manikin's. When he smiled, which he did now, shyly and uneasily, it was with his lips only. A faint crosshatching of barely perceptible white scars marred his cheeks.

None of them spoke right away. I began to feel foolish, like the revenuer in the Ozarks who gets the goods on the moonshiner and then is caught back of the still plowing a furrow with the moonshiner's willing daughter. Any minute now, I was sure, Papa Raoul would ask me if my intentions were honorable. What else could the family conference have been about? It would have been funny except that how I felt about Dominique, though pleasant, wasn't funny at all.

"I don't believe that I have had the pleasure of introducing myself to you," Raoul Guilbert said slowly in formal French. He got to his feet jerkily and pumped my hand once and sat down again. He looked very nervous.

I began to wonder if my intentions were honorable. I took a quick glance at Dominique, sitting primly on the edge of the bed next to her mother, and began to wish we were in Paris, or maybe Katmandu, alone, to work things out for ourselves. I smiled at her, tentatively. She didn't smile at me. Oh well, I thought, maybe she didn't want my intentions to be honorable.

"We have held a family conference," Raoul Guilbert said.

"Uh-huh. So I heard."

"In times of crisis, especially if a family is close, I am a firm believer in a family conference," he told me in his slow, formal French. "This family, as perhaps you have observed, is very close."

I thought of Nicole and her parking lot love scene. I remembered their argument afterward. "That's nice," I said.

"We have come to a decision," Raoul Guilbert said firmly.

"Well, look, it isn't that anything actually—"

"If you will allow me to finish, monsieur, then we would be able to discuss what is to be done."

"All right," I said, feeling more and more uneasy.

"It is our hope that you will consider your own course of action most carefully in the light of what will be said here."

"I'll try my best," I said.

"That pleases me," he said.

"It pleases us all," Nicole said.

No comment from Dominique. Gaston stood sullenly with his back to the door.

There was a long and uncomfortable silence. Raoul Guilbert looked at his wife. She nodded encouragement.

"This is not easy, what I have to say." Raoul Guilbert

cleared his throat. "Nevertheless, it must be said. You understand?"

I said that I understood.

He leaned forward in his chair. "All we can do is hope," he told me slowly, "that you have a mind as open and a nature as tolerant as the American who came here some months ago, the American named Jack Morley."

I wondered if the confusion showed on my face. "Jack Morley?"

"But yes. The Army investigator who visited Col de Larche in the spring. Jack Morley."

"Jack Morley," I repeated again, just to be saying something. It took only a few seconds for me to readjust my thinking. After all, I'd come to Col de Larche to learn why Jack had died. "What was he so tolerant about?" I asked.

Raoul Guilbert pulled a cheap theatrical trick, the kind that went out of pictures about the time they yanked the piano player out of the orchestra pit and let the screen do its own talking. He dropped on his knees in front of me, just like that, both knees going thud on the floor, and clasped his hands in an attitude of prayer. His face with the tiny surgical scars on it looked up. His eyes were wide and watery, and when he spoke it was in English.

"I throw myself at your mercy," he said, and as far as lines of dialogue go, that was pretty cornball too. He was almost blubbering. "I am not Raoul Guilbert. I have masqueraded as Raoul Guilbert for twenty years, ever since the real Raoul Guilbert died."

Who he was, then, was obvious, but I wanted to hear him say it. He spoke English like a Frenchman with a good command of the language or like an American who had spoken nothing but French for the past twenty years.

"My real name is Clay Bundy Jr.," he said and began to sob.

Nobody said anything else for a while. Nicole helped him to his feet, and he dropped like a sack of cement into his chair. Dominique was looking out the window toward the mountains. She didn't want to witness her father's breakdown. I couldn't blame her. If the attitude of prayer and the blubbering and sobbing were an act, being Dominique she'd feel nothing but contempt for her old man. If they were sincere, her father's manhood was being diminished right before her eyes, and when filial love turned to pity the family relationship was going to pot. I looked at Dominique's face and, for the first time since I'd known her, couldn't read it. Her face showed nothing.

"Let me tell you how it was," her father said, still blubbering.

Nicole had to take over for him. It only took a few minutes to tell, and the details were essentially as I had guessed them. She had saved his life by dragging him from the burning wreckage of his Mustang. Because her husband was then with the Maquis, she went straight to Dr. Auber. They hid Bundy in the cellar of the hotel while Auber did what he could medically for both of them. Convalescing, they were together constantly. Bundy suffered amnesia for a while and when it was over he had fallen in love with his nurse and fellow patient. His own personal war was over. He didn't want to go back.

Right around then, Nicole said, she got word that her husband had been killed fighting for the Maquis. The man who brought the news, possibly the only one who knew, died shortly afterward. Then the war in Europe ended. Then the war in the Pacific ended. Dr. Auber's plastic surgery gave Clay Bundy Jr. a new face. Nicole gave him, day after day, week after week, month after month while he was healing, every scrap of information she knew about her dead husband. He also learned French from Nicole, who was bilingual. Locked up in a cellar for over a year you could learn a lot of French.

When he emerged, he was Raoul Guilbert. They were the same size, except that he had had to gain a little weight. Nobody in the village doubted it. By then they hadn't seen Guilbert in almost three years.

"Then the Congressman, his father, came to Col de Larche," Nicole told me. "Despite everything, even despite the changed face, he knew his own son, of course. But Clay wouldn't go back with him. Why should he? He had a good life here, and he was raising Raoul's small children as his own. The village admired and respected him." She cast her eyes down. "He had a wife who loved him. He had learned to prefer the relaxed way of life of this small Alpine village to the frantic American pace. His father argued and pleaded. But Clay pointed out that his return, at that point, might ruin his father's career."

"Not if he claimed to have been a victim of amnesia all along," I said.

"Ah, but he wouldn't. It was the one weapon he could use against the Congressman. 'Leave me in peace,' he said, 'or I will admit to being a deserter.' His father saw that he meant that. Now he sends money. Otherwise, they have no contact. It is as if Clay Bundy Jr. is dead, and we wish to keep it that way."

Though it was what I had suspected, Nicole's story gave me a feeling of being let down. It was like reading a book in which you expected a snappier, surprise ending, only to find on the last page that there was no unexpected revelation at all.

Raoul-Clay blew his nose hard. At the door, his stepson was smirking faintly. Dominique's face still showed nothing.

"You sure have a swell way of keeping the family secret," I said. "First you tell Jack Morley, then me. Why don't you buy advertising space in the *Paris Trib*?"

"Ah, but you are mistaken," Nicole said. "Monsieur Morley had pieced together the essential facts himself. As, Dr. Auber advises me, you have done. Under the circumstances, how could you expect us to live with the sword of Damocles hanging over our heads? I ask you, could we lie in dread every night for the rest of our lives awaiting a knock at the door and a visit by the American CID? No; Monsieur Morley seemed a man of compassion. We told him the truth. Then he did a very strange and wonderful thing.

"As you know, he was an investigator for Graves Registration. His job was to close the books on men missing in action to the satisfaction of their next of kin. He looked my husband straight in the eye and he said—these were his exact words, monsieur—'You've got it wrong, pal. I'm looking for a dead man.'"

I thought for a moment and decided that was exactly the way Jack would have said it. But then, later, his conscience would have begun to nibble at his sympathy. Jack had been a guy with what the shrinks would have called an overdeveloped superego.

"We can only hope, now that we have thrown ourselves at your mercy as well," Nicole told me, "that you will prove as sympathetic." She glanced at Dominique and then back at me with a sly smile and added: "And there is also, shall we say, your own special interest in the family?"

I let that ride. Dominique bit her lip. I asked her stepfather: "Didn't you think Morley was blackmailing you?"

"We were mistaken. Gaston went to Paris and learned the truth."

"Did he? What truth would that be?"

"As you must be aware," Nicole answered smoothly, "Monsieur Morley was a heavy drinker. Naturally what he had learned here in Cal de Larche must have bothered him. We can only assume that he drank too much and began to—unburden himself."

"He must have talked too much in the presence of a man named Massicot," her husband said.

"And Massicot put the bite on you in Jack Morley's name?"

Nicole nodded. "We paid. We had to."

"But somebody wasn't taking any chances," I said coldly. "Massicot got himself poisoned and Jack got himself beaten to death. Why leave loose ends?"

Gaston came away from the door fast, in my direction. His mother waggled a finger at him. "You will stop, Gaston. That is a natural conclusion for Monsieur Drum to have reached—if an incorrect one."

"Then why don't you enlighten me?" I suggested. Gaston and I were eyeing each other warily.

"Massicot," Nicole said, "being the sort of man he was, would have had many enemies. And, as you would say in America, one of them caught up with him."

"That gives us an alternative for Massicot," I admitted, "But what about Morley?"

"Senator Bundy," Gaston said flatly.

His stepfather glanced up. "What are you saying?"

Gaston said contemptuously: "That the old man was being blackmailed too. By Père Massicot. In the name of Jack Morley. And that the old man, with his political career in danger, took appropriate measures."

225

Raoul-Clay said one word: "Never."

His stepson shrugged. "Believe what you wish."

"I can never believe that."

Nicole looked anxiously at her husband, and at her son, and back again. "There is another possibility. Tell us how Monsieur Morley met his death."

"He was beaten to death on the Seine bank at night."

"Ah then, you see? Paris . . . the Seine . . . at night . . . roving bands of hoodlums . . . pieds noirs from Algeria perhaps, déclassé . . ."

I walked to where she was seated on the edge of the bed and thrust my face close to hers. She looked alarmed. "Keep talking," I said, barely whispering the words but forming them carefully with my lips. I pointed at the door. I had heard a sound, a faint scraping. She frowned at me, confused, and then she got it.

She went on saying this and that about déclassé pieds noirs while I catfooted it to the door.

I yanked it open.

Amos Kidder was crouching in the hallway just outside. Quickly he untied and began to retie one of his shoes. The blood rushed to his head and made his face beet-red. His shell-rimmed glasses hung askew.

"Hi there," I said cheerily. "You must be the new neighbor they warned me about."

He finished tying his shoe. He studied the other one and decided to leave it alone. He tugged at a long-lobed ear and stood up, straightening his glasses. His face was still red. Suddenly he blinked at me, gave his own cheek a polite little slap and said: "Say you don't think I—" He let that one peter out. "This is mighty embarrassing," he tried a second time, "because it sure might look, it just might look like—" That one rolled to a stop too. By then Gaston was standing in the doorway watching us.

"You were eavesdropping, yes," he said to Amos Kidder.

"Who, me? You've got it wrong, son. My shoe, that's all. I guess I must have bumped into the door when I bent down to tie it. Me, making like a Peeping Tom?" He looked at me. "Like a shamus? Ha, ha, ha."

"You were eavesdropping," Gaston repeated.

Amos Kidder winked at me. "Well, I deny it, but where there's smoke there's fire, I always say. Yessir." He winked again. "I bet you were telling anti-Gaullist jokes in there. Ha, ha, ha."

"Your room on this floor?" I asked him.

"Why, sure. Right next door. I figured you knew."

"Just a minute," I said. "Don't go away."

I followed Gaston back into my own room. I shut the door. "False alarm," I said. "He was tying his shoe."

"He claims," said Gaston.

I ignored him. I ignored all of them, except Dominique. "Do you trust me?"

"We have put ourselves in your hands."

"Jack Morley kept your secret. He was my friend. Twenty years is a long time, Dominique. Who the hell am I to step in now and play God?"

"You won't regret your decision," Raoul-Clay said.

I was still looking at Dominique. "There's just one thing. I'm going to find Jack Morley's killer. I hope he's not in this room. But if he is, all bets are off. Do you understand?"

"Yes," she said.

"Then that's all."

They left the room, Nicole first, then Dominique, then Raoul-Clay, who shook my hand. Gaston brought up the rear. "I should thank you," he said, and I waited, and I realized that by his lights he had just thanked me.

I waited until the sound of their footsteps was gone. I went out into the hall. Kidder wasn't there, so I went next door and knocked.

"Come on in," he called. "But I better warn you, shamus, the joint is bugged. Ha, ha, ha."

He emerged from the bathroom with a pair of toothbrush glasses filled with whisky and water. He poked one in my direction, and I took it.

"Ain't you going to switch glasses with me?" he asked, grinning. "Seeing as how I'm a suspect?"

I switched glasses with him and drank off half my new drink. That almost broke him up.

"How much did you hear?" I asked, and he stopped laughing.

"You mean, outside your door? Something about pied noir hoodlums in Paris. What was going on in there, anyway?" When I didn't answer, he said: "Oh, I get it. Undercover work." He pulled at an over-sized earlobe. I wondered if that was how it had gotten that way. I held out my hand.

"Your wallet," I said.

"Huh? I don't get you."

"I want a look at your wallet."

His expression went from perplexed to pained. "Now wait a minute, shamus. If you figure I was really spying on you out there, say so. Otherwise lay off, will you? Is there a law against tying my shoes or something? Ha, ha, ha."

"The wallet," I said, and for an instant his eyes got the way I had seen them before, hard and depthless, and he shoved a hand into his hip pocket, came up with a thin pigskin billfold and slapped it on my palm.

It contained the usual junk, aside from a sheaf of franc notes: an American Express receipt for traveler's checks, a Diner's Club card in the name of Amos Kidder, Great Barrington, Mass., an auto insurance identification card, same name and address, a driver's license, ditto, two snapshots of a somewhat dumpy-looking faded blonde, one of them inscribed to Amos, with Love, a Kidder's Hardware business card with a line drawing of a face smiling inanely at you and the motto, *Your Business Is Our Pleasure—We Hope.*

There was only one more item, a narrow strip of paper maybe eight inches long and an inch and a half wide. Neatly printed on top was the legend: *Scratch paper for narrow minded people.* The silly note paper was so in keeping with Kidder's apparently vacuous personality that I started to smile—until I saw the single notation that had been jotted there in pencil. It was a Paris phone number: ELY 42-15.

Senator Bundy had given me that number at Fouquet's. It was his round-the-clock message center.

I hadn't spent any more time on the narrow minded scratch paper than I had on any other item. Replacing everything in the wallet, I returned it to Kidder. He looked indignant and self-righteous.

"Satisfied?"

"I guess so. Take off your glasses."

"My glasses?" he asked.

I nodded, and he shrugged and took them off, and I hit him.

It wasn't hard enough to knock him down, but the glass of whisky and water went flying out of his hands and shattered against the wall and he took two steps back on wobbly legs while his eyes tilted to plain white and then back again.

"Jesus Christ, what you go and do that for?" he wailed.

His nose had begun to bleed. He took out a handkerchief and dabbed at it. His blood was a healthy, bright red. "Once the sonofabitching thing gets started," he said, "it bleeds like a stuck pig." He sighed. "Just my luck I had to go and bump into a crazy private eye."

"ELY 42-15," I said, and waited while he snuffled blood back into his nostrils.

He sat down on a chair, put his feet up on the window-sill and gazed at the ceiling. "So that's the way it is," he said.

"How come you rate the Senator's private number?"

"Well for Chrisake you didn't have to poke me one."

"How come you rate the Senator's private number?" I asked again.

"That's a long story."

"I'm in no hurry. We've got until your nose stops bleeding."

He looked at his wrist watch. He looked at it some more, anxiously, during the next few minutes. I decided that meant he had an appointment.

"I'm doing a little job for the Senator."

"What kind of a little job?"

He considered that. He jerked a thumb toward the wall between our rooms. "I heard most of the conversation in there. That answer your question?"

"Why should it? They didn't say anything the Senator didn't already know. He's known it for years."

"Then search me. I guess he wanted it checked out again because somebody was putting the squeeze on him for some dough. What I hear, he's got plenty they could squeeze him for. Ha, ha, ha."

"Ha, ha is right," I said. "The Senator picking a hardware dealer to do his snooping."

"I wasn't always in the hardware line."

"No?"

"I used to be a private cop, same as you. In Boston. They pulled my paper on me two, three years ago, but I still manage to pick up an odd job here and there."

"Without a license?" I said. "For shame, Mr. Kidder."

"Yeah, your license and three francs fifty'd get you a carnet of tickets for the Paris Métro," he told me. He had me there. He looked at his watch again.

"Do any work for the Senator in Paris?"

He snuffled. His handkerchief was red all over. "Of a confidential nature," he said.

I smiled at him. It was a smile meant to worry him, and it did.

"Okay, okay. I tried to scare a guy for him. A guy name of Morley."

"That's all? Scare him?"

"That's all, and I guess he didn't scare easy."

"You didn't slug him with a blackjack?"

"Morley? I never laid a glove on him, not Morley."

"Then who?"

"A froggie. I never even knew his name. He got pointed out to me and I—"

"The word is fingered," I said.

"Hey, I didn't kill him. I just beat up on him a little bit. I hear he wound up in the hospital though," he added a little proudly. I figured that meant he was talking about the younger Massicot brother. "You tell anybody I said that and I'll just laugh my head off."

His nose had stopped bleeding. He took it into the bathroom and I heard the sigh, gurgle and splash as he drank water straight from the tap and washed his face. When he came back he didn't sit down. "Well, I guess that's it," he said, sticking out his hand. "No hard feelings?" He looked at his watch.

"Just a few more questions and I'll be on my way." I wanted to find out who he had an appointment with. The time was really getting him.

He still had his hand stuck out. "No hard feelings anyway?"

I started to shake, his hand closed on mine, hard. He had plenty of strength in his fingers. His left hand rose and came toward my head. The blackjack that led it made a swishing sound. I ducked, but not far enough.

Amos Kidder, Great Barrington, Mass., said, "Nobody takes a swing at me he don't get paid back," just as the top of my head got itself dusted by the blackjack. I started to fall. I wasn't quite out, but my legs had decided they knew their business better than I did. Kidder shoved me toward the bed and I alighted there obediently. I heard a sound that might have been a bomb exploding or a door shutting. I made it from the bed to the floor, on my knees. I got up, setting out for the window, thinking Kidder owed me that—pop me one, buddy, and I'll pop you one—but, maybe, what he really wanted was me in bye-bye land while he kept his appointment. Three falls and I reached the window. I leaned on the sill, both hands and my forehead. I got my head up.

A yellow Citroën 2CV was just leaving the parking lot. Kidder and someone else might have been in it. Maybe it was even the same 2CV that had driven off through the mud after Nicole and Dr. Auber had played their love scene. I hadn't seen any other in town.

Seventeen

I spent the next few minutes frisking Amos Kidder's room. He was a guy who traveled light. There was a Val-Pac on the closet floor, empty except for a few dirty shirts. Kidder's small wardrobe half-filled two drawers of the dresser, except for a single wrinkled drip-dry suit that hung forlornly in the closet. I found no other evidence that Kidder was working for Senator Bundy. I found nothing of interest to anyone but a sneak-thief until I went back to the closet and moved the Val-Pac to see if anything was behind it.

Nothing was behind it, but the Val-Pac felt heavy. I opened it and poked among the dirty shirts. Amos Kidder had hidden a brace of guns there: a .38 Banker's Special and a .25 target pistol with silencer attached. The .38 didn't mean much. Anyone in Amos Kidder's line of work would be inclined to carry an equalizer. I had a .44 Magnum in my own B-4 bag. But the .25 target pistol, complete with silencer screwed to its barrel, was something else again.

Nobody in Amos Kidder's line of work, or any line of work except one, needs a silencer.

Amos Kidder, Great Barrington, Mass., ex-private eye, was a hired killer.

I mulled that knowledge over for a while. Maybe he was a hotshot investigator too and maybe the Senator had hired him only for his investigatory skills. Maybe he had grown fond of the long-barreled target pistol; maybe like Mary's little lamb it went everywhere he went. Except that there is no civilized country in the world where the possession of a silencer is not illegal, and of course Kidder would know that, so I could assume he hadn't come to Col de Larche to use his target pistol to plink at tin cans in the backyard.

But what was he waiting for? He'd had plenty of time to nail his victim to the wall with a few well-placed .25 slugs. The longer a hired gun hangs around, the less likely it becomes that he can perform his function and get the hell out. The best contract kills are made in broad daylight on crowded streets by out-of-town guns who don't hang around long enough to wilt their shirt collars. Surely Kidder would have been aware of that.

Maybe, I thought, the kill was contingent on some item of information Kidder had come to find. He'd been prowling around, both here in Col de Larche and down on the Riviera. He'd even glued his ear to a keyhole, in the best tradition of the inept private eye. I wondered if he would be an inept killer too, and decided he wouldn't be. Senator Bundy was no fool.

Maybe Kidder was awaiting the final go-ahead from his employer. Or maybe, I thought suddenly, he didn't know yet who he was supposed to hit. That wasn't as crazy as it sounds. Somebody had been blackmailing the Senator, using Jack Morley's name. In my book Gaston Guilbert seemed the likely candidate; the Senator's hush-money would pay off his gambling debts. But it didn't have to be Gaston. It could have been Raoul-Clay, though the idea of him putting the squeeze on his own father seemed pretty farfetched. It could have been Nicole. Why should she settle for the Senatorial dole when she could get him by the short hairs and really make him pay?

The point seemed to be that Kidder didn't know who it was any more than I did. Once he found out, he'd have himself some target practice.

I went back to the window. No sign of the 2CV or of Amos Kidder. No sign of anyone except a khaki-clad postman bent over the handlebars of his bike and pedaling slowly by. He looked up, smiled and waved a greeting. "Bonjour, mademoiselle," he called, and I realized he was waving at the window next door, the window in my room.

For a moment I toyed with the idea of lifting Amos Kidder's arsenal. I decided against it. A call to the local gendarmerie, a jaundiced cop's eye view of that silencer, and Kidder would be put on ice as far as his activities in Col de Larche were concerned.

I went out into the hall and over to my room. The door was slightly ajar.

"Chet?" a voice called. It was Dominique.

I walked in there. "Hey, what's the matter?" I said. She had been crying. She looked up at me and sniffed once, and the tears spilled out of her eyes and rolled down her cheeks. She was all little girl then. She shook her head, angry with herself, and the tears flew. I took out my handkerchief and gave it to her.

"Here," I said. She blew her nose hard. "What is it?"

"Oh, I'm s-such a baby."

"Come on, tell me. You'll feel better."

"No. It would only make me feel worse."

Her whole face puckered up. She looked like someone trying her best not to sneeze. What she was doing was trying her best not to bawl. She turned her back on me so that I wouldn't see the effort she was making, and this feeling of protectiveness surged over me. She looked small and helpless and miserable. No matter what, I had to make her feel better.

I took the step that separated us and placed my hands on her shoulders. She canted her head a little to the right, and her cheek rested on my fingers. A tear fell there, but she didn't make a sound.

"You going to tell me or not?" I said, very tough outside.

"Leave me alone." But her cheek snuggled against the back of my hand.

"How old are you? You're acting like a baby."

"I already said I was a baby. I'm twenty-two."

"That's twelve years younger than me," I said, for no reason at all.

Her cheek moved against my hand, and I realized she was trying to smile. "Oh, that's ancient," she said. "You're prehistoric. I bet your joints creak and everything."

"Well anyhow I've had lots of practice cheering up lost little gamins. So stop crying."

"I'm not crying now. See?"

Her head came up and back, and those enormous brown eyes looking at me punched a couple of holes in my heart. Grabbing her chin between thumb and forefinger, I turned her the rest of the way around. She got up on tiptoe against me, lacing her hands in back of my neck. I could feel her heart galloping against my ribs. We didn't kiss.

I said her name: "Dominique."

And she said: "Mon Dieu."

And I said: "I'm falling in love with you."

And she said, against my mouth: "I've never been in love before, not like this."

We hit the bed in each other's arms. The lost little gamin went away then, and she was more woman than I had ever known.

"Be a little brutal first," she murmured. "And then be gentle."

I was both.

The sun was low. Twilight filled the room. She lay in my arms, sleek and spent, her breath fluttering against my throat.

236

"What is it like?" she said. "In the United States?"

"It's hard to say. I don't stay one place very long. And I'm kind of a loner."

"Yes, and the streets you walk on are not only lonely but savage as well. I could tell."

We lay there in silence for a while. Every now and then she would sigh happily. I don't know what she was thinking. I was thinking her hair smelled of the outdoors and youth and the orange blossoms they cultivate in Grasse between here and the Riviera for perfume. I was thinking of how her lithe little body filled her smooth, tanned skin. I was thinking of the shuddering cry of completion she had made into my mouth and of how her hands caressed my back and of the way her thighs pulled down and in. I was thinking that I had done the whole bit, with dreams of an ivy-covered cottage and all, only once before, and that it hadn't worked out and that since then I'd taken life one day and one night at a time, and I never thought it could happen this way again until here, now and Dominique. That was what I was thinking.

And then she said: "Now I can tell you why I came to your room."

I allowed as how why she had come to my room was a fact not without a certain amount of interest for me.

"I came here to tell you we must not see each other again until what you came to Col de Larche for is finished."

"Still feel that way?"

"I should. I don't. You know how I feel."

"Okay then. Stop worrying about it."

"But it's not fair to you. The way my mother looked at us, and she could tell, and she said you had a certain interest in the family. Oh, I hated her then."

237

"What I decided about your father's got nothing to do with us."

"If I could believe that."

"You can. It's the truth."

Her fingers stroked my rib cage. "You say that now because you are a man sated with love. But again soon you must be a detective."

I caught her hand. "If you don't cut that out I'll forget all about being a detective."

She laughed, deep in her throat, and didn't stop it. "Be a detective. I dare you."

So I said: "A yellow 2CV, with local plates. Who drives it?"

"Ann-Marie Auber."

"His wife?"

"Docteur Auber's wife, yes. Why?"

"Just wondering," I said. Her hand, which was still busy, left my rib cage.

"Now ask me another one. Harder." She chuckled again. "But I can tell you don't feel like being a detective now."

"How can you tell?" I asked innocently. I was looking down into her eyes then. The fading twilight was dim in the room, but I could see myself reflected there.

"Mon Dieu, yes," she said. "Yes, yes, yes . . ."

She cried out, and her lids covered those brown eyes and I never saw myself reflected there again.

When I awoke it was dark. My hand groped for Dominique but she had gone. I could still smell the fragrance of her in the bed though, and the other pillow was dented where her head had rested. I let my own head rest there. I think I smiled idiotically. I was in love.

I was also hungry. A look at the luminous dial of my watch told me it was just short of three o'clock. What had

Dominique said? *You are a man sated with love.* I was sated, all right. I had slept eight hours. If ever the going got rough as a private eye, I thought, I could always put Dominique on the market as nature's own tranquilizer. I felt completely relaxed. All the tension built up by a tough case had been drained out of me.

She was good for the appetite too. I was starving. I'll bet she's a great cook, I thought. All beautiful French girls who are magnificent in bed are great cooks. It is a law of nature, discovered by C. Drum. He won the Nobel Prize for it and lived happily ever after. Which reminds me, I went on thinking. Why not? Why not live happily ever after? I felt slightly drunk. Dominique had done that too. I'd have to take out a patent on her. At the very least I'd have to marry her. That was a tentative, small-hours-of-the-morning thought. I tried it again: I think I will marry her. For a honeymoon I will find us a cave and in it install the biggest bed in the world, on which we will romp for several years, turning out miniature Dominiques to the delight of all the little cave-boys in the neighborhood.

I definitely think I will definitely marry her, I thought. Who ever heard of marrying indefinitely? But what if she won't have me? She could always use her head and say no. But she won't. What kind of happy ending would that be? She'll say yes. Once I tell her about the factory for turning out miniature Dominiques, she'll say yes. It was the least we could do to make the world a happy place. And once in a while I'd even work, if the case didn't take me too far from the embrace of my Dominique.

I sat up and scratched a shoulder blade and smiled. I inclined my head and sniffed at the shoulder. Sure enough, there was Dominique's scent. Maybe the cave wasn't such a good idea. How selfish could a guy get? What I ought to do is buy us a sloop or a ketch or a schooner, and we'd follow the trade winds wherever the trade winds blew, and whenever we sailed into a port the smiling brown-skinned natives would line the quay and applaud Dominique's beauty and my good luck. We would become a legend. Nordhoff and Hall would write a story about us, or Michener. We would sail off into ten thousand sunsets, my Dominique and me.

My stomach rumbled. I was famished. I decided to slip into my pants and go downstairs and raid the hotel kitchen. Maybe Dominique was hungry too. Maybe we'd sort of meet there by accident.

I went into the bathroom, turned on the light and smiled at myself in the mirror over the sink. I combed my teeth and brushed my hair. Even the little knife scar on my right cheek looked good. Dominique was in love with me.

The knife scar made me think of the gypsy in the Paris Flea Market. She had recognized it as a knife scar. I scowled at myself in the mirror. She had refused to read my hand, and she had been gloomy regarding Dominique's future. The line of her life and the line of her love would meet, and end.

This is hard to explain, but a sense of foreboding came over me. I walk under ladders if ladders happen to be there, and some of my best friends are black cats. Ordinarily I am not superstitious, but ordinarily I have nothing to lose. Now I had Dominique. It makes a difference.

I scowled some more and called myself a name and padded back across the bedroom toward the hall door. Just as I got it open, I heard a scream, and then a second, and another, and it was Dominique's voice. Three screams, followed by a chilling silence and then footsteps pounding downstairs and a door slamming.

I started to run.

★ ★ ★ ★ ★

The family lived in a suite of rooms off the kitchen. The door was open when I got there. Lights were on all over the place. I saw Nicole Guilbert standing in a hallway. Her face was so livid you couldn't see the scars on her ruined cheek. She looked at me and pointed at a doorway and I went through it, into a bedroom.

Someone had turned the lights on in there too. It seemed as bright as a surgery, or maybe all the blood made me think so. There was a big, canopied four-poster bed and on it, supine, was Raoul-Clay. The covers were thrown back. He wore only pajama bottoms. He had been shot once in the forehead, between the eyes and halfway to the hairline, and once in the chest, from extremely close range. His chest and face were pitted with powder burns. Pillow and bedclothes were soaked with blood.

I hadn't heard any shots. I remembered Amos Kidder and his silencer. He'd come back. While I was making love to Dominique, while I was sleeping, while I was dreaming happy dreams.

A car started outside. Someone whipped it frantically into gear and it roared off. The sound of its motor faded. I didn't think of going out there after him, not yet. I only thought of Dominique and how hard, being Dominique, she would take this.

I was aware of Nicole standing behind me. "Dominique," she said in a flat voice. "In the kitchen. She wants you. I have called Docteur Auber."

"Your husband's dead," I said.

"Not for Raoul. For Dominique."

I went into the kitchen. The door of one of the two big refrigerators stood open. A half roast chicken was on the floor near it. The only light came from the refrigerator. It

241

spilled out across the red tile floor to where Gaston Guilbert sat with Dominique's head cradled on his lap. He looked up at me.

"I can't stop the bleeding," he said.

I stood there for a few seconds, and something which I would never get back drained out of me. I dropped to my knees near Dominique. She was wearing a peignoir, tied with a sash at her waist, and nothing else. It had come loose, exposing the firm mound of her left breast and a wound below it darker than the pale pink nipple. Blood pumped from it in small, terrible gouts.

Her eyelids fluttered. She looked up at me. "I was so hungry," she said, and tried to smile.

"Don't talk," I said. I thrust my hand against the wound. Blood seeped out around my fingers and down my wrist.

"A towel," I told Gaston. "Get me a towel."

"Hungry," Dominique said dreamily. "Oh, you will be awful for me, I will make love with you and become so fat."

I watched the blood pumping. Gaston brought a towel, and I wadded it against the wound. It became red very quickly. The bleeding wouldn't stop.

Dominique cried out suddenly. "My hand," she gasped, and she was a little girl again, a gamin alone and afraid. "Hold my hand."

Her fingers were cold. Her lips had no color in them. "Why?" she said faintly. "Why did he do it? The American. Mr. Kidder. I went to the icebox. I opened it. Chicken. For you. Oh, you would be so hungry too, I thought. He ran in. He looked at me. He shot . . . Why . . . ?"

She didn't know her father was dead. I didn't tell her. I just knelt there, holding her hand with one hand and pressing the towel against the wound with the other, though I knew it was no use. The blood wouldn't stop coming.

Except for the one time she cried out, she wasn't in any pain. The life just flowed from her. She tried to raise her head once but couldn't. "Oh, we would have been so happy, you and I," she said.

A harsh voice, not quite breaking, answered her. "We're going to be." It was my voice.

Her hand squeezed mine. "To all the hours," she said in a faint whisper. "To all the years . . ."

"To all the time in the world," the harsh, not quite breaking voice said.

She died with a gamin's smile on her lips. By then Docteur Auber had arrived. He just stood there, looking down at us. I kissed her mouth, Dominique's lovely mouth. The brown eyes were closed.

Eighteen

I remember faces. An Italian. Two of the beer-drinking Germans. I remember Docteur Auber giving Nicole some kind of injection. He looked at me and wanted to give me the same, but I shook my head. I remember Gaston guiding my steps away from his sister's body. Someone had covered it with a blanket, coarse and heavy so that the mound on the tile floor was almost shapeless. I looked at it but it wasn't Dominique any longer.

I remember checking the chambers of my Magnum .44. I don't remember climbing the stairs to my room for it. I was dressed and downstairs again. For a while I spoke to Gaston. He had spread a map on the reception desk in the lobby. He was smoking a Gauloises and peering down at the map through the smoke. The two Germans stood a little way off, watching us and whispering.

All of a sudden the conversation made sense to me. "Italy," I was saying.

"I agree," he was saying. "He will attempt to escape across the border." Gaston's finger poked at the map. "Route D-202 as far as Col de Vars, and after that D-100 through Larche itself to the border at Col de l'Argentière."

"What kind of road?"

"Mountainous. Twisting. And two high cols. Two mountain passes."

"What's he driving?"

We were outside. The map was under Gaston's arm. The .44 Magnum was under mine.

"He came down from Italy in a Fiat. Italian plates. I have a Peugeot station wagon," Gaston said. "It is faster."

"Not on a mountain road. Nothing but a sports car could beat a Volks around those curves. Come on." I led the way to my car. I didn't know if what I'd said was true or not. I wanted to do the driving.

Docteur Auber was standing in the darkness near the VW. "Good," he said to Gaston. "I thought you would go. I have not called the gendarmes as yet. I will wait an hour longer."

We were in the car. I started the engine. Docteur Auber jerked his head in my direction and asked Gaston a question. I didn't hear it, but I heard Gaston's answer.

"Because they were in love, this man and my sister."

"Get him," Docteur Auber told us both.

"We'll get him," I said.

I put the VW in reverse. The tires spun gravel.

It was almost dawn when we left Col de Larche, but the road to the Italian frontier plunged down into a valley and it was night again. Only high above us the peaks were pink with the first light of day.

Then the road began to climb, twisting back on itself, toward the high pass of Col de Vars. I took each switchback in a controlled skid, letting the rear of the VW fishtail and whip us around. Kidder would make better time on the straightaway. We had to overtake him on the curves, and he had a fifteen-minute head start.

If he had come this way, I thought suddenly. I wanted to see the map again, but didn't want to stop to see it. Maybe there was another way to the frontier. No, Gaston would know. But maybe Kidder had outsmarted us. Maybe he figured we'd chase him toward the Italian frontier. Maybe he'd gone the other way, deeper into France toward the Rhône Valley, or south to the Riviera. A boat might be waiting for him at some little town near Cannes. At Théoule or Cap Roux or Agay. Maybe he'd driven down to the Riviera the other day to arrange it. But no, he hadn't been ready to make his move then. He'd been digging into the background of the Guilbert family, same as I had done. I wondered if he had learned anything in Cannes that I had missed. But what difference did it make? Dominique. He had killed Dominique. That was all that mattered.

A road sign informed us that we had reached the top of Col de Vars. Elevation 2483 meters. It was full dawn again. I cut the headlights and peered below us to where the narrow road serpentined down the mountainside until it was lost in the gloom of a valley.

"There he is," Gaston said.

I looked where he was pointing. Half a dozen switchbacks below us, a tiny bug was crawling along the thread of the road. It might or might not have been a Fiat. I felt my lips drawing back in a grimace. I felt the weight of the Magnum under my left arm. One thing I knew for sure about the VW. There is no better downhill car in the world. You work your way down through the four forward speeds. You don't have to brake. Downhill a Volkswagen can over-take anything but a Grand Prix racer.

Down we went. Pretty soon I needed the headlights again, for we had plunged from morning into gray pre-dawn. Gaston sat very straight, not saying a word. Every now and then his left foot would move from a clutch pedal that wasn't there or his right for a nonexistent brake. I shifted from fourth to third as the pitch of the road in-creased. I used second only for the hairpin curves, and that was when Gaston went for the brake that wasn't there. The engine and the big air-cooling fan roared and whined be-hind us.

The road straightened and knifed into a valley. *St. Paul's-Ubaye,* the road sign said, and some farm buildings sped past us and then a high stone wall on either side of the road and some shuttered shopfronts. We left the village be-hind. More farm buildings and the sharp, strong scent of manure.

A cock crowed.

I saw taillights ahead of us. I floored the gas pedal and we began to gain. Two hundred meters, then a hundred. From the rear the car had the square lines of a Fiat. At fifty meters our headlights picked out the nationality plaque above the license plate. "I" for Italy. My lips made that gri-mace again.

Half a minute later I felt sure. It was a Fiat, and when I flipped my headlights on high beam I could see the silhou-ette of the driver. He sat hunched over the wheel, alone. I kept the headlights up and pulled out to pass him, then cut back in sharply. He swerved off the road, braking hard. I stopped in front of him and got out on the run, the

Magnum in my hand. It never occurred to me, then, that he might sit calmly waiting, and draw a bead on me with one of his two guns, and fire. All I could think was this was the man who had killed Dominique, and we had overtaken him.

"Climb out of there," I called. I heard Gaston's shoes kicking up gravel on the road shoulder behind me.

The door opened and a small fat man scurried out of the Fiat. He said something angrily in Italian, his voice almost a falsetto. When he saw the Magnum, his hands flew over his head. I had never seen him before.

He began to jabber excitedly when we turned our backs on him. In the VW again I thought: a minute lost, a precious minute. Amos Kidder would be a mile closer to the frontier.

I slammed the door and started driving.

After a while it becomes almost automatic. A VW handles like a bicycle. You turn the steering wheel a little way and the front wheels respond instantly. You touch the gas pedal and, although there is not much power in the rear engine, it accelerates at once. You climb and you turn, and the tires thump into potholes and out. On the turns your headlights pick out wind-stunted pines and larch, and soon you have driven up into the dawn again and you don't need lights. Then the stunted trees are gone. You are above timberline. There is a growth of scrub and lichen on the desolate rocks. You can see your breath in the cold air. The high peaks glitter pink with snow.

And you think: Dominique is dead. Your fingers feel stiff with her caked blood. You'll never see her again. You'll never see that smile flash, or hear that laughter. She passed through your life, and she is dead. You loved her. She was twenty-two. She is dead.

247

You flip a cigarette out the window into the slip stream and watch the flying sparks. You have lit another one, unaware. The smoke is harsh in your throat. Then for a while you forget her. There is only the road and the speed and the high Alpine country. There is only the man you are pursuing. But soon the car skids on a tight curve, and for an instant it is out of control, and next to you Gaston cries out, "Mon Dieu," and it is so much like his sister that she surges back at you.

We came upon the Fiat without warning. One moment there was only the road ahead of us, climbing steadily, switching back on itself to reach the top of Col de l'Argentière, the high pass straddling the frontier. The next, we swung around a switchback and there it was.

Kidder had parked on the shoulder, his right front fender only inches from the guardrail. The hood was raised. Steam rose from the open radiator. He had pushed his car too hard. In the thin Alpine air the boiling point of water is less than at sea level. The Fiat had overheated. That might have happened to Gaston's Peugeot too, but not to the VW with its air-cooled engine.

A hundred meters beyond the abandoned Fiat, the road disappeared into the side of a mountain. There had been no way to lay a roadbed over that final precipitous peak. They had tunneled through it.

We got out of the VW. A sheer cliff rose from the left side of the road and a sheer cliff dropped from the right side. We were well above timberline. There was nowhere for Kidder to hide. He had gone into the tunnel on foot.

"The frontier," Gaston told me. "A kilometer beyond the tunnel. No more. The French douane."

We walked past the raised hood of the Fiat. The radiator

cap and a work glove were laid out on one fender.

"Can he get water around here?" I asked Gaston.

"In the tunnel perhaps. There are runoffs. Depending on the time of year. Depending on how much snow fell last winter." He shrugged. "We had much snow."

The morning sunlight was brilliant in the thin mountain air. By contrast, the tunnel entrance was pitch black. We crossed the road on the run. On the right side, silhouetted against the sky, we would have made perfect targets. If Kidder was watching. On the left, against the gray and dun of the cliff, we'd have a chance.

I drew the Magnum and went forward fast, with Gaston almost on my heels. He was unarmed. I didn't see what good he could do.

"Wait here," I told him.

He only smiled. It wasn't a smile, really. It was like the grimace I had made while driving. He kept coming behind me.

The tunnel entrance yawned ahead of us. A sign above it said: *Allumez vos phares.* Put on your headlights. It was going to be dark in there, especially in the first few moments.

Walking in, I heard a scuffling sound behind me. Gaston was sprinting to the opposite wall of the tunnel.

At first the darkness was complete. I shut my eyes and waited, giving them time to adjust. I felt a crawling sensation down my spine. Kidder could have taken us then.

I opened my eyes and could see the yellow dividing line of the road for a distance of ten meters. The walls of the tunnel were roughhewn. There was the sound of water, not dripping but cascading down. It was very cold and damp in the tunnel.

We advanced along opposite walls. From ahead twin

eyes appeared, the amber headlights of a French car coming through from Italy. They grew bigger. In the confines of the tunnel, the engine roared. I flattened myself against the wall on my side as the car approached. It was a sleek Lancia, and it glistened wetly. Somewhere ahead there was a water runoff in the tunnel.

I stepped away from the wall and waved. The car braked to a stop. Its driver looked startled.

"Is there anyone else ahead on foot?" I asked him in French.

He opened his mouth to answer, and then he saw the big Mangum in my hand. He hunched over the wheel. The Lancia leaped forward and away. I breathed its exhaust fumes and started walking again.

After a while I saw a patch of light ahead. A ventilating shaft had been cut into the roof of the tunnel. A waterfall plunged down from it, splashing noisily on the roadway. There were mountain torrents up there, still carrying melted snow down into the valley below.

If Kidder had come into the tunnel to fetch water for his overheated radiator, this was where we would find him.

At first I saw nothing. Only the waterfall and bright sunlight piercing the ventilating shaft. And then that grimace twisted my face again. On either side of the ventilating shaft I saw niches in the wall, where a man could hide, where a man could stand, partially protected from the fall of water while filling a vessel from it. I began to feel better about the impulse that had made me enter the tunnel on foot. Gaston hadn't questioned it. The VW might have given us some protection in the event that Kidder was lying in wait for us, but driving through we might never have spotted him.

He wasn't lying in wait for us. He was standing in one of the niches, on the left, on my side. Only his arms showed.

He'd probably got there only moments before we had. He was holding a four-liter oil can out under the water. His arms were in sunlight. His sleeves were rolled up. We were so close I could read the label on the can. *TOTAL,* it said. His arms were hairy and wet. He hadn't seen us coming. He hadn't heard us. We had him.

We had him.

And then we didn't. Gaston leaped across the width of the tunnel, splashing in water almost ankle deep. The oil can disappeared. Gaston got as far as the yellow dividing line.

"Look out," I shouted, and Kidder fired just once.

The sound of the gun going off was deafening in the tunnel. Kidder had used the big Banker's Special. The slug ripped into Gaston's middle, jackknifing him and slamming him against the far wall of the tunnel.

I fired a single shot toward the niche to keep Kidder back and went at a crouching run to where Gaston had fallen: I dragged him toward the darkness. Kidder fired once more. Rock chips flew whining past my ear. He didn't fire again, and neither did I. We were two old pros. Our ammo, unlike TV ammo, was not unlimited. He couldn't see me in the darkness. I couldn't see him in the niche in the wall. If I advanced on him, into the sunlight streaming down the shaft, he'd hit me with a single well-aimed shot, the way he'd hit Gaston. If he tried to leave the niche, I'd hit him. Check and countercheck. All we could do was wait. Maybe one of us would get nervous. Maybe one of us would develop a twitch.

Nineteen

It was just short of eight o'clock on the luminous dial of my watch. An hour and a half had passed. No more traffic had entered the tunnel from either direction.

Gaston lay on his back, close to the wall. There was nothing I could do for him. There was nothing they could have done for him in the Bethesda Naval Hospital with a team of gunshot experts. The .38 slug had taken him low in the abdomen, between waist and crotch. The wound wasn't bleeding much. I might have tried carrying him out of the tunnel, but it was several hundred meters and the pain of it alone would have been enough to finish him. He was dying. It was only a matter of time.

He'd gone into shock almost at once. He lay there, shaking with chill, bathed in cold sweat, his teeth chattering. I had covered him with my jacket but it didn't help.

At seven-thirty he'd become delirious. He opened his eyes, which were glassy. He knew he was dying. He began to speak French, gasping, fighting to dredge each barely audible word up. "Confess me," he said. "Father, confess me. For I detest all my sins."

He repeated that several times. I had to lean close to his face to hear his choking whisper over the roar of the waterfall. Finally I placed a hand on his shoulder, and he thought I was the priest. "Father," he said, "I have sinned. Confess me, give me absolution, Father, for I . . ."

His voice ebbed and flowed with a lifetime of sins, real and imagined. I was only half-listening. My eyes never left the niche in the wall, beyond the fall of water.

Then, just before eight o'clock, I began to really listen.

"I gambled, Father. A streak of bad luck. I borrowed. Again I borrowed. It wouldn't change. Each time I thought surely. Surely it must change. It never did. It was a fortune. My life. There was danger to my life. If I did not repay my debt. Still I did not despair. Is despair not the one unforgivable sin, Father? So you have always said, and I did not despair."

His mind wandered through the years of his life. ". . . I am a fornicator, Father," he said, and went on to confess a youthful adulterous affair with the wife of a villager. ". . . I am a blasphemer . . . I am an avaricious man . . . I am a glutton . . ." For each sin named he submitted a confession, but his life had been like most men's lives, neither all good nor all bad, and I listened, not really listening, and I waited for Kidder to make a move, and the dying man's words, spoken with such intensity as he revisited the sinful milestones of his life, all ran together so that what I heard was a gasping drone without meaning until all of a sudden these words jumped at me:

". . . I am a sinner against my own father . . ."

I waited, but he gasped and said: ". . . I am an apostate who dares not hope for the grace of Mother Church . . ."

"How could you sin against your own father?" I asked, my voice low even though I doubted Kidder could hear anything above the splash and roar of the waterfall. "How could you sin against him? The man who died today was not your father. Your father died when you were an infant. That man took his place. That man was an American."

He tried to raise himself on one elbow but fell back. "That man was my father. Who was with the Resistance when the American crashed in Col de Larche. Who returned two years later with his face ruined, as the American's face had been ruined. Who came back to find that the American was living his life. Who regained his identity the only way he could."

So I laid my hand on his shoulder once more, firmly, and I asked: "How can that be? Only yesterday the American masquerading as your father admitted it. You were there. You heard him."

And Gaston said: "He admitted it once before to the other American, to the one called Jack Morley. But it was not true. There was danger both Americans, the one called Morley and the one called Drum, might learn what really occurred. So my father told them what they wanted to believe." His voice was faint, and there were long pauses in what he said. "My father was clever and except for one thing long ago a good man, and still I sinned against him."

"What did they want to believe? The Americans?"

". . . sinned against him . . ."

I had to bring him back. I had to know. "What did they want to believe?"

"That he was their countryman. That he had deserted and then lived a good life for twenty years. That, for them, his nationality and the good life he had led exempted him from punishment. They are sentimentalists, the Americans. My father knew that."

"What was the truth?" I asked.

"Everybody believed my father was dead. Killed fighting with the Maquis. Then the American came. He was more dead than alive. For a long time my mother nursed him. They . . . loved. He feared going back. His war was finished. He deserted. He would live the life of my father. With a new face, who would know?"

"Your father," I said. "If your father was alive, he would know."

"He was alive. But he did not come back for a long time. He suffered a loss of memory and was living in Orleans. Meanwhile, when the war ended, the Congressman, the

American's father, came to our village. He saw his son, who refused to go back. That was . . . just as well for the Congressman. His career would be ruined by a son who was a deserter. He went back to America. He sent money to my mother, through a lawyer in California.

"One night my father came back. His face all bandaged. He had lived for that moment. It was a dark night and raining. Raining hard. No one saw him come. He found them, the American and my mother. In each other's arms. He had hoped for . . . everything. And came back to that. For a moment he was crazed. He killed the American with a kitchen knife. He . . . stayed. Docteur Auber helped dispose of the body. For a long time my father was like . . . a dead man. Docteur Auber operated on his face. My mother wouldn't go near him.

"But in time she learned to . . . live with him. To tolerate him. The flow of money from America was everything to her. If she betrayed my father, it would stop. She did not betray him."

"Who did?" I asked. "Was it you?"

". . . against my own father . . ."

"How? How did you betray him?"

"The American called Morley came here. We told him what we had to. He went back to Paris. His lips would remain shut. But me, I had this debt. This truly enormous gambling debt, and so I thought . . . I was desperate . . . they threatened my life . . ."

"Using Morley's name you blackmailed the Senator," I said.

"Unless he paid, I would reveal that his son was still alive. It was not true. But he had no way of . . . knowing that." Gaston's lips curled down in bitter self-contempt. "My father and I, we never got along. I heard him argue with my mother once, when I was young. I heard the truth. I think he was a little . . . afraid of me. And I did not wish to spend my life here in Col de Larche. The sin of ambition, Father . . ."

"So, still using Morley's name, you blackmailed your own father," I said.

"This time with the truth. He paid. They both paid. There was a man in Paris, Père Massicot, who was collecting for me, from the Senator. He was a man who could do many things. First he obtained a counterfeit American passport for me, in the name of Jack Morley. So I could collect the money he sent at Poste Restante in Cannes. But Massicot, he became greedy. He would reveal who I really was, he said. Unless I let him keep all. All."

Though I prompted him with questions, he said nothing else for a while. I listened to the flow of water down the ventilating shaft. I waited for Kidder to make his move. I saw the pain twist Gaston's face. A gut-shot man dies slowly, and in torment. At last he spoke again, his voice very faint:

". . . I am a murderer, Father . . ."

I waited.

"Père Massicot. First I went to him and agreed to let him keep the money, all of it. But my sister Dominique . . ."

I felt my fists clench at the sudden mention of her name. And then Gaston was speaking once more: ". . . From things she said, I was afraid she suspected that I . . . that it wasn't Morley . . . that I was blackmailing my own father. She wasn't sure. I wanted to show her she was wrong. Massicot hired some Algerians for me. That would show Dominique, I thought. They were only supposed to beat Morley. They went too far. They . . . killed him."

"But first you poisoned Père Massicot," I said.

"Oui," he said, and then he spoke some words I couldn't understand, and he chanted a Hail Mary with my hand on his shoulder, and his voice grew fainter and fainter, and I sat there watching him die and thinking:

That gives me all of it, all of it except Amos Kidder, all of it except Senator Bundy. But he was a politician, and he'd probably had a fat political thumb in a lot of dirty political pies, and in one of them maybe the lawyer who was paying off Nicole was involved. I knew that was as close to the truth as I could get, but it was close enough. The lawyer. It had to be the lawyer. For some reason he turned on Senator Bundy. He had the investigation into Clay Bundy Jr.'s missing in action status reopened, and that brought Jack Morley into the picture.

For the Senator that much would have been bad enough, but then Gaston began to put the bite on him. The Senator's career was in double jeopardy, and the one man responsible, the one man at the root of it all, was his own son. Or so he thought.

Which was when Amos Kidder entered the picture on the Senator's behalf.

Who was he? What would his instructions have been? He was an international assassin, a hired gun with probably half a dozen identifies. All his papers I had seen would be false, of course. There was no Amos Kidder in Great Barrington, Mass., or anywhere. He would cross the Italian border. He would have a new identity waiting for him.

And his instructions? Go there and learn what you can learn. If there is no other way, silence him. Silence my son Clay permanently.

Hit him in the head.

What Kidder had learned, from Docteur Auber's jealous

wife, was the final irony. There was no Clay Bundy Jr. Clay Bundy Jr. was dead. A man named Raoul Guilbert, French, no relation, thank you, was responsible for the Senator's little old problem. Masquerading as Clay Bundy Jr., masquerading as himself, he was just as dangerous as the real thing.

And Amos Kidder had struck.

I watched Gaston die. He died in pain and he died alone, as every man does, and then I was alone with Amos Kidder. He must have known time was working for me. I could afford to wait, and he couldn't. He had waited this long because if he emerged from the niche in the wall I'd have him. But he knew, as I did, that sooner or later the gendarmes would come. They would walk into the tunnel from both ends and it would be all over.

I didn't want that to happen. I wanted Kidder for myself. In a cold, unreasoning way, I was just as desperate as he was. But there was no way he could know that.

He made his move when a car entered the tunnel from the Italian end. I saw its headlights, the amber French lights, and I heard its tunnel-confined roar. It was a low-slung Citroën DS, coming fast.

I watched it pass, on the far side of the narrow roadway. For an instant my eyes retained the after-image of the red taillights. Then dimly I saw a dark shadow move.

Kidder had come out behind the car. He fired twice and I fired once. Something hot and heavy seared and slammed my left hand with enough force to half spin me around. He fired again, but his sight also had been impaired by the bright lights in the tunnel. I saw the muzzle flash of his Banker's Special, very close. I only heard it the first time, an enormous blasting sound in the tunnel. My left hand hung limp at my side. Nothing else had hit me.

Then his face came close, the bland bespectacled face, and I chopped at it with a barrel of the Magnum. His cheek was laid open from temple to jaw. The glasses sat crooked for an instant below the bridge of his nose, then fell off. I chopped with the Magnum again. The Banker's Special jumped from his hand. He didn't have the other one. The little target pistol that had killed Dominique.

That had killed Dominique.

He staggered back toward the ventilating shaft, toward the fall of water. I don't remember tucking the Magnum in my belt, but I could feel its weight there. I hit him with my right fist, the only one I could use, and he fell down. Water drenched us both. He got up with his hands in front of his face. He hit me, and I slipped to one knee in the water. I got up and hit him again, and his head jerked back very hard, and he fell down again.

He got up slowly. I backed him against the wall, where the fall of water was heaviest. I jacked him against the wall with my left shoulder and hit him. He couldn't go down. I had him pinned there. I kept hitting him. I couldn't stop. His face changed. It was like beating a clay statue that hasn't been fired yet with a hammer.

I was still hitting him, lunging awkwardly with my whole body, no longer striking methodically, when the gendarmes came. They tore me away from him. I fought them. Three of them had to hold me. A couple of them bent over Amos Kidder. One of them said something. At first I didn't hear it, but he said it again.

"His face. Have you seen his face?"

And another one said: "He is dead."

They went easy on me. After all, I had caught their killer for them. All they'd had to do was pick up the body, and when they are after a murderer who is cornered and will fight for his life, no cops anywhere will object to that.

I stayed a couple of days in a hospital in Briançon. I had a bullet hole in my left palm, a clean wound with no complications. Every knuckle on my right hand was broken.

The only one who made the papers back in the States in a big way was the one who almost got away.

When I left the hospital I went to Paris and stayed a week. I dictated a deposition which Jill Williams typed in duplicate for me. I sent one copy, airmail, to Senator Bundy, who by then had returned to Washington. I kept the other copy. With the Senator's copy I enclosed a note. Copy number two, it said, was on its way to the *Washington Post*.

That wasn't true. Somehow I wanted to keep Jack's secret, even if he had had it wrong, but the Senator didn't have to know that.

I flew home. Senator Bundy had made the headlines of the first paper I picked up at Dulles International Airport. He had jumped or fallen from his office window on the eighth floor of the Senate Office Building.

He had been working eighteen hours a day under tremendous pressure, the paper said. He never stood still. He was a guy who sacrificed his personal life to help keep the world safe for democracy.

That's what they said.

About the Author

After serving in Korea, Stephen Marlowe spent a solid apprenticeship in the last of the pulp market and in the new paperback original market. As the reviewers agreed virtually unanimously, Marlowe was slated for bigger things, however. And time has certainly proved their predictions true.

Born in New York, educated in Virginia, Stephen Marlowe founded the writer-in-residence program at the College of William and Mary. After writing popular fiction for many years—and after living on and off in Europe—Marlowe began writing serious literary novels. He is now an acknowledged master of his craft, having won the esteemed French literary award *Prix Gutenberg du Livre* in 1988.

But Marlowe has never forgotten his roots—nor have they forgotten him. In 1997 he was awarded the Lifetime Achievement award from the Private Eye Writers of America.